the
Predicteds

the Predicteds

CHRISTINE SEIFERT

sourcebooks fire

Copyright © 2011 by Christine Seifert
Cover and internal design © 2011 by Sourcebooks, Inc.
Cover design by RD Studios
Cover image © Iulian Dumitrescu, model: Iulia Vacaroiu

Sourcebooks and the colophon are registered trademarks of Sourcebooks, Inc.

Published by Sourcebooks Fire, an imprint of Sourcebooks, Inc.
P.O. Box 4410, Naperville, Illinois 60567-4410
(630) 961-3900
Fax: (630) 961-2168
teenfire.sourcebooks.com

Library of Congress Cataloging-in-Publication data is on file with the publisher.

Printed and bound in the United States of America.

VP 10 9 8 7 6 5 4 3 2 1

For my mom

PROLOGUE

THE ROSE-PATTERNED CARPET OF THE ROOM REMINDS ME OF the guest room in my grandmother's house. When I was a kid there, I used to hop from petal to petal. If I landed on white space or a leaf, I had to start over again. Everything in my grandmother's guest room—*my* room, I called it—was the same purplish-red of the roses in the carpet. Even the little ball on the end of the chain I pulled to turn the light on and off matched the flowers.

I can't remember if this room matches, and I can't see much of anything. The side of my face is smashed against the carpet, and I can feel a hand pressing hard on the other side. "What are you going to do to me?" I ask, but I doubt he can understand me, because my cheeks are sucked in like a little kid doing a fish impression.

"Shut up," he says, but he's good-natured about it, like we're just fooling around.

"Please," I say, and the pressure on the side of my head eases.

I lift my head as much as I can, my neck straining, my hands bound behind my back.

"Why are you doing this?" I ask.

He's quiet for a moment as he releases my head, but as soon as I struggle to a sitting position and glance wildly around the room, he smashes my head back to the ground, grinding his knee into my face.

"We should've known this would happen," he says. "It was predicted."

PART I
divided

CHAPTER 1

Attention: There has been a shooting on school grounds. The building is currently under full lockdown. Please check back here for updates.

—Quiet High website

OH, DEAR," MRS. MCCLAIN SAYS, HER LIVER-SPOTTED HAND unhelpfully lingering on the fire extinguisher.

"Gross," a girl who is actually named Lexus says when I finish. She shakes her smooth cap of hair in disgust.

"Somebody get this girl some water," Mrs. McClain calls, finally moving into action.

"I'm fine," I say. "It's just my first week of school." Blank stares all around. What they don't know is that this happens to me *every* first week of a new school, even though this is my ninth new school since kindergarten. It's not always *this*, exactly, but it is always something. The first day of second grade, I threw up in Mrs. Horvath's purse. The third day of fourth grade, I sneezed so hard, I broke a blood vessel in my nose and spewed blood all over some kid whose name I can't even remember. In seventh grade, I leaned against the fire alarm and set off the overhead sprinklers. Tenth grade? I hit an icy patch with my car and drove over the assistant principal's left big toe (and lost my learner's permit). This time around, it was the choking.

I was just sitting there, chewing gum, trying to make it through a coma-inducing demonstration on balancing chemical equations, when I felt the fruity chunk slip down my throat. Suddenly, there was no air at all. After a brief moment of panic, I stood up and staggered around, not knowing for sure what to do. My feet got caught in the strap of my bookbag, and I staggered, zombie-like, from left to right, spilling the bag's contents. Finally, the guy in front of me jumped up and moved toward me. One, two, three, then four painful Heimlich maneuvers later—under the watchful stare of twenty-two pairs of eyes, including Mrs. McClain's rheumy gaze—I spat out the gum and took a giant breath.

Shortly after, I threw up on my savior's shoes.

Hello, Quiet High. I've arrived!

"Get her some water!" Mrs. McClain yells again. My rescuer appears in front of me. "You're going to be okay," he says reassuringly. I nod. "I'm Jesse, by the way." He sticks out his hand as if we are at a cocktail party chatting over meatballs stuck with toothpicks, instead of standing with a puddle of my vomit between us. "Pleased to meet you," he says without any sign of sarcasm.

"Ah, thanks," I say to this kid, this odd misfit among the cowboys and jocks who populate Quiet High. What else can I say? *Sorry that I spewed stomach bile on your Skechers?* I expect him to be insulted by the bite in my voice—or too grossed out to be near me—but he gives me a half-smile and then leans over to set my bookbag upright. I bend down with him. Up close, I notice that behind his sleek, plastic-framed glasses, he has shiny brown eyes and eyelashes that curl up. Around his neck is a skinny tie, knotted loosely.

Mrs. McClain herself finally hands me a cup of lukewarm water. "It's going to be okay, honey," she croons, her warm bony hand delicately patting my back, her coffee breath spreading over my cheek. Her wrinkled face suddenly crumples as she looks at the floor. Her voice changes. "You'll need to clean this up immediately. Health code standards," she adds sharply. Her bony hand now feels like a cold claw inching across my shoulder blade.

"Oh," I say. "Where are the—?" I stop when I realize I have no idea what tools I'll need to clean up barf. How about a hazmat suit?

"Over there." She motions toward a supply closet in the corner of the room. "Mops, buckets, paper towels, sanitizer, rubber gloves, sand, everything you need." *Sand?* What do I need sand for? What exactly does she expect me to do?

I reluctantly head for the closet as conversation resumes around me. Skinny Tie trails behind me, following me to the supply closet. I give him a little kiss-off wave, part "Thanks for saving my life!" and part "Please don't ever speak to me again, because I'm mortified!" I step inside the clammy darkness, close the door behind me until it latches with a satisfying click, and take a deep breath. Just enough light from the classroom filters in underneath the door so that I can easily find my way to a floor-to-ceiling shelf unit in the back. It's towering with textbooks and assorted junk: beakers, test tubes, cleaning supplies, and a strange collection of what appear, upon closer examination, to be *Star Wars* figurines. There's a small sink on the left side, and I lean over it, lapping up the cool water like a parched dog. I rinse and spit a few times before I wash my face, and then squint at the tiny mirror. It's too dark to see if I look as rotten as I feel. I consider flipping on the light switch by the door but decide against it. The darkness is soothing.

The dull murmur of the class barely makes it through the heavy wooden door. Away from the lull of McClain's scratchy voice, I feel kind of relaxed. It's sort of nice in here, kind of like how I imagine a morgue would be, only warmer and less creepy. I move to a Red Cross bucket in the corner and tip it over to make a comfy seat. Why rush to clean up puke? Maybe if I wait long enough it'll disappear. Or maybe I'll disappear. I prop my feet on a stack of books and lean against the shelves. I drift someplace between awake and asleep, a pleasant middle ground that has no good name.

Sometime later—seconds or minutes, I don't know—I hear the screams, the abrupt scuffle of desks and feet, and a sudden chorus of pained cries. "Help!" someone yells over the din.

And then as quickly as it all begins, silence resumes, and I wonder if I've imagined it. My paralysis lifts quickly, and I scramble to the door, tipping the bucket over in my haste. I trip on the handle and catch myself before I land on my face. My hand is on the doorknob when I hear it: Mrs. McClain's voice is plain, calm, and strangely indifferent, like she's talking about her bunions.

"He's got a gun," she says. "Nobody move."

CHAPTER 2

Being able to see a person's future. That's what we were after all along. We wanted to know what makes a good kid good and a bad kid bad. Can you blame us for that? So we spend years and years of research trying to figure out what makes people tick. And then what happens? We find an astoundingly, marvelously simple answer: The brain isn't so much a complicated machine as it is a crystal ball. If you look into it, you will see everything you want to know.

—Dr. Mark Miliken, senior researcher at Utopia Laboratories

A PIERCING SCREAM CUTS THROUGH THE CLASSROOM. IT almost seems to travel, slithering under the crack of the supply closet door and landing on me. I physically jump when I feel it touch me. A cacophony of observations rise up out of the room:

"He's heading for this room! I can see him down the hall!" Someone is brave enough to look out the door.

"Barricade the doors!"

"The tables are bolted to the floor!"

"The door doesn't lock!"

"He'll see us! Don't go out!"

"Stay quiet! Nobody talk!"

Shrieks transform into whispers. Sobs turn to hiccup-y, snotty sniffles.

"He's almost here." Strangely, this last observation is punctuated with an eerie giggle.

I hear rapid staccato pops. It could be a Fourth of July round of Black Cats, competing snare drums, a carburetor backfire. Only it's a gun. Long pauses between shots make me tremor all over—successive pops are almost reassuring. He's still far away. He isn't here. Yet.

I am frozen, my hand still glued to the door handle. Suddenly, I realize that the popping has ceased for a long time—at least a couple of minutes.

"He's gone! I can't see him!" The voice is strong but tentative. It's coming from the lookout, the kid who is manly enough to try to protect the whole class. I know who it is: Sam Cameron, the blond giant who sat across from me before the choking incident—the man of the family.

I ease the door open, my hand steady and firm. Slowly, slowly, the door inches open, but my view is blocked. A strong back fills the opening. Hands are placed on either side of the doorframe. I couldn't get out if I wanted to. It's a sentry—a skinny-tied sentry. "Stay back," Jesse says to me now.

And then it seems to all happen at once: the shots, the window breaking, the voices intensifying, the "Oh, god" moan rising above it all. Someone shrieks, "He's coming through the window!"

Why doesn't somebody stop him? I think. *Where are the cops? Push him out the window! Punch him in the face! Do* something!

"Let me out," I order Jesse. It's not rational. Why would I want out now?

He's coming. "I want to see," I whine, feeling more scared because I can't see what everyone else can. Wouldn't it be better if I could just see the shooter's eyes, the barrel of the gun, the fear in the eyes of the girl who is crying so loudly I can't hear myself think?

"Stay," Jesse barks at me. "Please," he adds, his voice softer, protective.

That does it, the *please.* It's the last nail in what feels like my coffin. *I want out!* There's not enough air in here. Panic rises inside of me, and I feel it whooshing through my nose. I just want some air, some light, some space. "Let me out!" I cry and push hard against his back, so hard that my wrists burn. But nothing happens. He doesn't move even a millimeter. I push harder, and then, suddenly, he turns. I fall forward, catch myself, take two surprised steps back. And then he's in the closet with me. The door is closed and his back is against it. He grabs my shoulders. "Shh," he whispers. "He'll hear us. He's in the room now. I can hear him out there. He didn't see me. I'm sure he didn't see me."

Inexplicably, my head clears, my heart slows down, my hands stop shaking. I can breathe. He's in here. It's already done. Somehow, it feels better. I breathe through my nose. In and out. In and out. "Good," Jesse says. He drops his hands and takes hold of my fingers.

"What's going on out there?" I ask. Jesse turns to the door, presses his ear against it. He keeps one hand awkwardly gripping my right pinky. "He's talking." Jesse listens. I move forward, silently, and lean my ear next to his.

The shooter's voice is low and gravelly. *He has a sore throat,* I think to myself. "I hate dumbfucks," he's saying. "I hate all the dumb people, the retards, the people who screw everything up for me. I'm too good for this. Too good for this shitty world. You know? Nobody is ever going to truly get me. I'm all alone." *He's crazy.* "Death to socialism!" he says now, triumphantly. "Death to politics and the establishment and the so-called authorities!"

"Hey, buddy." A voice in the corner tries to soothe him. It's Sam again, taking over.

"Shut up!" the shooter yells. "You all need to remember this! Everybody look at me! Look at me! I want you to remember what it's like to watch me—to watch me shoot. It'll never get more real than this. So pay attention!"

Before I can react, Jesse shoves me hard. His hand is wrapped tightly over my mouth, so I can't make a sound. He moves me almost gracefully to the sink at the side of the room and pushes me hard on my shoulders.

"Who's there?" the croaking shooter yells from the classroom. "Who's there?" He is getting closer to us, closer to the closet. "Do we have volunteers in there? Volunteers who want to know what it's like to die by my hands?"

Jesse pulls open the cupboard under the sink. "Get in," he hisses. He gives me a hard push when I hesitate.

"I can't," I say, eyeballing the tiny cupboard in the dark. "I'll never fit." He puts his hand on top of my head and forces me to crawl headfirst into that tiny space. My shoe falls off. He barely misses my toe when he slams the cupboard door shut. I can barely breathe in the tight space. Sickening pain takes over in my spine, my legs, my arms. I'm bent in ways I didn't think my body could physically bend. My neck aches. My cheek is pressed against my sweating ankles.

A knock sounds at the supply closet door. "Come out," the shooter singsongs. "Come and see the greatest thing you'll ever see!"

Jesse is moving quickly and desperately right outside the cupboard. I can hear books falling, the *Stars Wars* figurines breaking beneath his shoes, the metal shelving scratching on the cement floor. *He's going to block the door,* I think hopefully.

The doorknob jiggles. "Son of a bitch," the shooter says. "It's jammed."

Jesse is still scrambling. I can hear him mumbling under his breath as things continue to drop off the shelves. I want out of this horrible cupboard where the sink is leaking on my head and the smell of rusty pipes fills my nose, but I can't move. "If that's how you want to play it," the shooter calls, "then we'll play. Very smart, by the way. But not as smart as I am. Not by a long shot."

Sirens are blaring outside. How long have they been there? How long has this been going on? Seconds? Hours? Days? I can't remember anymore.

"Come out of there," the shooter yells, angry now, "or I'll start shooting out here! Your choice: you or them. Feel like a hero today?"

"Don't," I say, but I can't get enough air to my lungs to be heard over the sirens and the clatter in the closet. Jesse is pulling on something. I can hear him grunting. "I'm going to count to three. *Uno, dos...*"

Thwack! The sound reverberates. A sense of relief streams through me in that cupboard, even though I don't know what has happened. Still, I feel calm.

But then the gun goes off, so loud my eardrums ache. "Help," I try to say, but who's there to hear me?

CHAPTER 3

Bullied? Are you kidding me? He wasn't bullied. He was the bully.

He was a weird kid, kinda scary sometimes. He liked guns. Obsessed with death. Hated most people because he thought they were all dumb. I could kinda see where he was coming from.

We worked at Pizza Heaven together. He was pretty cool. I think he worried a lot about being such a failure with women. He talked about that a lot.

I didn't even know him. Was he new here?

I heard he had a hit list.

His parents are responsible for this mess. They should be in jail right now.

—Interviews with Quiet High students and teachers

ARE YOU SURE?"

"Of course," I say, annoyed. "I'm totally ready to go back to school, *Mother*." I emphasize the last word because I know it will get on her nerves. Long ago, she insisted we move to a first-name basis. "It's much more mature," she'd told me. I was five at the time.

Melissa just gives me a sympathetic look now, the kind she reserves for when she feels sorriest for me, like the time I broke my toe or the time I came in third in the science fair. It's always a sign she's way more freaked out than I am.

It's been a week since that day, and I'm sick of sitting around the house. Quiet High has been closed for seven long days while the staff and community volunteers have worked to repair the broken fixtures and windows, clean the hallways and classrooms, and fill in the bullet holes with plaster. "A good coat of paint, and it'll be just like new," the school board president insisted in a news interview.

"I don't know," Melissa says skeptically. "You've had a terrible trauma."

Trauma. If I hear that word one more time, I'm going to scream. Melissa sounds like the woman with the frizzy feathered hair who has been here twice to compel me to talk about what happened. "You are experiencing a flashback, aren't you?" she asked when I stared past her flipping hair wings and tried to tune out her high-pitched voice. I don't feel much of anything, and I don't want to talk about it. But Melissa has been expecting me to fall apart ever since Jesse led me out of the school that morning, my legs so numb I could barely walk. Jesse had to hold me up, and I leaned against his chest, feeling his heart beating hard and sure.

Jesse truly was the school hero that day. When the shooter burst through the closet door, breaking the lock with ease, Jesse whacked him over the head with a metal shelf that he'd pried from the wall. The shooter collapsed in a daze, the gun pointed at the floor. This is how I imagined it, at least. The rest I heard about from Melissa, who watched the news religiously for days.

They recreated the whole thing using cute animated diagrams, a clip-art boy stalking the hallway with scattered X's meant to represent the rest of us. I didn't watch much of that, but Melissa told me how it all went down. In the very end, it was Jesse standing over the shooter when he raised his gun, his arm shaking violently, Jesse stepping backward toward the cupboard under the sink, Jesse standing in front of me. That's when the shooter pulled the trigger.

But he didn't shoot Jesse. The shooter killed himself. After all of that, all of that swagger and destruction and fear, he just killed himself. I was pissed when I found out. There was something not right about that. Now I'll never get to say to him, *Why?*

For the first few days, the local and the national news camped outside our house, but I never came out. They had only one picture of me, taken right after Jesse pulled me out of the cupboard. In the photo, I am under one of his arms, the metal shelf is under the other. There I was on the front page of the *Quiet Daily News* with a red, sweaty face, looking baffled and tired, like I'd just run a marathon I didn't know I was in.

"What's the latest report?" I ask Melissa now as I reluctantly shovel a spoonful of lukewarm oatmeal in my mouth. I wipe the edge of my lips, and stamp my right foot, which now has a tendency to go numb with no provocation. Melissa says it will go away soon.

"Three more released from the hospital. It's really amazing." Melissa is referring to the death toll: a grand total of one. And that is the shooter himself. Lucky for us, he was either a terrible shot

15

or he just preferred to aim at things rather than people. Bullets smashed trophy cases, battered lockers, tore through banners, and decimated the stuffed armadillo mascot's head hanging above the main office. Of the twenty-five people injured, all of them were hit indirectly, either by debris or ricocheting bullets. So far, only two remain in the hospital: a sophomore who broke his leg when he slipped on water from a leaking water fountain, and a secretary who had a mild stroke during the shooting. She was actually at home, sick with a cold, watching the coverage on television.

The news is calling the whole thing a miracle, like it's some stroke of luck that a psycho with the hand-eye coordination of a street monkey brought a gun to school and terrorized everyone. "Just think what damage he *could* have done." It's a constant refrain that confuses me. Why would I want to think about that?

The yellow wall phone rings, and Melissa grabs it with her free hand—she's holding a wooden spoon with the other, trying to scrape a layer of oatmeal off the side of the saucepan.

"Yes," she says patiently into the phone. The oatmeal tastes like paste. I appreciate Melissa's efforts to be more motherly, but her cooking skills suck. She looks over from the phone and smiles at me. She points at my spoon. *Good, huh?* her eyes say. She's so proud of herself that I take an enormous bite to give her an extra thrill. She probably needs it. This week has been hard on her too.

Melissa's used to being immersed in her research, not making pasty oatmeal and worrying about me. She lets the spoon clatter in the sink and tries to put on a faded corduroy jacket while she's holding the phone with her shoulder. A fake poppy sticking from the buttonhole pokes her in the eye. She is one of those rare people who can pull off hippie chic. On her, a vintage T-shirt with her ugly flowery skirt looks secondhand and classy at the same time. I've definitely borrowed her style sensibility, but I never look half as good as she does. Plus, she looks a tiny bit like Julia Roberts, only Melissa never wears makeup and she's short—a lot shorter than I am. Still, she has that same Julia Roberts chestnut-brown hair and mile-wide smile. She's also the smartest person I've ever met. She graduated from high school when she was sixteen, had two Master's degrees before she was twenty-one, and was the youngest person to ever get a PhD from MIT. I've often thought that if I had somebody else for a parent—say, some other brilliant scientist who also happens to be morbidly obese or plagued by an unfortunate skin rash—I'd be a lot better adjusted.

She's still muttering, "Uh-huh, uh-huh, uh-huh," in the receiver with no inflection, but now she stretches the long cord to the living room and her voice gets lower. I can't hear her at all anymore, which, of course, intrigues me. Melissa usually isn't so secretive—in fact, she's the kind of person who has no filter. I cringe just thinking about the time she told the Walgreens cashier that I had "begun menstruating" while she waved a box of pads in front of his nose.

"Call me back in a minute," I hear her say in a normal volume. She clunks the heavy phone—a remnant from the previous owners—back on the wall. "You sure you don't want me to walk with you?" she asks.

17

"I'm pretty sure that I'm capable of making it to school by myself."

"Well…" she says skeptically, but she's already thinking about other things, I can tell. She grabs a bruised pear from the counter. "I'm going to take a few calls from my office, okay?" I know she means the space she's converted out in the garage, not her office at Quiet State College. She hardly bothers to go there—she hasn't even removed the former occupant's nameplate from the door. For all who pass by, Melissa is Dr. R. K. Phillip Rathbine. (R. K. is, apparently, in a nursing home now and hasn't the slightest idea who he is. Melissa was his mid-semester replacement.) "You know where I'll be," she says, heading for the side door.

The first thing Melissa did when we moved into this house was set up her office. It's what she does every time we move, only this time, she got the bright idea that the garage would be a good place to *spread out* and *get some privacy*, like I've ever shown the least bit of interest in whatever boring scientific thing she does out there.

"Who was on the phone?" I ask, eyeing the Lucky Charms. Once she leaves, I can dump the sodden clump of oats.

"Nobody," she says. Then she adds, "It was just the school."

"What do they want?"

"They have questions."

"For me? Because I've already told everything I know." I sigh loudly. I've been through the story a zillion times. At least.

"For me," Melissa says. "They have questions for me."

"Why you? What are they asking you?" Melissa's not a grief counselor, like that frizzy-haired creature. She's a neuroscientist with subspecialties in computer science and genetics—stuff that requires zero people skills. Before we moved to Quiet, she worked at Utopia Laboratories in Saint Paul, Minnesota, developing some boring computer program that models brains. "Why would the school want to talk to you?"

"No reason," she says, and I glance at her with suspicion. Melissa couldn't be deceptive if her life depended on it.

"What's going on?" I ask her.

She adjusts her fake poppy. "Nothing. Let me worry about it." Then she practically runs out the door.

Worry? What's she worried about?

The phone rings again, and I let it go for three loud rings. Melissa will pick up the extension in the garage. On the third ring, I get annoyed. Why can't we use cell phones like normal people? Melissa seems to think *old-fashioned* means *morally superior*. I push my chair back and grab the stupid phone. But before I can say hello, I realize that Melissa has already picked it up. Instead of hanging up my end, though, I listen, mostly because I hear my name: "Daphne doesn't know about any of this," Melissa is saying.

The person on the other end talks quietly, with phlegm stuck in every word. I recognize the voice immediately: Mrs. Temple, the principal at QH. I met her the day Melissa registered me for school, just a week before the shooting. Mrs. Temple had wanted me to skip to my senior year, because I was *so far ahead of my*

19

classmates, but Melissa insisted that I needed to remain a junior for my *social development*—this coming from someone who would suggest to total strangers that they *might consider investing in a treadmill to combat corpulence.*

"We are going to have to announce these results. Publicly. We have no choice," Temple is saying. "I thought you should know."

"Give it some time," Melissa says, a faint hint of pleading in her voice.

"Please note that I'm not asking for your permission. I'm aware that this is no longer your project; your company made that quite clear. I'm simply being courteous by telling you what's going to happen. Whether you like it or not, I will be making some changes at Quiet High. I simply must do so for the safety of everyone here, including your own daughter."

I hang up the phone after Melissa does.

I get a weird feeling—a feeling I haven't had since I heard the first shots fired that day. What is going on here?

CHAPTER 4

PROFILE is the name of a computer program so revolutionary that you won't believe it until you see it. It will change the way we think, the way we live. And that's a promise we can keep.

—Utopia Laboratories marketing copy

One day, scientists will be able to predict everything about every individual. We'll know what an individual is going to do before she even thinks of it herself! It'll be a new world where everything is predicted before it ever happens!

—Dr. Melissa Wright, quoted in *Minneapolis-St.Paul Magazine*

HI," THE ONE WITH THE CURLY HAIR SAYS. SHE STICKS HER hand out. "Desdemona, but everyone calls me Dizzy, because I kind of am. It's really supposed to be Desi, because, you know—short for Desdemona. But Dizzy fits. Don't you think?" She smiles and wavers back and forth, like she's about to fall over. Her curly hair is in neat ringlets held back by a thick, black leather headband, like a girl whose mother did her hair for picture day. Only sexy. The others follow suit, sticking out their hands toward me.

We are back in chemistry class, although Mrs. McClain is out indefinitely, because her *nerves are frayed*, and we're also in a new classroom, a meeting room in the library, formerly used for school board meetings. Crammed around a tiny, rectangular metal table, I feel like a sardine. And it isn't helping that Dizzy and her brood of followers are crowded around me, fighting to introduce themselves. It seems that being *the girl from the cupboard* has made me a kind of celebrity.

"Let me introduce you," Dizzy says, slapping her hand against the table. The substitute teacher is wandering around the room, trying to find a dry-erase marker. Nobody is paying any attention to her pleas for help. "This is Brooklyn Bass." I look at the tiny little girl called Brooklyn. She is one of those pinch-faced girls who probably irons her socks and alphabetizes her panties by color. "Brooklyn," Dizzy tells me, "is the star pitcher on the girls' softball team. And," she adds proudly, "she's a professional pageant girl."

"Oh," I say to Brooklyn.

"I'm Miss Calf Fry," Brooklyn reports.

I obviously look confused.

"Calf fry is an Oklahoma delicacy: deep-fried bull testicles," Dizzy explains.

"Oh, how nice," I say, making a face.

I try not stare at Brooklyn's sparkling tiara, but I obviously fail, because she reaches up to her head and says, "It's just for show," in case I was under the impression that she was the reigning queen of the library.

"Shhhh!" the substitute teacher says, trying to get us all to shut up. Dizzy just talks louder. "And this is Lexus Flores." Lexus waves and scoots her skinny butt into the tiny space next to me in my chair. "Hey, girl," she says.

"We've met," I say, thinking about that first day of school.

"Lexus has a golden retriever, loves the color purple, and just got a brand-new car for her birthday—a Lexus, of course!"

"How wonderful for you," I say without meaning it. It seems clear that Dizzy is going to continue with this party chatter until she's properly introduced each girl at the table. I count five more besides Brooklyn, Lexus, and the current girl she is introducing, a ditzy, giggling thing named Cuteny.

"You know, I really have some things to do," I say suddenly, interrupting Cuteny's introduction. "It was nice to meet all of you," I lie. I scoot my chair back, grab my coat and my backpack—we still don't have lockers until the new paint dries—and walk toward the door. The sub doesn't even notice. The girls watch me leave.

How can these girls act like what happened that day was no big deal? Sure, everybody is talking about it, but it's like something that happened to other people, not to us. Nobody says *his* name. He's just *the shooter* or *that psycho*, or sometimes, just *him*. That part is fine with me, because I don't think he deserves a name. But I can't just forget about what happened. How is it that they can?

A safe distance outside the classroom, I flop into a chair between two racks of paperbacks. Surprisingly, it doesn't take long before I feel myself drifting off, sleep coming faster than it has in days, a welcome relief. Curled up with my red raincoat as a blanket and my backpack as a pillow, I kick my plaid Rocket Dog shoes to the floor and use the small table in front of me as a footstool. The chair is old and squishy, broken in by hundreds of lazy students before me—a chair meant for napping. But the library itself feels like whoever designed it wanted to ward off any restful thoughts or happiness. Everything is gray—including the librarian's face. The high shelves are loaded at the tops and bottoms, with the middles mostly bare, as if someone wants students to have to really stretch or crouch for books.

I jump when I feel my backpack moving under my head. My coat falls to my feet. "Hey!" I exclaim loudly, sitting up and stomping my bare feet on the ground. "What's going on?" The librarian sends me a warning shush.

"It's okay," a gentle voice behind me says. I twist around. Standing there is a girl with blond, matted hair that she's braided into small pieces and haphazardly arranged on her head with tiny, hot pink butterfly clips. Her face is pale, and her eyes are kind of sunken, the way eyes are on people who are too skinny with their bodies shriveling away. Her nose seems to be the only thing that sticks out of her form. She may be the saddest-looking human being I've seen in recent memory.

"Sorry," she says. "I didn't mean to wake you. I was just going to put this under your head." She holds up a folded sweatshirt.

"Why?" I ask.

"I like to hang out here."

What? How was that an answer to my question? Who is this

girl? Does she patrol the library looking for people who need pillows? She smiles wanly at me as she throws the sweatshirt over my shoulder, tosses my backpack to the floor, and then throws her own bag on top of it. She comes around the side of my chair, shoving my legs out of the way with her own, and flops on the chair next to me. I pull the sweatshirt off my shoulder and hand it back to her. "Thanks," I say, "but I'm just leaving."

"Mind if I hang out with you?"

I do mind, but I don't know how to tell her without being totally rude, so I just don't answer. I stifle a yawn and taste that horrible taste you only get when you've been napping. I snap my mouth shut and wish that I had a Tic Tac. I gather my coat and my backpack and scout out another empty chair, but the girl leans across me and pulls a thick book from the shelf nearest me. I pause and strain to see the title. I can't help myself. If someone else is reading a book, I need to know what it is. *Outlander*, the cover says.

The girl spots me peering over at her, and she lowers the book. "A romance novel about time travel," she says. "It's pretty predictable, and the sex scenes are boring, but I like the idea of disappearing and ending up in some other time, far away from here. Did you know that in the world of time travel, you can never stop what's going to happen? The universe is a cruel master." She says this very seriously. "In case you were wondering," she adds in a tone that suggests I've been wondering for ages, "I leave the book on the shelf and read some of it every day. Did you know that in over a year, nobody has checked it out?" She turns back to the book before I can respond, so I assume she's done talking. She drums her fingers militantly on the wooden arm of her chair.

"Well, enjoy your book," I tell her, stepping over her feet, which are covered by strange blue and yellow polka-dotted peep-toe heels.

"Sorry," she says, grabbing my arm. "Stay. I didn't mean to bother you." She looks so pitiful that I hesitate. She sees the opportunity. "Come on. What else do you have to do? I know you're ditching class." We both look toward the classroom. I lower myself back in my chair. "I won't say a word," she promises. "You go back to sleep."

Convinced that I'll never be able to sleep, even though my lids are heavy, I end up drifting back into that half-asleep state where the idea of getting up seems like more work than I could ever muster. Eventually, my eyelids flutter open, and I find the girl standing with her little round nose about three inches from my face. I jump. "What are you doing?" I exclaim, scrambling in my chair.

"Post-traumatic stress," she says definitively. "You've got it."

"What are you talking about?" I say loudly. The gray librarian looks up from her post at her desk and calls—far louder than I did—"Second warning, Missy. Keep it quiet."

"What are you talking about?" I whisper.

"Post-traumatic stress," she whispers back, leaning in closer to look at my eyes. I swat her away, catching one of her butterfly clips in the palm of my hand. "You are jumpy," she says, "because of the shooting."

"Maybe," I say sarcastically, "I'm jumpy because you are in my face."

She nods as if to say, *Good point*. "Did you know him?" she asks after a second.

The odd thing is that I don't have to ask. I know immediately that she means the shooter. "No," I say, realizing that for just a second, I hadn't thought about him. "I didn't even see him," I tell her now. I don't have any idea what he even looked like. I haven't even seen a picture of him. And I never will. I don't want to know. Giving him a face is more generous than I feel like being. I prefer to think of him as a blurred-out entity, like a mob witness.

She nods. "Lucky."

"How about you?"

"I was outside. Cut class for a cigarette. I missed the whole thing."

"Must be karma," I say.

"Yeah," she replies bitterly and tugs at a frizzy piece of hair, pursing her shiny pink lips. "You're Daphne Wright, right?"

"How did you know?"

"I'm psychic," she says, tossing the book on the table in front of us. A little orange construction-paper bookmark falls out.

For a split-second, I'm charmed by her. "Oh, really? What am I thinking right now?" I smile tentatively, half-friendly, half-making fun of her.

"Not that kind of psychic, silly."

"I didn't realize there were different kinds of psychics."

The girl rolls her eyes. "I can tell you everything about you."

"I already know everything about me."

We are at an impasse. Do I like her, or do I want her to suddenly come down with a case of laryngitis? It's always a toss-up with me. Melissa says I'm a misanthrope in training. The girl's eyes move to the open double doors of the library room from where I've just escaped. The noise is louder, the sub looks even more harried. She'll never make it through the day.

"How do you know my name?" I repeat.

She points at the freshly printed schedule clipped to the top of my notebook that is sticking out of my backpack. I've been carrying it around since the first day. *Daphne Wright*, it proclaims. "Oh," I say.

The girl slinks down in her chair so low that she looks like a puddle of goo melting. Her earrings—hideous dangly things that look like blue peacock feathers—move violently as she whips her head, peering one way and then the other.

"What?" I ask, growing nervous. *Is he back? How could that be?*

She's staring at Dizzy and her friends. They've come out of the classroom and are standing a few feet from the paperbacks, just out of our earshot.

"Them?" I ask. "I just had the pleasure of meeting them. Mean girls, huh?" I've already written them off. I've been to enough schools to spot these kind of girls a mile away. It's best to be polite but distant. Never get too close, or they'll figure out how to torture you.

Dizzy sees me in the chair and waves. She gives some sort of hand signal to the others, and they all began walking toward us. *Great*, I think.

"Shit," the butterfly girl says as she sits up quickly. "I'm outta here." She grabs her bag and makes a run for it, a skinny flash scampering out the library doors.

"Nice to meet you," I call in spite of these facts: (1) the librarian is practically apoplectic over the noise we are making; (2) we technically didn't meet; and (3) I'm not sure it was nice meeting her at all. She's definitely weird, like the trying-too-hard weird type.

Dizzy leads her troops over. "Hi," she says kindly. "You're obviously new here, so we don't expect you to know this, but you really should avoid talking to people like her." She points in the direction that the butterfly girl scurried off.

"At least, don't do it in public," Brooklyn amends.

Dizzy elbows Brooklyn in the shoulder. "Shut it, Brook. You're going to make her think we're horrible bitches. What she's saying," Dizzy continues with a smile, "is that certain people at Quiet High are better left alone. It's not worth the hit you're going to take to your rep, you know?"

I don't smile back. "Well, thanks for the information regarding my rep," I say coldly, "but I'll probably take my chances." I'm not a big fan of being told what to do.

Lexus flips her shiny hair out of her eyes. The hair flip is obviously her signature move. "January is a total nonentity at QH. She's *persona au gratin*."

"I think you mean *persona non grata*," I correct.

"Whatev. Point is, I'm pretty sure you don't want to associate with someone like her. Not after what happened."

I say nothing, because I know she wants me to ask.

"The shooter," Brooklyn tells me. "Don't you know who that was?"

"Do you want to know who you were talking to just now?" Dizzy asks gently. "January. January Morrison. Sound familiar?"

"It was her brother who did it," Lexus supplies. "Genetics," she says, shaking her head, as if she has spent much time wrestling with the topic. "You never know what people are going to do."

"And if he was such a psycho, January will be too. These things run in the family, you know," Brooklyn ends with a quick pageant smile, like she's just told me that she wishes for world peace.

I don't know what to say.

"Come on, Brook," Dizzy says quickly. "She's new here. Let's give her a chance to get acquainted." She flops herself down beside me just as I stand up. "So," she says, "the only question now is who *you're* going to be. One of us? Or one of them? We're going to need to see your PROFILE score," she laughs then.

"My what?"

"PROFILE," she says. "You know...PROFILE."

"Not helpful," I tell her.

"Where did you come from? Another planet? How can you not know what PROFILE is? Can you believe it?" she asks the others. They shake their heads solemnly.

"Obviously, I don't know what it is," I say with exasperation. "Maybe you can tell me."

30

"You're serious," Dizzy says, her eyes wide.

"Yes, of course I'm serious. Why wouldn't I be? What are you talking about?"

"What do you think I'm talking about?"

"Oh, forget it," I tell her, planning to go back to the classroom. Maybe the sub will have figured out what she's doing by now.

"Wait," Dizzy hisses. "I'll tell you." I turn around and she looks conspiratorially around us, as if she's going to leak top-secret information. "You swear to God you really don't know what PROFILE is?"

"Either tell me or don't, but stop asking me that," I say.

She breathes heavily through her nostrils. "Well," she says to Lexus and Brooklyn, "I guess these tests are as secret as they promised." She turns back to me, plainly dying to dump the secret. "PROFILE will tell you everything you need to know about anyone. PROFILE is what is going to save us all, what is going to keep us from ever having to go through what happened last week again. We've all been tested—we're a test school." She says this proudly. "PROFILE," she continues, her voice now growing louder and stronger, like a televangelist gearing up for the hard sell, "can tell us who we're going to be." She looks at me triumphantly, as if waiting for my jaw to drop, my head to spin, my legs to give out. None of that happens, because I turn on my heels and walk out, the same way January did moments ago.

I need to talk to Melissa.

CHAPTER 5

Utopia Laboratories is striving to make your life better, one future at a time.

—Cover of a brochure explaining Utopia's mission
mailed to every student at Quiet High

WHOA," HE SAYS. "WHAT'S THE RUSH?

I haven't talked to Jesse since the day of the shooting. Seeing him right here, right now, is weird and unsettling—like running into teachers outside of school, irrefutable proof that they exist off of school grounds.

Or maybe it's like seeing deer graze in the parking lot of the Quiet Walmart, something that absolutely floored me the first time I saw it. Deer and Walmart seem like two things that exist in different planes of reality. Jesse exists in that cramped closet, not here in the hallway, not right next to the giant cross that the Warriors of the Lord club erected to "remember our humanity."

"Hey," I say breezily, not quite friendly. I feel uncomfortable with him, like I revealed too much of myself that day. "I'm okay," I say, realizing too late that he didn't ask me how I am. I tug on the end of my hair and stare blankly over his shoulder, pretending I didn't just say that.

He smiles. "Well, that's good to hear."

I half-smile, a trick I do easily and often: I move one side of my mouth into a garish grin while keeping the other half perfectly straight. Melissa tells me I look like a crazed clown when I do it. It's my way of dismissing people without having to say so. "Well, see you," I say, moving toward the front double doors.

"Where are you going? Don't you have geometry?"

"Are you stalking me? Because stalking is hardly funny." It's a line I've heard Melissa use before. When tongue-tied, I quote the weirdest, most socially inept person I know. That's just great.

The obnoxious, bleating bell signals the end of the period. We ignore it.

"Actually," he says, "we're in the same class."

"Oh," I say, slightly embarrassed. I shake my head and stick my pink beret, a remnant from Saint Paul, over my unruly hair. We stand there staring at each other, even though people are pushing around us, trying to get past. They are like aisle salmon, pushing the wrong way against the crowd. The silence gives me time to stare, to really take him in for the first time. I'm surprised when my brain processes him as a cross between Angel on *Buffy the Vampire Slayer* and a Greek god: dark-haired, heavy lashes, and a perpetually creased forehead. Probably full of himself, I think. The kind of guy who doesn't have to bother with a decent personality. Probably.

Yet there's something soft in his eyes, in the way he bites his lower lip while he's thinking, that makes me think he is kind. Fundamentally kind. An image of his face, shadowy and vague in the supply closet, flashes in front of me. I think of the way he led me to the cupboard, the way he insisted I stay inside while he faced the shooter. "Well," I say abruptly, "I'm actually cutting class today. I'm going home."

"Are you sick?" he asks with a hint of worry.

"I just want to…" For one ill-considered second, I contemplate telling him the truth. *You see, there were these bitchy girls in the library, and they were talking about this thing called PROFILE, which got me thinking about something. Melissa—my mom—created that computer program. She wrote PROFILE's program. But when I asked her about it, the day we left Saint Paul, in fact, she denied it. So what's up with that?* Instead, I take the easy way out: "I'm just going home."

"You walked here this morning."

What the hell? Is this guy recording my every move?

"I saw you. I drove past you on my way in," he says sheepishly. "Let me drive you home." It's raining. He points toward the window, where the gray sky has lowered itself like a big parachute. "If you're sick, you shouldn't go out in the rain."

"I'll be fine," I tell him. "I just really need to get out of here." I flip up the hood of my red raincoat, a vintage find that makes me want it to rain indefinitely, just so I can wear the thigh-length shiny coat with the belt knotted tightly at my waist. I slip on my sunglasses, just because I don't feel like looking into those soft eyes of his anymore.

"Hey," he calls after I walk away. I stop and turn just a few feet from him. "I'm glad you…" He trails off. "I'm glad you're okay."

"Me too." I look over the tops of my sunglasses. "Me too," I repeat.

◼◼◼

I walk home, taking every shortcut I can find, cutting through the Walmart parking lot, the busiest place in Quiet at any given time. When it starts to really pour, I speed up to a jog on the shoulder of McElroy Street, a busy road with two lanes and an almost nonexistent shoulder, until I find a side street that goes through to the Quiet State College campus. From there, I'm just a block or so from home.

Panting for breath, I slow to a walk as I maneuver precariously on the edge of a ditch, dodging sodden litter and mud-filled potholes. The whole town of Quiet is brown and ugly—murky and saturated now. Everyone warns me that it will turn scorching and gritty when summer arrives. Great. Something to look forward to.

Right now, Quiet looks like it's just taken a beating by a big, mean bully. Evidence of the last tornado, which hit over three years ago, is everywhere, especially on the outskirts of town, where piles of broken fence and other debris make up a giant garbage heap. If you drive out of town a ways, which I did recently when I was daydreaming about what it would be like to just leave this place, there are rolling hills and acres of farmland. Everyone says it's beautiful in the summer. Green Country, they call it. But right now, it just looks like a vast expanse of nothing—a prison with no walls.

36

Once I get to the house, my hair is soaking wet, but my red raincoat has kept at least part of me dry. Regardless, I change into faded jeans and a dry T-shirt—a washed-out, threadbare thing that I've had forever. I wrap my hair in a worn bath towel and peer out the front window to see if Melissa's car is parked in its usual spot, half on the curb directly in front of the house. It's not.

It's almost silent in the house, save for the sound of rain pounding against the roof. I try to remember Melissa's teaching schedule. In the kitchen, I find the bright orange index card attached to the fridge with a Papa John's magnet. She wrote out her schedule, supposedly so that I will always know where she is. Personally, I think it's the only way that *she* can remember where she's supposed to be. I scan the card. She doesn't have class on Mondays. Where is she? The gym? Recycling club? A save-the-feral-cats meeting? In the Monday column on the orange card, she's simply written *Intellectual Development*. I roll my eyes. That's *so* Melissa.

Digging through my backpack, I find my soggy class schedule. On the bottom is the number of the school office. I pick up the scruffy yellow phone and dial the number using the old rotary dial. When the secretary answers, I use my Melissa voice, a slightly higher pitch than my own with a hard edge on the vowels, and explain, "Daphne is ill and won't be returning for the day."

"Oh," the secretary says sympathetically, "we do hope she's not feeling too badly." I contemplate correcting her incorrect use of an adverb, as Melissa undoubtedly would, but end up simply saying thank you and hanging up the receiver.

I flop on the scratchy plaid couch, a junk store find, and stare at the brown water mark just to the right of the light fixture. I flip on the old radio Melissa keeps on the end table—it's already tuned to National Public Radio. I'm a total junkie. There's something soothing about all that news delivered in intellectual monotones, sort of like Melissa reading me a bedtime story. I'm probably the only sixteen-year-old on the planet who has a favorite NPR foreign correspondent.

I let the dull drone of the radio take over while I think about PROFILE, the word rolling through my brain like ocean waves. *PROFILE.*

The day we left Saint Paul was so cold it *couldn't* snow, but you could tell the snow was out there. Waiting. On our second day on the road, while Melissa was checking out of our *quaint* motel room—the kind of place that made the Bates Motel seem all right—I rummaged through the trunk of the Accord and found Melissa's locked, fireproof box, one of the few things we took with us. Melissa had everything else shipped directly to our new house in Quiet.

Melissa is a total space case and would lose her eyeballs if they weren't tight in their sockets, so I had no trouble finding the key—taped to the box itself. A quick turn, a swift riffle of papers, and there it was: The letter from Utopia, the one that arrived in the mail three days before we left. The one that I pulled from the mailbox myself and handed to her with my very own hands. And it was I who watched her open the letter, read it, and then put her hand on the side of her head. "Well, screw you too!" she said to the letter. "Just try running PROFILE without me!" And that was it. The next thing I knew, we were in the Accord, heading down tornado alley. I stuffed the letter in my coat pocket and read it in a smelly rest stop bathroom someplace between Iowa and Kansas.

I roll off the couch now and go to the coat closet by the front door. When I open the door, books and papers, winter scarves, a Frisbee, a single snow boot, and various other detritus falls at my feet. Melissa is the most unorganized person I know. All of this stuff arrived in boxes in the mail. Melissa opened each box and dumped the contents into whatever space she could find. "We'll worry about it later," she'd said dismissively. I dig through the junk. At the bottom of the pile is my Columbia ski jacket, the coat I wore when we left Saint Paul. I haven't worn it since the day we arrived. Stuffed in the pocket is the letter, exactly where I put it that day. It's folded into a tiny square and curled up at the edges. I unwrap it carefully and read it again.

Dear Dr. Wright,

We have reviewed your request, and it is with regret that we report we will be unable to halt upcoming research trials any longer. Regular PROFILE testing will resume at the designated test location. We ask for your cooperation during the testing process. While there is no question that you are architect of this program, you cannot halt progress simply because you suddenly feel "ethically reluctant." You may be the "mother" of PROFILE, as you say, but your "child" is now ours.

Any further disturbance or hindrance of PROFILE testing will result in your immediate termination. Consider this a first warning.

Best wishes,

Gordon Davidson

CEO of Utopia Laboratories

I'd asked her about it later, in a roundabout way, after we'd settled in the house in Quiet, casually leaving out the part about stealing her personal mail. Instead, I posed a direct question: "Did you get fired at Utopia?"

"Of course not," she'd said—no twitching, no difficulty meeting my eyes, no catch in her voice.

"What were you working on at Utopia? What was your big brainchild?" I'd asked after that, pretending to be conversational, fooling no one.

That's when she'd looked a little alarmed, a tiny bit rattled. The last time I'd seen Melissa like that was when I was in the sixth grade and I told her I might be a Republican.

"Nothing," she'd said. "Nothing that's any of your concern." Her voice was cold, even a little bit mean. Very unlike Melissa.

I didn't ask about it again.

◼◼◼

"I'm home!" Melissa yells.

I wake up with a start, my face smashed against the side of the brown couch, NPR droning in the background. I stretch my legs and feel a charley horse gallop up my calf. "Ohhhhh," I moan, limping pitifully to the kitchen, where Melissa is pushing the door shut with her foot, chattering loudly.

"I went to a lecture on campus and got stuck at a pointless faculty reception afterward. I ended up having to listen to a history professor rhapsodize about his research on medieval cooking pots. Ugh." She flops across a kitchen chair and then looks at me suspiciously. "Wait, what are you doing here?" She looks at her watch. "It's Monday, isn't it? Why aren't you in school? Are you sick?"

"Something like that," I say. I use both hands to smooth my messy hair, which I can tell has dried in an odd-shaped horn on the side while I was sleeping.

Melissa sticks her head in the fridge. "The lecture was *so* awful," she tells the empty egg trays. "An entire forty-five minute speech on thirteenth-century cookery without a single reference to Ibn Razin at-Tugibi." She shakes her head in disgust. "I swear, some people don't even bother with primary research anymore. It's sad, really."

I make a face at her back. She can be so pretentious sometimes. I know better than to just come out and ask her about PROFILE. When Melissa doesn't want to talk, she doesn't talk.

"Are you hungry?" she asks me now. She's been worried about what I eat (or don't eat) lately—ever since the shooting, I just haven't been interested in food. Eating seems too ordinary, something we did before the incident. *B.I.* Now it just doesn't seem important. "Eat this." Melissa tosses a pear at me that I catch and then drop on the avocado-green kitchen linoleum. I pick it up and run my finger over the bruised skin.

"I need to work," she tells me. "I'll be in the garage." Only

Melissa would fail to ask me what I'm doing home in the middle of the day.

"What exactly are you doing out there?" It's a question designed to get her talking, to lead into my larger question: What is PROFILE?

"Nothing big."

"Hey," I say, feigning that I've just thought of it, "tell me something. Why'd we really leave Saint Paul?"

It's obvious that it has something to do with that letter, something to do with PROFILE, but she doesn't take the bait. She yanks open the door and sighs louder than she needs to. "Things happened. I promise, Daph, if it was something you needed to know, I would tell you. Right now, I just need a little bit of time to sort things out."

"Does this have something to do with your work? Maybe something to do with—what's it called?—PROFILE?" I play dumb, like I'm pulling the name out of the far recesses of my brain.

"What are you talking about?" she says innocently, her eyes wide and guiltless. I study her carefully. Usually when she lies— like when she told me that Grandpa was going to be okay, even when he was dying of cancer—she rubs her palms together, making a loud swooshing noise. Her hands are on her hips now, planted firmly.

"PROFILE?" I repeat, quietly this time.

"Never heard of it," she says, then smiles and walks out the door. Just like she wasn't lying through her perfect white teeth.

CHAPTER 6

I've always thought of Daphne and me as a team—partners. But I've also made a practice of separating my work from my relationship with her. There are some things she just doesn't need to know. I don't want her to look at everyone around her and think she knows who's inherently "good" and who's inherently "bad." I just want her to see people. And I never want her to look in the mirror and think that who she is has already been determined. That's why I didn't tell her about PROFILE. I don't want her anywhere near that stuff.

—Dr. Melissa Wright, from her research journal

LEAVE FOR SCHOOL SUPER-EARLY, BARELY AFTER SEVEN. MELISSA is sound asleep in her bedroom, which I tiptoe past. I didn't hear her come in from the garage last night. In fact, after our conversation yesterday, I didn't see her for the rest of the day, not even for dinner. I stewed in my room, finally falling asleep after midnight.

The sun is just rising as I walk toward school dressed in one of my favorite spring outfits: baggy white capris and a soft, yellow, patterned, three-quarter-length-sleeved shirt with a vintage knitted brown cardigan. I pull my hair back in an antique hair clip, a yellow dragonfly set in gaudy rhinestones.

When I slam my freshly painted and barely dry locker shut, with my chemistry books tucked under my arm and my laptop bag strung across my shoulder, Jesse is standing there.

"You're early," he says.

"So are you."

"Tennis practice." He holds up a racquet. "Walk with me." He grabs my laptop before I can protest and throws the bag over his shoulder. I'd planned to go to the library before chem lab to think and surf the Internet in privacy, away from Melissa.

We walk toward the new gym, where there are two indoor tennis courts—practice courts for when it's too dark or cold or wet to play outside. The gym is part of New QH, a large addition that opened just this past year that everyone is thrilled about. It's gorgeous, largely because it looks nothing like a school—the blond wood, the thick carpeting, and the abstract murals on the walls make it feel like some kind of futuristic doctor's office. The whole contemporary feel takes me back to the wide hallway that ran past Melissa's corner office at Utopia. I can almost hear the elevator music. The air here in New QH isn't yet filled with the smell of depression—chalk dust, sweat, and red Oklahoma dirt, which is what I smell every time I walk in the front doors of Old QH.

We stand at the edge of the gym, inside of which the gym teacher, Mr. A., is yelling military commands at whoever is unlucky enough to be in there with him. "About face!" he yells, his voice more dictator than public educator.

"I keep thinking about that day," I tell Jesse. It pops out of my mouth before I realize what I'm saying. When he doesn't respond,

I keep going. "I close my eyes, and that's what I see." I slide down to the floor and sit with my back against the cold brick wall, my feet stretched in front of me and my chemistry books resting by my side. I wiggle my blue toenails in my sandals. Jesse sets my laptop messenger bag beside me and then slides down to the floor too. He's wearing QH shorts—purple nylon things with a picture of an armadillo on the lower part of the right leg. His legs are thick and tan, like he's been at the beach for a week.

"I think about it too," he says. "You have nightmares?"

"Do you?"

He nods. "Only when I go to sleep. But I'm not sleeping much."

I bend over and adjust the strap of one woven sandal, kick the wedge heel against the floor. "I can't dream," I say. "I sleep like I'm dead. Even when I'm awake, I feel nothing—less than nothing. I just feel like, *What's the point*, you know? What's the point of anything if you're just going to end up in a closet waiting for some psycho to kill you?" As soon as I say the words, they are true, even though I haven't thought about any of this before. Saying it makes me feel better. Much better, actually.

"I know," he says, tapping his racquet against the carpeted floor.

Mr. A.'s voice floats out to us. "Fall in!" it says.

Jesse looks at the mural across from us. I keep talking, because he's listening. "So there's this journalist who spent years embedded with soldiers, reporting on the war he was in. Nearly every day, there were explosions and bullets flying and land mines. Death and mayhem everywhere. And when people weren't dying, they were waiting for it to happen. When he got back to the United

States, to his normal life, he couldn't live—not the way he did before the war. The stakes were too low. How can you ever sit through a movie or take a nap or play tennis"—I point at the racquet—"after something that big? Nothing matters anymore." Is it too dramatic to say this? I pull my legs up to my chest. "Do you feel like that?"

He breathes in heavily, lets the air out slowly. I look at him, his hair falling over his eyebrows. "No," he says definitively. "I want to live. I don't want this to be my defining moment." He touches my thigh briefly, accidentally, and when I jump, he moves his hand quickly to my laptop bag.

"Thanks," I tell him after a while.

"You would've done the same thing. I just did what I had to do when he showed up at the door."

"I didn't mean that," I clarify, stretching my legs out again, turning my eyes from him. "I mean for this. For listening."

He nods. We sit quietly for a long time, listening to Mr. A. yell his dumb commands. Eventually, we can hear tennis balls thwapping against the court—tennis practice has officially started.

Jesse finally says, "You know, it's better this way, actually. We won't ever have to *not* know. We'll never be surprised like that again."

"What do you mean?" I turn my head. "What do you mean, we'll never be surprised again?"

When Jesse moves suddenly, I assume he's getting up to go play tennis. But he's not. He grabs my cute, brown and pink flowered messenger bag and pulls out my computer. He flips the thing on without even asking. "What are you doing?" I ask.

"I want to show you something." He moves the bag to his right side, scooting closer to me. He sets the laptop on one of my legs and one of his. His warm thigh rubs against mine. I debate scooting away an inch, but I don't. We both stare at the screen while the computer boots and finds a wireless connection. "You don't know about PROFILE, do you?" he asks.

"How did you know that?"

"You're the only person at QH who doesn't talk about it nonstop. Also," he adds self-consciously, "Dizzy told everyone."

When the browser appears, Jesse types *PROFILE* into the Google search bar. He types perfectly, his index fingers expertly hovering over the *F* and *J* keys. I lean closer to the screen. Two and a half million hits: instructions for getting financial aid; a tool for "pimping" my MySpace profile; a blog about profile racing; an invitation to join a professional network; companies; and a Wikipedia definition that appears like magic. Jesse clicks on it and then hands the computer to me.

PROFILE (an *acronym* for Predictive Readout of Foreseen and Illustrative Life Effects) is a software application designed by scientists at *Utopia Laboratories* in order to identify the likelihood of criminal and *antisocial behavior* in tested subjects.

PROFILE synthesizes the results of various established tests, including *personality inventories*, *IQ tests*, and *psychopathological exams*. PROFILE compiles those results and compares them with detailed analyses of *cognitive and neurocognitive systems* of *the brain*.

PROFILE then examines the results of this information using a complex mathematical formula that yields a *predictive score*. That score indicates how likely an individual is to commit a crime, engage in addictive behaviors, and/or behave in socially problematic ways in the future.

Testing of subjects must occur between the ages of approximately fourteen and fifteen. This is the optimum age when enough neuropsychological data exist, but the subject hasn't been overly impacted by his or her environment and…

I stop reading to give myself a second to think. "So PROFILE predicts people's future behaviors? How is that possible?"

"Welcome to twenty-first-century science. No more waiting and wondering," Jesse says. "We know. We can predict exactly who is fated for a life of crime, a life of drugs—everything."

"So how come nobody stopped the shooter?" I ask skeptically, although I already know the answer. I think about that letter from Utopia, about what I overheard when Melissa was on the phone.

"Test results weren't released. Nobody knew—nobody but the researchers, those people from Utopia Laboratories who did the testing here."

"Melissa," I say out loud.

"Melissa?"

"Never mind." I go back to the screen again and click through the rest of the entry. I read some of it out loud. Jesse sits with his hands on his legs, watching me closely.

Approximately three thousand high school students have been PROFILEd thus far at an undisclosed test location. The test results in the first nine rounds of testing were kept strictly confidential. Not even test subjects or their parents were aware of the results.

While PROFILE is still being tested, researchers have made every effort to keep the test and the results as top-secret as possible. Many argue that keeping the results private is a mistake.

"Wow," I say out loud to myself, but the word doesn't seem to do justice to what I am thinking. *The shooter. They knew. Nobody told us.*

And that kid who opened fire at a crowded mall somewhere a couple of years ago—he might've been stopped. All those school shooters could have been stopped—a new one every year, it seemed like. PROFILE could have told everyone before all those bad things happened.

Everything with Melissa made more sense now. She developed PROFILE—it was her baby. And then she backed out, didn't want to do the testing anymore. That's what the letter I stole had said.

Now? That was part of what I still didn't know. What was she doing in the garage? Why did she want to stop the testing? She could've changed things. And she didn't. Why not?

"He could've been stopped." I say it softly. What I really mean is, *Melissa* could've stopped him. She knew. I feel a weird sensation in my stomach.

Betrayal.

"The next one *will* be stopped," Jesse replies. "I promise you."

She's in the garage office.

I jog around the house and slink up the driveway. The stealth is probably unnecessary since Melissa can't see me unless I'm standing right in front of the window at the little side door. I crouch underneath the window and slowly rise to sneak a peek through it. She's sitting at her computer at the edge of the garage, staring into space. The room itself is Spartan: just her desk, an office chair, a safe, a filing cabinet, a small fridge, and a bookcase almost empty of books. I've never, ever gone into the garage before. I've never really been interested before, so I take a deep breath and turn the doorknob. "What the hell is going on?" I demand as soon as I enter.

Melissa jumps and then reaches over to casually close the window on her computer. "What are you doing here? Have you quit school altogether?" she asks lightly. It's meant to be a joke.

I stomp over to her, accidentally kicking the metal trash can in the process. "Damn it," I mutter, my toe smarting.

"Daphne," she says, growing alarmed, "what is it? What's wrong?"

"Why do you always treat me like a baby?" It's not what I intend to say, it's just what comes out of my mouth. It's my bad habit to think after I speak.

She sighs. "Is this about your car?" She's referring to the one I had in Saint Paul, the one she sold before we moved. "I told you that I'm sorry we sold it. I didn't think we needed two cars, what with all that gas guzzling, and the Honda gets better gas mileage, so I just thought—"

"This isn't about the stupid car!" I practically scream at her. "Damn it, Melissa! What aren't you telling me? Why won't you explain to me why we left Saint Paul? What are you working on all of the time out here? Why are people at school—people I hardly know—telling me about PROFILE instead of you?"

Melissa leans over and rests her elbows on her knees. She sighs with resignation. Her eyes are sort of puffy, and I notice for the first time that she looks very tired. "We've been over this—"

"Yes, I know! I've heard it all before!" I pick up a binder sitting on the edge of her desk and hurl it at the wall. Canary yellow sheets of paper fly out and rain down on us. I stand in front of her, my hands on my hips, the first time that I've truly had a tantrum. Not even when I was a child did I act like this. I'm feeling wild, almost scared of myself. "It's what you always say— you'll tell me what I need to know!" I mimic her. "When are you going to start treating me like an adult? You can't keep bad things from me forever. It isn't fair, and I don't think—"

"Daphne!" She interrupts me. "Stop! You're right."

"I am?"

I flop down—somewhat deflated—on the metal folding chair next to her desk. I had intended to have a much longer argument. I was working up to (unfairly) using my fatherless status for a guilt trip.

"You are," she says firmly. "What do you want to know? I'll tell you. I give up. I can't fight with you anymore. You *yelling* at me,

51

telling me what I already know to be true, is worse than having to tell you the truth. You're right. You deserve to know. I've wanted to protect you, especially in light of what happened at school. But maybe I can't always shield you."

"Is that why you lied to me?"

"I didn't lie. I just didn't want to tell you the truth."

Melissa is very literal sometimes. "And you'll tell me now?"

"I don't have much choice, do I? I'm afraid you'll decimate the place." She points at the open binder on the floor. *Decimate* is a bit of an exaggeration.

"How do I know you won't lie to me again, just like you did last night?"

"You don't."

She's so irritating sometimes. I try again. "What does it mean to be predicted?"

"It involves a complex analysis of genes, personality, behavior, and predilections that can identify a person as a future criminal. But I'm guessing you've figured that much out already."

"Who is predicted at QH?"

"I can honestly say that I don't know. I left Utopia before we had the last set of names. And I don't remember any of the early lists. We tested at Quiet High for quite a few years. I never really paid attention to the names."

"So your subjects aren't even people to you?"

"Don't be silly, Daphne. That's not what I said."

"Why Quiet High?"

Melissa leans back in her desk chair, crosses her legs, and

steeples her fingers underneath her chin, like she is my psychiatrist. "We needed a test site. Most schools wouldn't hear of scientists coming in to do psychological profiling. Quiet High jumped at the chance—Utopia offered the school board a lot of money. You know the new addition at QH?" I nod. "Paid for by Utopia. And parents at QH signed permission slips, allowing their kids to be tested without raising a single question. It was a dream situation, actually. And then I did a couple of rounds of testing at Academy, just because we had access there—because of you and all the other kids whose parents worked at Utopia. We wanted to make sure that our results weren't skewed, because they were all obtained in Oklahoma."

"Do you believe in it?"

"Believe in what?" she asks as she scoots back in her rolling chair and plops her feet on her desk, knocking over a cup of coffee. She ignores it and kicks off her "good" shoes—ugly brown Mephisto sandals that she's had forever—onto the floor. She wiggles her toes.

"Do you believe that this program, PROFILE, can predict people's behaviors?"

"Of course!" She seems offended that I would suggest otherwise. "The brain is not as complicated as it might seem, Daph. PROFILE simply allows us to see inside of it. Once we're in there, it's not hard to predict how it's going to work. And from there, we simply take note of what's going to happen."

"What can it tell you?"

"What do you want to know?" she asks, incredulous. "The

criminal predictions are the most useful, but in most cases, we can also identify antisocial and persistent problematic behavior. Cheating, lying, stealing, drug abuse—that kind of thing."

"And when will people who are predicted do the things they are predicted to do?"

Melissa leans over and picks up the empty coffee cup. "We don't know that much yet. With more research, maybe we could tell. Right now, we just know what people are *going* to do, but we don't necessarily know when. We aren't psychics." She laughs, which seems kind of insensitive, given what we are discussing.

I remain serious. "But can't people change? Don't you think that you're influencing people? Like maybe someone wouldn't be all of these awful things, but now he thinks he is, so he just gives in? How can you live with that, Melissa?"

She covers her eyes with her hands and rubs them. "Why do you think I left Utopia?"

"You were fired?"

"Don't be silly. I left by my own accord. I just wasn't sure that we'd fully considered all of these angles. And without me, the research is pretty much at a standstill."

"Am I predicted?" I ask.

She opens her eyes wide and then sits up straight, her feet flat on the floor. "Absolutely not! Did someone tell you that?

"No. Have I been PROFILEd?"

"Yes, from when you were at Academy. Remember all those interviews with the counselors?"

I do. I remember all the dumb questions I had to answer: *Would you rather murder someone or be murdered yourself?* What kind of question is that?

Melissa stands up and puts her shoes back on. "You are not predicted, Daphne. You aren't even at risk for smaller negative behaviors. You are perfect. Just as we've always known…but not everybody is like you. PROFILE helps us see inside minds."

"That sounds wrong. How can a computer program know anything about what a person is like on the inside? I can't believe you, of all people, would be willing to let technology define humanity." I feel triumphant. That last phrase sounds exactly like something Melissa herself would say. "PROFILE is just plain wrong," I say petulantly. "It has to be."

"I don't know," Melissa says. "I'm not sure I know anything anymore."

She sniffles. I hesitate and then pat her on the back. She looks so sad all of a sudden.

I soften a bit. "I know how much your work means to you." I go from being mad at her to feeling sorry for her before I even realize it. Melissa has a way of turning me into an ally, even when I want to run away and never talk to her again. I pat her back gently, annoyed that I feel sympathy for her.

"You should know," she says slowly, "that they will be releasing the predicted lists at Quiet High very soon. I don't think we can avoid that. Not after what happened. I've been talking to your principal. There's nothing I can do to stop these names from becoming public. You'll need to be prepared for what happens."

"What do you think is going to happen?"

She laughs bitterly. "I wish I could predict that. But honestly, Daph, I have no idea."

CHAPTER 7

Releasing the predicted lists will ease a lot of minds. I'll feel better when I know which of my daughter's classmates are capable of barbarity.

—Marianna Bass, mother of Brooklyn Bass

You look fancy," Melissa tells me when I come out of my room. She's in the kitchen making tuna salad. "Want some?" she asks.

"No, I'm going out."

She drops the mayonnaise spoon in the metal bowl. "*My* Daphne? Going *out?* In Quiet? And on a Friday night? This is news. You've never *gone out* here."

"Yes, well, I'm full of surprises."

"Who is he?" Melissa says, picking at the spoon with her fingertips.

"What makes you think there's a *he?*"

She points at my skinny jeans, my brown ankle boots, and my jade-green top, the one with the scoop neck and a lace insert; I've thrown a soft cardigan over it. I top it all off with chunky beads and a silver-studded barrette to hold back my long bangs. "You're dressed to impress."

"Well, you're wrong," I say defensively. "I'm hanging out at the lake with a bunch of people from school."

"Yeah? That doesn't sound like your speed at all."

It's not. In fact, I don't really want to go, but it's what everyone talked about at school all week. I was sort of invited as an honored guest. Dizzy caught me in the hallway Wednesday and begged me to come. She actually got down on her knees and begged, claiming it was *soooo boring* going to the same parties every week with the same people. I'm a fresh face, new ears to fill with her gossip. I relented only so she would get up and stop embarrassing both of us.

"It's so *not* my speed," I say to Melissa.

"By the way, I'm glad we had that talk on Tuesday. And I'm glad you are speaking to me again. The past week with you has been lovely. I feel like you've completely outgrown all of your teenage drama. I love it. Maybe you've turned into an actual adult now. A real little person."

I smile flatly. Melissa's pseudo-compliments are generally tinged with enough traumatic subtext to keep me in therapy for years.

"I'm taking the Accord," I say. It feels weird to share a car, when just a few months ago I had my own and I could leave anytime I wanted to without fear of leaving her stranded.

"I don't care," Melissa says. "I have my two feet if I need anything." I head for the door. Unlike any normal mother I know, Melissa refrains from saying anything about being careful or about being home by eleven. Instead, she tells me to pay close attention to the sky. "Mercury is in retrograde!" she calls excitedly.

▪▪▪

58

Lake Vernon is on the edge of town, just behind the boat motor factory. I read about it online—it's a human-made lake, built a few years ago to increase the value of the property surrounding it. Last year, some guy was fined for releasing his pet piranha into the lake. The piranha then ate a bunch of the fish that the city stocked in the lake for fishing. The year before that, a couple of swimmers got some gross parasitic worms from the lake. Now there are signs all over telling people not to swim in the lake and/ or dump garbage or animals. Only in Quiet would you have to tell people this.

The lake is a welcome interlude between the dust fields on one end of town and the rundown buildings of downtown Quiet on the other. If not for the humidity hanging in the air and the red dirt peeking up from newly awakening grass, it could be Minnesota. I squint my eyes, willing the place into submission, making it into what I want it to be.

The lot I park in is almost full—people are spilling out of their cars into the cool night air. It's finally stopped raining, and there's a summer-like feeling tonight. Everyone seems happy to be outside. You'd never believe that barely two weeks ago, we were all held hostage by a guy who is now dead. With the exception of a giant cross in the hallway at school, it's almost like nothing happened and that monster never existed in the first place.

Dizzy sees me before I see her. She takes a running leap for me, wraps her arms around my back, and shrieks. "You came! Let me introduce you."

She rattles off names—mostly people I recognize from school, although I know I'll never remember all of their names. One of the guys, a bulky, sandy-haired kid named Bucky Roy (that's his first name), says, "Aren't you the new girl who threw up in the chem lab?"

"Yeah, that's me."

"The new girl is here!" Bucky Roy yells. Some people stare.

You can spot the ranch kids—the cowboys like Bucky Roy—because they drive Chevy or Ford pickups, eat homemade triple-decker steak sandwiches for lunch, and belong to the FFA (Future Farmers of America). The guys almost always have a telltale round imprint in the back pocket of their Wranglers. I recently learned that's their *chaw*—chewing tobacco. I find clumps of it in the water fountains and all over the sidewalks by the parking lot. The cowboys date the *farm girls*—the girls who have belt buckles of their own and who have, at some point in their lives, entered a homegrown vegetable in the state fair competition.

In contrast, the popular guys live in town. They like sports, video games, beer from a keg, and illegal fireworks. They wear jeans or cargos. Their baseball caps are ever-present and pulled low. They seem nice enough, although they are constantly joking around, accusing each other of being gay, something that no guy would ever have done at Academy in Saint Paul. Dizzy introduces me to one of these guys: Sam Cameron, the guy from chemistry who tried to talk to the shooter. When he's standing up, I see that he's got to be well over six feet tall. He's a curly-haired, blond giant, all athletic skill and muscle wrapped in a boy-next-door package. "Hey," he says, sticking his hand out to me. "Really nice to officially meet you. Glad you could make it."

He gives me a once-over, and I feel like barfing—he's totally not my type. I'd wager money that his mother worships the ground he spills corn nuts and Mountain Dew on. "Hey," I say.

"Come on," Dizzy says. "I'll take you to Brooklyn and the other girls."

Sam holds up a Miller Lite in one hand and a Diet Coke in the other. "Which one?" he says to me. I point to the Coke, and he tosses it to me. "Hope to see you again, Daphne," he says and smiles broadly.

Dizzy giggles as we walk away. She grabs my arm. "He likes you," she whispers.

"Great," I whisper back sarcastically.

She leads me to a group of girls who are standing around someone's open tailgate. "*Hola, chicas!*" Dizzy yells. Some of the girls run to hug her, like they haven't seen her for weeks, when in reality, she'd only walked away for a few minutes.

Lexus Flores, the girl with the shiny cap of hair, gives me a tiny wave. "You look hot, Dizz," she says. "Did I say that already?"

Dizzy does an exaggerated model pose. "This old thing?" she says with mock dismissal. She's wearing a tight, short black skirt, a billowy pink sleeveless top with a clunky black necklace, and black lace-up boots with super high heels that she's tottering in. Most of the other girls are wearing jeans.

Cuteny—the petite girl with two blond pigtails whom I also

met in the library—pretends to bow down to Dizzy. "Bestow upon me your fashion sense, Dizz."

Dizzy waves it all away with one hand, though it's obvious that she's delighted by the attention. Brooklyn, the tiara girl, is there too. "Hi," she says. "Have you met Ruth and Stephie?" She points at two of the other girls, a tall one wearing a soccer sweatshirt and a shorter one clutching a tube of lip gloss that she applies and reapplies to her already shiny lips.

"We saw you talking to Sammy, Dizz. What's going on there?" This comes from Cuteny.

"Nada," Dizzy says. "He wasn't even remotely interested in me. Not when Daphne here is around. You should see the way he looked at her!"

Everyone yells, "*Woooo*," at the same time, the way that fourth graders do when they see people kissing.

"Sam's just friendly," Brooklyn says. "He's not interested in you." Behind her, Dizzy mouths at me, *She wants him.*

"I'm not really looking for a relationship anyway," I tell Brooklyn.

"Good," she says firmly. She turns around to face the lake until chatter resumes. Everyone but me is deep in the middle of a conversation about whether it's appropriate to wear pajamas in public when Brooklyn yells, "Oh my god!"

We all turn to look. "What?" Dizzy asks urgently.

"What's wrong?" Lexus chimes in.

"There she is! I didn't think she'd come. Poor thing." Everyone stares toward the bank of the lake, me included. Two shadowy figures are standing side by side, passing a cigarette between them.

"It's January," Cuteny says quietly.

Oh, the others say under their breaths, much the way they might react if they'd just come across a squashed puppy on the highway.

When she moves under a streetlight, I see that it is January. She's wearing the same basic getup she had on that day in the library, except she has some kind of weird, cape-like sweater over it all. Next to her is a short, rodent-like kid with a pale blond mustache threatening to overtake his top lip. I know him from one of my classes. He's Nate Gormley, one of those outcast kids who seems to always be smoking or skulking around, making you think he's just done something illegal.

"Poor thing," Lexus also says. "She really deserves our pity."

"She's the sister of the shooter," Ruth tells me.

"I know," I say. I study January in the distance. She's so skinny and tiny, she looks like a winged fairy in that oversized sweater cape. But something about the way she holds her head, the way she squares her shoulders, makes me think she is far cleverer than she lets on.

"Poor girl. With genes like that, who knows where she's headed," Stephie says, smacking her lips.

"Personally," Brooklyn says, clearing her throat, "I do feel sorry for her, but I don't want to be around her. You just don't know what a person like her will do. Those people who come from that kind of genetic stock are like wild animals. You just never know. We should be kind, of course, but we need to avoid people like January and that awful Nate Gormley. Let them stick together.

Then when they snap, they'll only hurt each other and not innocent people like us."

I stare at her with a gaping mouth. Is she serious? I wait for someone to respond, but everyone just sort of nods reverently.

"I can't believe you would say that," I tell Brooklyn myself when it's evident no one else is going to speak up.

Her eyes widen. "What? I'm just telling the truth." She turns to the others, waiting for them to defend her. Nobody does. "Fine," she says eventually. "I'm going to say hi to Sam." Then she stalks off toward the boys, shooting me a dirty look in passing.

"Brooklyn is kind of excitable," Dizzy says to me when she's gone. "She thinks everyone is genetically flawed."

"That shooting has everyone on edge," Lexus say. "Let's try to forget about it, though. No use obsessing about it. Once we know all of the PROFILE results, we'll know exactly who to avoid."

"Right," Dizzy says confidently.

Then they change the subject—so quickly that it takes me a minute to catch up. When I do, I realize they are talking about Dizzy's ex-boyfriend, some guy named Josh Heller. Dizzy points at him in the distance for my benefit.

"Isn't he hot?" Lexus says.

I guess I could see how he might be attractive to some, but the baby face and wavy red hair don't quite do it for me. In the dim light, he looks like he could be Pippi Longstocking's older brother. "Not really," I say honestly, but everyone ignores me. They all watch him move toward the lakeshore, a beer in each hand. He stops near January.

"Josh Heller's mom has more money than God," Ruth says to me. "Not that I care. But ever since she married David Kable, she's rolling in it."

"Jesse's dad," Dizzy supplies for my benefit. "Have you met Jesse yet?" She sucks in her breath. "Oh, yeah. He was in the closet with you that day. I'm sorry."

"It's okay," I say. "He seems pretty..." I search for the right word. "Pleasant." It's not really what I mean, but I can't find the words I want.

Dizzy laughs. "Pleasant?"

"You obviously don't know about his past," Lexus says as she runs her fingers through her hair, her head tipped backward.

"What about it?" I ask. More gossip. These girls are absolutely full of it.

"Well..." Dizzy says, giving Lexus a complicated look. "It's all just rumors. Be quiet, you guys. Jesse saved her life. She doesn't want to hear this."

"Yes, shush," Cuteny says. "Besides, it's rude to talk about people behind their backs."

Lexus laughs loudly. "When did that ever bother you, Cute?" She turns back to me. "There's been a rumor going around, since forever ago, that Jesse was stalking this older girl who broke up with him. She had a restraining order against him."

"Allegedly," Cuteny notes.

"Allegedly," Lexus repeats. "It's probably not even true. You know how rumors are." We all nod.

"I don't care if he *is* a stalker. Because Jesse is *yummy!*" Cuteny yells. Everyone giggles. "And Sam," she adds, doing a fake make-out session with her hand in front of her face. Clearly, this girl wants every guy at QH. I wonder how she feels about Bucky Roy.

Suddenly, I feel really tired and startlingly out of place, like a zoo animal, or some kind of unusual Minnesota wildlife—a black-tailed prairie dog on display for these Oklahoma predators.

I walk away. Nobody stops me.

I walk down one of the docks scattered around the lake. In the night breeze—with the noise of the party behind me—I feel like I can finally relax. I can think out here. I let my feet dangle, the bottoms of my heels skimming the lake water. A breeze ruffles my hair, and I reach to adjust my barrette.

"Hey," someone says.

I whip around. "Oh, hey," I say, struggling to stand up.

"No," Jesse says. "Stay there." He walks toward me and takes a seat a few feet from me.

He brings one leg up, squaring his foot on the dock, moving his body away from mine. We don't say anything at first. I play with a rock that I've found on the ground.

"Who are you here with?" he asks me.

"Nobody. Just hanging out with Dizzy and company."

"Ah," he says knowingly.

"And you?"

"With January."

"Really?" I say, surprised. Jesse doesn't seem to fit into the three major groups I've identified at QH. He's definitely not a farm boy, but he isn't preppy and All-American like Sam either. And he's certainly not a stoner loser, like that kid Nate Gormley. So what's he doing with January, who is, by Brooklyn's standards, anyway, a total genetic land mine?

He must read my mind. "We've been friends for a long time. Since we were little kids." He sounds defensive, even though I've said nothing. I just nod.

It takes a second to dawn on me. "So you knew the shooter."

He doesn't answer, at first. "Yeah," he finally says. "I knew him."

"Did you know that…I mean, did you ever suspect that he would do something like this?"

"We were friends. At least, I thought we were."

We listen to the voices in the distance, the tinkling of beer bottles clinking, cans crushed in fists.

He breaks the silence first. "I try to keep an eye on her. On January. She's depressed. You know, this whole thing with her brother has been really hard for her."

"I can imagine."

"She's been drinking too much—she's getting herself into dangerous situations. It's weird to see her like this. She used to be so—sweet. Full of life. Smart. Funny." He stares wistfully. "Now she doesn't care what happens to her. She's…" He trails off, as if he can't think of what to say. She's what?

He starts over again. "I just wanted you to know that…" He pauses. I throw a rock in the lake and watch it sink into the blackness of the water. "I just wanted you to know that she's not my girlfriend. But we are very close."

"Oh," I say. It's the answer to the very question I wanted to ask. Not that I ever would have asked. It's too forward. I make a point never to chase guys. It's a policy I live by. We sit for a long time without talking before we both get up to leave.

On the walk back to the parking lot, Jesse swings his hands, making fists as he walks. He pauses abruptly when we pass some geese nosing around the sidewalk. It's past eleven now—not a time you usually see geese out—but all the artificial light and noise and people must confuse them. They are like college students, vampires, or night-shift workers: the absence of sunlight is hardly cause for sleep. "Hey, there," Jesse says, bending over. The geese are obviously tame, used to people feeding them. One of them pecks at his open palm and squawks angrily when she discovers there is no food. "Sorry," he says to the goose in a voice that is tender and soft.

The sounds of squawking geese are replaced by a girlish scream in the distance. It echoes. It's not a scream of a girl in danger so much as a scream of a girl who is trying to get a guy to notice her.

"That's January," Jesse says.

"Do you think she's predicted?" I wanted to ask the question before. It's rude to ask it now, but I can't help it.

"We'll find out eventually."

"I know," I say, thinking about what Melissa told me. They'd be releasing the names publicly. Sometime soon. "But do you think she is?"

"Yes," he says plainly. "I do."

"And who else?" I throw out the question before I realize that it's probably rude and gossipy to ask. I don't want to be like

Brooklyn. "I'm sorry. It's none of my business." We both start walking again, faster this time.

"No, it's okay. I think we all suspect the same people. Her brother is a suicidal school shooter. Her dad drank himself to death. Got drunk and wrapped his car around a telephone pole. Not even an original way to go." He pauses. "What can you expect? That's what we're all thinking. Trapped by genetics." We walk a little farther.

"Can you imagine?" I ask. "Thinking you are *destined* for something like that? I can't even fathom it."

"No, you wouldn't know. You can't imagine what…" He stops talking and crosses his arms, looking over his shoulder at the parking lot. "I'm sure it's really hard," he finally says.

The crowd is dwindling. People are saying good-bye, driving away. They are going home or going to drink someplace else. I've heard about the old train car just outside of Perry, thirty-five miles south of Quiet. Apparently, it's an abandoned car: open, creepy, shadowy, remote. Everybody under the age of twenty-one—so the rumor goes—drinks out there. It's haunted, they say. Sometimes the ghost of a little old woman appears, and people think she's the wife of a man who killed himself and her in that very car, back before any of us were ever born. I don't buy it. But it does make for a good creepy place to hang out, I guess.

Jesse is looking intently at me now. I look away bashfully, very unlike me. He reaches out toward my face, but he stops before he touches it. "You look real," he tells me suddenly. "Like a real person. Not like any other girl here." He closes his eyes. Before

I can respond, we hear that scream again. It's January in the distance. His eyes snap open, his expression changes. "I really have to go."

He's off, jogging toward the parking lot, toward January.

I stand there, staring, unable to move until I realize what's bothering me: *You can't imagine*, he'd said.

Did that mean *he* could?

PART II
together

CHAPTER 8

We had a connection right away. Before we even talked to each other, I knew. I don't even know how to explain it.

—Jesse Kable, quoted in the book, *The Future of the Predicted*, publication forthcoming

YOU *HAVE* TO COME TO DELL'S," DIZZY SAYS FOR THE eightieth time.

"Dizzy, I don't know any other way to say no."

"Good," she says, "then you're coming." She grabs my hand and drags me off the porch. "I'm going out," I call to Melissa, who is in the front room, reading medical journals. Fortunately, Dizzy lets me grab my flip-flops from the doorway, but I don't have time to change clothes. I feel like a total slob in a baby pink Gap hoodie and faded jeans so long they practically cover my feet.

Brooklyn is waiting in Dizzy's car, a shiny BMW. Nice. She's obviously not keen on the idea of me coming with them—I can tell by the tight smile plastered on her face—but it doesn't keep her from dominating the conversation on the ride over. Apparently, she's scored a major coup. After the lake party, she went home with Sam, where they hooked up. "We're pretty much dating now," she tells me confidently.

"Congratulations," I say sarcastically. Brooklyn strikes me as the kind of girl who needs a boyfriend to feel good about herself. I should probably have some sympathy, give her a chance, but I dismiss her easily, simply because I don't like the way she narrows her eyes when she talks, like everybody smells bad.

I've always avoided Dell's Diner on Main—it's the kind of place that you wouldn't feel right entering by yourself, kind of like the prom or a wedding chapel. Walking through the crowded parking lot with Dizzy and Brooklyn, I discover my suspicion was right: it *is* like a private party. Everybody from QH is at Dell's, the place to be when it's too hot, cold, early, or wet to be at the lake; the only thing to do in Quiet on a Sunday night. We are still talking about Sam when we walk into the diner and practically run into him. He's dressed in a football jersey and cargo shorts.

"Hey, girls!" he calls. "Daphne, right?" he says to me.

Brooklyn says to him, like she has a bite of old cauliflower in her mouth, "Daphne agreed to come with us. Aren't we lucky?" She gives me a pageant smile and a hug that actually hurts. She hates me. Well, at least it's mutual. Dizzy and Brooklyn flirt with Sam while I stand there, mushed between what feels like a zillion people in the main entryway. I stare impassively out the diner window to the parking lot. Under the streetlight, Nate Gormley—the kid I saw at the lake with January—puffs hard on a cigarette and runs his fingers through his tangled, greasy hair. January stands near him, a long trench coat covering her body, her skinny arms crossed against her chest and an inflexible scowl on her face.

"Girlfriends!" Dizzy crows, running toward Lexus and Cuteny as they step through the doors. With them is Dizzy's ex-boyfriend, Josh Heller. He's wearing plaid shorts and a baby pink polo with the collar flipped up.

Josh raises his hand to Sam for a high-five. They lock hands in guy solidarity. "What's up, ya big wussy?" Josh says to Sam with obvious affection.

"Nothing. I see you're still dressing like a clown, you stupid prepster."

They bump shoulders, side to side, forcing everyone else to step around them and give them room.

Somebody get me a barf bag.

"Hey," Josh says. "How come they got to go ahead of us?" He points out two women—probably in their late twenties or so— who walked in behind us, but who are now being led to an open table by the large windows. "That's discrimination," he says. He turns to the crowd milling behind him. "Right?" he asks.

"Right," a few voices respond.

"Don't start something, Heller," Sam warns, but you can tell that Sam doesn't mean it. "I've seen you in action." He laughs.

"And we won't stand for it!" Josh yells.

"Right." The voice of the crowd is growing smaller and less indignant.

"We demand to be treated with respect." By this time, Josh is laughing obnoxiously. He's drunk. He reminds me of my great-uncle Freddie, who used to walk around carrying those tall cans of beer in a paper bag, like a bum.

"You're such an idiot, Josh," Dizzy says to him. She's playful, so I can't tell if she's serious or not. Did she actually like this guy?

"Is this a job for Lefty?" Josh asks, flexing his left arm. "Or Right-Man?" Neither "bodyguard" looks particularly impressive to me.

"I'm calling my dad," Brooklyn says, pulling her cell from a giant, metallic-gold purse. She dials while Josh and his buddies snicker. Brooklyn gives a measured wave back at some girls who have just walked in the door. "Lexus," she screeches while she waits for her dad to pick up her call, "I need to tell you about the Miss Chitlin Pageant. It was a disaster. Daddy?" she says into the phone. She pauses for a moment. "I know you are busy. I know. But this is important. I'm being discriminated on." She looks meaningfully at an older waitress with a hairnet who is carrying coffee and slices of pie from the display case to a table of diners.

"*Against*," Josh says, between fits of laughter. "You're being discriminated *against*, not *on*."

She waves her hand dismissively at him. By the way she pouts, I guess that Daddy must not share her outrage. "Fine!" she says and slams the hot pink phone shut.

"Can you believe this?" she says to me, as if I am likely to be upset. "My dad is an attorney, and he is going to be so pissed when he understands what happened here tonight."

"I can imagine. It's a complete violation of our civil rights!" I realize too late that I'm totally making fun of her, and unfortunately, she figures it out. After a twenty-second delay.

"Who asked you anyway?" Brooklyn demands, her little fake-tanned face scrunched into a pouty frown. "You know, I wasn't going to say anything, but as long as we're here, I might as well tell you: I don't like you the way you flirt with Sam. It makes you look…desperate." She crosses her arms triumphantly. "And I don't like the way you talk to all of us. You think you're better than we are."

Sometimes, the truth is hard to admit. So I pretend I don't hear that last part. I stay focused on the part about Sam. "What? I've talked to the guy like, once. How could I be flirting with him? Trust me. I'm not the least bit interested in Sam." I give Sam a quick glance. He's standing with his hands in his pockets and staring at the ground. "No offense," I say to him. "I don't even know you."

"Come on, Brooklyn," Sam says good-naturedly. "Don't be silly."

Brooklyn purses her lips, looks from Sam to Josh to Dizzy to me. "I don't like you," she says gravely. "I can't fake it anymore. There's something about you. I have a sick sense for these kind of things. There's something not right about you"

"*Sixth* sense," I say. "You mean a *sixth* sense. Not a *sick* one."

Josh lets out a howl of laughter. Nobody else dares speak. "Come on, Sam," Brooklyn says, tugging at his arm. "This place is for cool people only. It's not for losers." She seems to be on the verge of forming the shape of an *L* with her fingers, but she catches herself, perhaps realizing just how lame and outdated that gesture is. I need to close my eyes to keep them from rolling in my sockets.

I swear, Quiet is twenty years behind the rest of the world.

Regardless of my commendable restraint, her now-aborted gesture causes me to make another grave tactical error: I laugh. Not just a subtle laugh—a guffaw. It's not directed at Brooklyn, per se. It's just me getting a case of the nerves, cracking under the pressure of everything, I guess. Brooklyn puts her hands on her hips and wrinkles her noise as if something smells bed. "That is so rude, Daphne."

She's right. It is. But that doesn't mean I can stop.

As everyone gets quieter and turns to look at me, I laugh even harder. It's something about the way Brooklyn is standing with her arms crossed, her lips pursed, and her head cocked to one side that makes me feel like laughing for days. I could easily stop—I'm not prone to laughing fits—but it feels kind of good, releasing all that tension from PROFILE and January and the shooter and everything else into the air. So I keep going, even when someone lightly pokes me in my ribs and tells me to knock it off. "I'm sorry," I say to Dizzy, who is standing with her eyes scrunched in a confused expression.

"Calm down," she tells me. "Brooklyn is trying really hard here."

As I'm standing there almost doubled over, holding my gut, laughing like a maniac, I feel a *whoosh* of air through my hair. Brooklyn is furiously winding up her giant gold purse above her head like it's some kind of medieval weapon. She lets loose, and I duck just before the bag can smack me in the head. I stand there stunned, because I'm truly amazed that someone would use her oversized purse as a weapon.

In the millisecond it takes me to contemplate the oddity of this whole scene, the giant bag makes its way back around to Brooklyn's side, taking out Josh, who is standing behind her staring out the window. He falls forward on the fake-leather bench, across the laps of an old man and an old woman. The old lady fans a Kleenex over him, as if he's a too-hot dish or a bowl of soup with a fly in it. Dizzy runs to him.

Naturally, the entryway erupts in uncomfortable laughter, save for Brooklyn, who stands with her hands on her hips. "Get up," she tells Josh.

For a second, I think that he's laughing too, but when he slides off the old people, stepping on the old man's shoes, I see that he is pissed. "You bitch," he says, and I look to Brooklyn to gauge her reaction to this. It takes me a second before I realize that it's quiet and everyone is staring at me, including the couple on the bench, who look far too old to be eating dinner this long after sunset.

"Oh," I say. "You mean me. She's the one who hit you." I point at Brooklyn.

That doesn't seem to matter to Josh. He moves toward me. I can tell he's trying to look threatening, but it doesn't come off as all that tough. He's actually sort of staggering toward me like a reanimated corpse. Instead of moving, I just stand there. Like an idiot.

"God," Brooklyn says, because that's her go-to phrase. I wonder if she realizes what a stereotype she is.

I'm about to back off and apologize for my ridiculous laughing when I have (another) moment of insanity and decide that I really have nothing to apologize for. "I think you owe *me* an apology," I say, looking at Josh.

"I don't think so," Josh says stepping up to me. He's so close that I can smell alcohol and cigarettes and some other strange smell, like maybe Cheerios. I'm pretty sure Great-Uncle Freddie poured beer over his Cheerios. Maybe Josh does that too.

Sam steps closer to me. Lexus, dressed in a purple miniskirt, closes ranks around Brooklyn, surprising me by saying, "Come on, Josh." She pulls on his shirt. "The food here tastes like dog doo-doo anyway." I wait for people to laugh at Lexus's choice of words, but nobody does. I shoot her a *thank-you* look. I glance at Sam, but he just shrugs his shoulders and moves a half-step behind Dizzy, who has crossed her arms firmly across her chest. The crowd at the door is murmuring, and the older couple has gone back to whatever they were doing before a teenage boy landed across their laps. Josh walks away from me backward.

I'm bored with this whole thing now. I'm thinking about how hungry I am and how it would be better to just turn away. I'm about to do just that, when I feel myself falling. I have no idea what's happening. I don't even feel my feet under me—just a huge crack as my head and shoulders smack the glass doors of the entryway. Everything goes black for a second, and the next thing I know, I am reclining on the floor, my head sort of angled to the side, like I've just stretched out for a little nap. "What happened?" I try to say, but the words won't come out right. It sounds like gibberish, even to my own ears.

Not as lucky as Josh, I haven't landed on any soft elderly lap. I'm on the dirty floor. The first thing I do is check to be sure that I'm not wearing a skirt, since I can feel that I haven't landed gracefully.

Phew. Jeans.

There's a rush of people around me. I try to sit up, but someone yells, "Don't let her move." And then hands are pushing me back toward the cold floor. I put my own hand to the back of my head, where I can feel a stinging sensation. My hair feels a little sticky.

"Be careful of that door," someone warns. "The glass is cracked, so it might shatter. Nobody use it."

"Give her my sweater," someone says, and it must be the old lady on the bench, because I immediately smell geriatric perfume as the sweater comes near me.

"She's bleeding," I hear someone else say.

Brooklyn is crying. "He didn't mean to," she yells to everyone. "He didn't mean to!"

"Yeah, I got pushed by someone in the line. God, are you okay?" Josh says above me.

My vision clears, and I note that Dizzy is kneeling beside me, her corkscrew ringlets almost touching my face. Sam is hovering behind her, with Brooklyn practically wrapped around his waist.

"Oh, Daphne," Dizzy says with the same tone you would use if you just found out your dog had been hit by a mail truck. "Sam, get me some towels or something."

"I'm fine," I announce, but I can't quite work up the energy to try sitting up again.

"Sam! Go get some towels. She's bleeding."

"I'm fine," I repeat, but it's clear that nobody believes me. "Really," I tell nobody in particular. "I'm totally okay." I pull my hand away from the back of my head and notice that it has blood on it—not a lot, but enough to make me woozy.

I close my eyes. I don't actually feel that bad—just a little sleepy.

"Call 911," a voice over me says.

It takes me a second to realize that it's not Dizzy anymore. "Where is she?" I ask. "Where did Dizzy go?"

I open my eyes to see the owner of the voice taking off his jacket and rolling it up to put underneath the side of my head. It's Jesse, but he looks different somehow. His eyes are darker in this artificial light: deep brown, the color of melted dark chocolate chips. His shoulders are broad but hunched up slightly, like he's preparing to fight. The way he holds his lips tightly pressed together with his jaw clenched and his eyes focused directly on me tells me he is worried. And that makes me worry that maybe I'm hurt worse than I realize. I panic for about ten seconds, and then I go back to surveying Jesse's broad shoulders, his wavy, dark hair, his—

Jesse interrupts my thoughts. "She went with Sam to find towels."

"Who went with Sam?" As soon as I say it, I realize that we are talking about Dizzy. Jesse frowns at me and pats my arm gently. I let him think that the accident caused my short-term memory loss. What can I say? *I was just thinking about how hot you are, and I forgot that we were even having a conversation.*

I change the subject. "No," I protest, trying to get his coat out from under my head. "I'll bleed on it."

"Shhh," he says. "Call an ambulance," he yells again over his shoulder. "And tell Dizzy I need that towel right away."

"Tell her to keep her eyes open," a female voice says from above me.

I look up and see a girl with pink streaks running through her hair. She runs short blue fingernails over her head. It's January with her coat off, wearing a dress that looks like it's made out of a cotton bed sheet.

"It's just so weird here," I say out loud. "Why are you here?" It sounds perfectly clear in my head.

"She's not making any sense," January says.

"Get her some water," Jesse tells January, and she steps around me and heads toward the seating area.

I actually feel okay, save for the stinging sensation in my head. "I didn't even really break it," I tell Jesse. "The window, not my head," I add, pointing to the cracked window behind me. "Not that my head is broken," I clarify, wondering if I sound as idiotic as I feel.

The goateed manager, in a stained white shirt and a green apron, is busily at work behind me. He opens the undamaged door and yells to a crowd that has clustered outside to observe what must be the most exciting thing to happen in Quiet in a very long time. "Hey, make room for the ambulance. As soon as we get her out of here, we can let you in." He shuts the door, and then opens it a crack and yells, "Soup of the night is catfish gumbo! Chicken-fried steak is the special!"

I snicker, but it must sound like something else, because Jesse grabs hold of one of my hands. "You're going to be fine," he reassures me. "Don't move. Just stay still." He gently pushes me back down so that my head is on his coat. I feel like taking a nap. I mumble something, but even I can't understand what I'm saying. I drift away for a second, feeling like I'm floating on water. I'm feeling woozier now.

"Here," one of the servers says, holding out a white towel from the kitchen. Jesse takes it before I can, and he leans over me, holding the towel against the side of my head.

My eyes open, and I feel almost normal again—except for the humiliation. That's still there. "I feel like a bird that flew into a glass window."

"You did," he says. "I've never seen anyone fly like that." He is still holding the towel against my head.

"Pretty impressive, huh?" I ask.

"Yeah, I wish I could've caught it on camera. It would be viral on YouTube by the time you leave the emergency room."

When he moves the towel away from my head, it's got blood smattered on it, and his hand glistens from some of it. "Gross," I say. "Is that totally gross?"

"What?" he asks. "All this blood? Nah, I always begin my meals tending head wounds."

"I usually try to crack my head open at more convenient times, like *after* dinner."

"That's probably wise." He smiles at me.

"I don't suppose I can just get up and quietly slip away, can I?"

"Probably not," he answers. "I think you're going to have to make a grand exit. But you sound better. I think you're going to live."

"I mean, I wouldn't want to ruin Brooklyn's night or anything." I'm sarcastic now. That's a good sign. I'm talking to him the way I'd talk to a guy under normal circumstances, if I weren't sprawled on a restaurant floor, bleeding from my skull. The dizziness is coming back again. I let my eyelids drop closed and begin to enjoy the hum of the diner around me. The stinging sensation in my head feels so distant now.

"Keep your eyes open," someone says. I wearily open them again. There's an EMT standing over me. He has green lettuce stuck in one tooth, but I don't tell him.

"What's your phone number?" the EMT says. I recite it three times in a row, just in case this is a test.

"Good," says a fat guy with garlic breath standing over me. Then he asks me questions like what is my name and how many fingers is he holding up, which is super-annoying when you feel mostly fine. I let him and some other people heft me onto a stretcher.

In the parking lot, Melissa comes running to the stretcher, which just feels silly. "I don't need to go to the ER," I tell anyone who will listen.

"Of course you do," Melissa says. "They called me. I got here in record time." Melissa runs her hand through her hair while she bites the left side of her lip. She's worried, and for a second, I'm afraid she's going to cry. Then she says, "What did you do? I sprinted here like a marathon runner." She breathes heavily.

"I'm okay," I mumble, but I don't think it comes out right, because she seems even more worried after I speak.

It's not until right before they lift me in the ambulance that I see Jesse again. Melissa has already wandered away to talk to Goateed Manager and two cops, probably the whole Quiet police force. She is undoubtedly lecturing them on something, because that's what Melissa does in times of crisis.

She also does that in times of no crisis. It's kind of her signature move. You get used to it after a while.

I look at Jesse hovering over my face, and I instinctively press my lips together to see if I still have lip gloss in place. Yes! Thank goodness for the long-wear stuff. Without lip gloss, I'd probably look like a corpse. He looks as if he's going to say something, but he doesn't.

"Can you imagine it?" I ask. I'm referring to the conversation we had at the lake, when we were talking about what it feels like to be predicted.

"I'm not sure what she's talking about," he says to someone.

"Yes, you are," I argue. "Were you trying to tell me something?"

He doesn't answer. He just steps away when the paramedics hoist me into the ambulance. Before they shut the doors, I look up and see him standing in the parking lot, January Morrison next to him, his arm draped around her. Their heads come together like hands in prayer.

CHAPTER 9

January Morrison puts out for anybody. I should know.

—Writing on the boys' bathroom wall at Quiet High

AT JUST BEFORE MIDNIGHT, THE PHONE RINGS. I EXPECTED him to call. I knew he would find a way to get my number. Guys like Jesse are good at that kind of stuff.

"Hey," Jesse says smoothly. "I hope I'm not calling too late. I just wanted to check on you. Did I wake you?"

I play it cool. I make a habit of not letting guys think I've been sitting around waiting for them. I yawn before I speak. "Actually, no, you didn't. I'm wide awake. I somehow managed to sleep through most of Monday and all of last night. Today, I was up for a few hours in the morning, but I fell asleep this afternoon."

"I'm not surprised. You had quite a night on Sunday."

"Yeah, quite a night," I say sarcastically. "I'm actually pretty mortified. Did you know that Nell—the granddaughter of Dell of Dell's Diner—called here to request reimbursement for the cracked window? Because, you know, apparently Nell thinks I should be held responsible for recklessly throwing my head against the glass door."

"Well," Jesse says seriously, "I can understand her concern. If she doesn't make an example out of you, all the kids will be doing it."

"It'll be the new craze," I agree with a laugh.

"As soon as I first saw you, I knew you were a trendsetter. Let me guess—now everyone will come to school with stitches in her skull, a shaved patch of hair, and a gauze bandage on her head. I heard all about it."

I groan and touch the back of my head, remembering that they had to shave a very small circle of my hair at the emergency room. It turned out that the cut wasn't that bad, nothing a couple of stitches couldn't take care of. And the bald patch is small enough that I can just comb my hair over it. I was home before midnight, and then I zonked out for the next twenty-four hours. "How did you know about my new bald patch? Did I make the cover of *Cosmo* again?"

"No, but you did make the Quiet High news. Mrs. Temple announced it to the whole school today."

I cringe inwardly. Now I'll be known as the Girl with the Head Injury. I'd rather stay The New Girl. Or just be invisible.

"I called and talked to your mom this morning," Jesse says. "She said to try back late tonight, when you might be awake. She said you had to get up sooner or later. How do you feel?"

"Like I put my head through a glass window."

"Poor Daphne," Jesse says sincerely.

"What happened after I made my grand exit?"

"Same old. Hanging out at the diner, drinking coffee, followed by a rousing evening of loitering in the parking lot until it was time to go home. Typical night in Quiet Rock City."

"Wow, sounds like almost as much fun as I had," I say.

"Well, it was slightly more exciting than usual because we had your injury to discuss. Are you aware of how emotionally scarred Brooklyn is over this?" Jesse says this with enough sarcasm to make me laugh.

"I'm sure it was really rough for her."

"She *almost* got blood on her shirt. Furthermore, if that glass had shattered, she might have been injured! She was standing right by you!"

"I'll try to be more aware of her whereabouts next time I crack my head open." Then I ask, "And January? How is she?"

"She's fine." It's a simple declaration. No secret yearnings that I can detect. Just a plain sentence. I stretch the long phone cord and wander out into the living room. Melissa's bedroom door is closed, and her lights are off. I switch phones and go into the kitchen, where I see a note by the fridge: *Plate of food for you, if you wake up hungry. Jesse and Dizzy called for you. Dizzy says she is "like, seriously concerned about you." Wake me up if you want to talk.* It's signed by Melissa. She's been waking me up every couple of hours. I can't imagine what she thinks I might have to talk about.

"And you?" I ask him.

"What about me?"

"Blood doesn't freak you out?"

"Nah, not even a little."

I pull the plate of food out of the fridge—fried chicken from the grocery store deli with a damp lump of mac and cheese and a side of withered green beans—and eat it cold while Jesse and I talk. It's one of those conversations that's completely seamless: no pauses, no awkward silences, no weird places where you talk over each other or misunderstand what the other person is trying to say.

At three o'clock in the morning, I'm back in my bed, drowsy and full of chicken. The phone is cradled next to my ear. I start to fall asleep, and I'm just about in total darkness when I hear Jesse say, "I'll let you go back to sleep. Can I call you again?"

"Ahhh-hemmm," I say, my tongue unwilling to move, the phone dropping lower and lower as I loosen my grip.

The last thing I hear him say, or *think* that I hear him say, is this: "There's something I have to tell you, Daphne." It sounds ominous. Or maybe just melodramatic. I try to laugh, in case it's a joke—part of our flirtatious conversation—but I'm just too tired. The phone slips out of my hand.

I fall asleep, happy for the first time since before the shooting.

The next time the phone rings, I am sleeping deeply. It feels like I've been sleeping for days, and I kind of have been. Except to eat and go to the bathroom—and take a quick bath—I've pretty much been in bed since Sunday. I pick up the phone after five long rings. Melissa is home and can hear the phone, but she never answers unless she thinks it's for her. She's probably been up for hours already. Melissa is one of those annoying people who thinks that getting up before the birds is a sign of some kind of moral virtue. I, however, am a night owl—and I can sense that it's late morning already. My head is aching, and I feel like I've been hit by a truck. "Ughh," I groan, instinctively reaching for my head.

I manage to croak out a greeting that probably sounds something like hello, and a loud voice on the other end says, "Can you meet at eleven? I was thinking the mall. The one in Quiet. Not that it's much of a mall, but it's a place with stores that sell things, and I desperately need to find a swimsuit. It's almost pool weather. What if I don't find a suit? What does yours look like?"

"Who is this?" I'm totally confused.

"It's Dizzy." I half-expect her to add *of course*. She seems put out that I don't recognize her voice and that I can't seem to pick up this conversation, which feels like it started much earlier. Without me.

"You know we don't have school today, right?" she asks suspiciously.

I look at my clock radio as if it can tell me what day it is, and then I remember that it's the Thursday before Easter. We're out until Monday. I sigh in relief. Honestly, I am probably feeling well enough to go, if I could just get out of bed. Knowing that I don't have to sit through classes makes me smile.

Dizzy has resumed talking. "I got your home phone number from the office. They should really keep those private. What if, like, a stalker got your number? By the way, Daphne, you are the only person on this planet who doesn't have a cell phone. Do you know that? You live in way-back-world. Land-of-no-technology."

I mutter under my breath. Not having a cell phone is a sore spot with me. Melissa thinks cell phones promote narcissism.

"How's your head? That was so hysterical when you cracked it on that window in the diner."

"Yeah," I mutter, "I'm a riot."

"Brooklyn is so pissed at you," Dizzy says. "It's all she can talk about. But listen, I'm sure you two can patch things up. She's kind of hard on newcomers, but that doesn't mean you can't win her over. Once you get to know her, you'll like her. She's just a little bit…dramatic sometimes."

"Let's not talk about Brooklyn."

"Sam is really flirtatious. Brooklyn thinks he has a thing for you."

"I don't even know the guy."

"Oh, I know," she says so quickly that I'm almost insulted. "So are we on?" she asks. "Are you ready to go?"

"To the mall?" I ask, just to make sure I'm following this strange conversation.

"Duh."

"I'm still in bed," I tell her. "Right where I was when I picked up the phone." She seems surprised that I haven't been showering and performing other hygiene rituals while we talked.

"Well, get off the phone then," she says. "I'll be at your house in fifteen minutes. Thirteen if I run the stop signs." Then she adds, "Just kidding. I'm a very safe driver."

Before I can confirm the plan, the phone is dead, and I realize I better get in the shower.

By the time I dry off, blow-dry my hair until it's just damp, brush my teeth, put on a tiny bit of lip gloss, and throw on jeans and a hoodie, Dizzy is already in the kitchen. Everything is taking me a bit longer, because I start to feel a little woozy if I stand up too long. I sit on the edge of the bathtub, but I can still hear Dizzy talking to Melissa, who is responding in very serious and well-timed "Uh-huhs" that indicate she is either intensely interested or intensely appalled by Dizzy's chatter. I run out of my room to the kitchen in case it's the latter.

"There's our girl," Dizzy says when I appear. "Tell me you didn't spend more than five minutes getting ready. Because, don't get me wrong, you look fine, but that is not the look of someone who took more than five minutes. Seriously, though, with twenty, you'd be a knockout. We can cover that bald spot." She reaches up and tries to touch my head, but I flinch. "And just a wee bit more makeup would do wonders." I stare at her caked-on look. Her eyelashes are so heavy with mascara, she looks like she's going to nod off at any moment.

Melissa smirks. She's one of those people who takes about two minutes to get ready in the morning, and she still looks better than most people because of her milky-white complexion and her Mount Everest cheekbones. She says she doesn't have time to worry about hair and makeup—that's for people who don't have anything else to do in a day. It's an attitude that only someone who is naturally attractive can afford to have. If Melissa had a mustache or hair that naturally grew in the shape of a mullet, she'd be singing a different tune.

"But seriously, Daphne," Dizzy continues, as if I haven't been serious so far, even though I haven't even spoken, "I was thinking that I could take you to get a haircut. We can do something about that…" She searches for the word "stuff." She points at my hair. "I know this great place. Well, it's not great. It's in Quiet, so don't expect miracles, you know? But it's pretty good. The guy who cuts my hair, Lightning Rod—that's his name, funny, huh?—can do wonders with anything. Any. Thing. Even me. Awesome, huh?" She glances at Melissa for confirmation of the awesomeness of Lightning Rod, then wrinkles her overly made-up nose at me and blows me a kiss.

I'm about ready to back out of this whole thing, which Melissa can tell, so she grabs her wallet and pulls out some cash that she hands to me. "Don't bring her back until she has a haircut and some new clothes," she says to Dizzy.

"I wasn't planning to bring her back before then," Dizzy says very seriously.

Melissa must be losing it, because normally she praises me for being the kind of girl who is not obsessed with being a girl. When I was five, I asked Melissa if I could have a Barbie doll, and she gave me this huge lecture on the dangers of encouraging girls to play with dolls. It causes little girls to romanticize motherhood while preparing them for caretaker roles, she argued. So she bought me a plastic hockey stick instead, which I broke the first time I took it outside and tried to hit a Super Ball. I ended up cracking the hockey stick against the side of the house.

I take the money anyway.

∎∎∎

The mall sign says *The Mall*, as if it is the only mall in existence in the entire world. "Pretty cool, huh?" Dizzy looks from me to the mall. "It's all new. Before this, we had to drive to Tulsa or Oklahoma City to shop. Then we got our own mall." She beams at it.

"Yeah, pretty cool," I say, thinking about how many of *The Mall* could fit into the Mall of America, where I used to shop back home.

Dizzy parks near the salon where Lightning Rod is waiting for us. He turns out to be this middle-aged guy with the beginning of a beer gut whose real name is Rodney. "Lightning Rod" is a nickname he earned for how fast he can cut hair—which I don't necessarily think is a positive attribute for someone wielding scissors near my head.

While he cuts my hair, he keeps making this joke where he says, "Oops, oops, oh, crap, I'm so sorry." And then he and Dizzy laugh. I can't see what he's doing, since Dizzy insists that they surprise me with a haircut she picked out of a magazine. Still, I can see long chunks of hair raining down around me. Instead of making me feel sad, it makes me feel powerful, like each hunk of hair is one less thing I have to carry around. Lightning Rod has to work much slower than he'd like, he tells me. He has to carefully cut and comb around my stitches, which are still sore and tender. I grit my teeth every time he gives my hair even the slightest tug.

I'm also a little nervous, because even though Dizzy is what I imagine guys think of when they think of sexy, her hair is kind of a disaster. She's playing with it now, pulling it out of a braid and putting it up into two curly pigtails that look cute but are not exactly my style. I grew out of pigtails at birth.

When Lightning Rod is done with what he calls *his masterpiece*, I finally get to have a look. When I turn around, all three of us examine it in utter silence. "Well, say something!" I finally plead.

Lightning Rod places his hand over his mouth. "Oh! Oh, oh!" he says. "I'm going to tear up. I'm going to, right now." He shakes his hands in front of his face.

"Me too," Dizzy chimes in. "I can't believe it!"

"It's unbelievable," Lightning Rod agrees.

At this point, I'm contemplating a wig. I mean, it looks fine to me, but if this is the kind of reaction I'm going to get, I might as well forget about showing it to anyone else. "That bad?" I ask, thinking that my taste must be seriously off. The longer I look at it. the more I think it's kind of cute.

"Bad?" Dizzy yells. "It's awesome!"

"You look like Louise Brooks," Lightning Rod says.

"Who?" I ask, wondering if I even want to know.

"She was a silent movie star, a pinup girl. She was…something else." Lightning Rod blows a kiss into the distance. "Hot. Sexy. Out of this world. That kind of girl."

Dizzy pulls out her BlackBerry and quickly finds an image. I stare at the black and white photo of Louise's sleek, shiny crown of hair. I do kind of her look like her, I guess. My hair is longer than hers, falling just below my chin, but I can see that we have the same dark eyes, pale skin, and bow-shaped lips.

I smile at the mirror and then at Lightning Rod. "You think I can pull this off?"

"Honey, if you were ten years older, or I were ten years younger, you would be my dream girl. I love it!"

Dizzy squeals and hugs me for about the hundredth time today.

The only word I can think to describe it is *cool*. That's how I feel. I don't even feel bad about the hunks of my long hair lying dead on the tiled floor.

"This is exactly what you needed," Dizzy tells me. "Now you are finally you!"

After the haircut, we buy two pairs of jeans, some makeup, and a pair of dangerously high heels with silver studs for me. I blow through Melissa's money quickly, and I have to reach into my purse for the few dollars I've saved from Christmas and birthday money that my grandmother sends to me. Lightning Rod doesn't come cheap. And buying stuff at the mall, I realize, is seductive and addictive. I'm enjoying the idea of being a different version of me, someone who has clothes from the mall, rather than just the hippie-esque things that Melissa gives to me—undoubtedly, someone's thrift store castoffs.

We end the shopping marathon by picking out Dizzy's swimsuit, a daring two-piece in chocolate brown with gold rings on both the top and bottom. She looks incredible in it. Dizzy is one of those people whose good looks sneak up on you. One minute, she looks like a little girl playing dress-up—someone who packed on her mother's makeup—but if you look at her for a few minutes, you realize she's actually sort of amazing, with

97

curves in all the right places. Even with those pigtails, she can pull off a bikini in a way that I could only imagine. I try not to act too surprised when Dizzy twirls around.

"When does pool season begin?" I ask.

"Oh, not until May, probably. Josh is having a pool party for his birthday then, and if you don't get a suit early, all the good ones are gone. Come on," Dizzy says after she pays for the little brown swimsuit with a credit card. "Let's get food."

We get pizza slices—glossy-looking pieces that have obviously been under a heat lamp for hours—and look for a place to sit in the tiny and crowded mall food court, a depressing circle of chairs and tables beside a foul-smelling waterfall. It's almost three o'clock, but there's no sign of the lunch rush dying down. The few chairs are loaded with Quiet High people, and many of them rush over to Dizzy to greet her or chat with her, so it takes us a long time to finally sit down at a table in the corner, right beside the window that overlooks the vast parking lot of The Mall. *Is the lot ever full?* I wonder. *Where would that many people come from?*

Dizzy talks a lot—and it's all frustratingly fast and incredibly loud. I have to be quick if I want to jump in and get something out before Dizzy interrupts. She's not trying to dominate the conversation or anything—she's just the type of person who has so much to say that she can't manage to keep her mouth shut for very long. After much chatting about pool parties, she switches topics with no warning. "So do you have a boyfriend at your old school? Are you a virgin?" she asks, without the slightest hesitation. My jaw drops.

"No, no boyfriend," I say, ignoring the virgin question. "I went out with a few guys here and there. Nothing special. Just dinners, a couple of movies, that kind of thing."

Dizzy laughs until she chokes on her rubber pepperoni. "That's so old school! Dinner dates!" She turns to the people sitting next to us—two women with small children. "A dinner date!" she tells them. "Can you believe it?" They move their children closer to their table.

What I don't tell Dizzy is this: I've never met a guy that I could see myself being with for more than a few hours. Nobody has ever caught my attention in that way.

"I'm a make-out slut," Dizzy tells me in a softer voice. "I have a running tally." She pulls a notebook out of her giant pink purse and slaps it on the table. Names neatly written in different colors of ink litter the page.

"Wow!" I say loudly. One of the little kids starts to cry.

Dizzy slams her hand down on our table, sending plastic silverware bouncing off our plates. "Thirty-three just this year!" she yells with glee, and the kid cries harder. The mother shoots us an irritated look.

"What about Josh? You were with him at the diner."

"Eh," she says. "We're on-again, off-again. We're not like some of the couples at Quiet High. Old married people." She makes barfing noises. "What do you think of Sam?" she asks suddenly.

I shrug. "I don't know. Seems okay, I guess."

"Almost every girl at QH has a thing for Sam Cameron, but he's pretty particular about who he hooks up with. Brooklyn is pretty lucky," she says. "I know girls who would kill to be in her pointy pageant shoes."

I refrain from saying that Sam can't be too picky if he's with Brooklyn. "You act like Sam is a celebrity."

"He sort of is. He's Sam Cameron. Every school has a guy like him. He's our very own Brad Pitt."

"Sam's not really my type," I say, surprising myself. I am not really aware that I have a type until the words come out of my mouth.

"What?" Dizzy says, holding her ear, pretending that she's heard me wrong. "Did you just say that Sam Cameron is not your type? What, for goodness sake, then, is your type?"

I'm thinking of an answer when I see January's pink-streaked hair in the distance. She's carrying a handful of shopping bags, and she's talking animatedly to the person walking with her. I squint into the distance. It's Jesse. He's looking through the glass of the pizza case. January keeps talking, putting the shopping bags on her wrist and using her hands to punctuate. Jesse suddenly moves his head slightly in our direction. I feel silly saying that The Mall suddenly gets quiet, but I swear that it does. His eyes lock on mine—he smiles, a genuine smile that covers his whole face. I force myself not to look behind me. I give him a half-smile back, just in case there's a crowd of people behind me who are waving at him. Jesse touches his own hair and then points to me. He gives me a casual nod. I give him slight head turn, a modest *Who me?*

Dizzy, oblivious to the fact that I've been ignoring her, is hard at work sawing at her pizza, running her plastic fork against the tough skin of cheese. "Wow," she says. "That settles it. You're crazy."

Then she proceeds to explain the history of every relationship of every person at QH, pausing only to make sure I'm following the complicated soap opera plot. Apparently, everyone dates everyone else. "Within reason," Dizzy says. "One of us is not going to date someone like him." She points her fork at a table behind me, where a cowboy-hatted, Wrangler-wearing boy eats, holding a fork like a shovel. He smiles at Dizzy, unaware that she is holding him up as Exhibit A: Cowboy Eats Chick-fil-A Coleslaw.

"I see," I say, turning back around to face her.

"Hey, Dizzy." January and Jesse appear at our table.

"Oh, hi, January," Dizzy says in a fake sweet voice. "Jesse," she says, nodding at him, giving him a million-dollar smile. She turns back to me and raises her eyebrows. Obviously, she's trying to speak to me in some kind of secret code, but I have no idea what she's saying. I just nod.

"I hardly recognized you, you look so good," January says to me.

"Gee, thanks."

"Awesome, isn't it?" Dizzy says proudly, as if she did it herself. "The bald spot is practically invisible." My hand goes immediately to my scalp, and then I wince when I touch the stitches.

"You look incredible," Jesse says boldly. We all turn to look at him. We exchange smiles that seem laced with undertones. *You didn't call me last night*, he says with his eyes.

I didn't know I was supposed to, I say back with mine. My cheeks feel warmer. I reach my hand out and touch my new, smooth hair—it feels like the satin edge of a blanket. It's weird not having it draped down my back, feeling hot and sticky.

"It's different," I say.

"It suits you," Jesse says.

"What's going on? What are you two up to today?" January asks.

"Bathing suits," Dizzy says, reaching for her bags. "Check this out." She extracts the brown top and waves it in front of her face. "Cool, isn't it?" she says to January in a pleasant tone laced with pity. She's being nice to January because she feels sorry for her.

"God, I'm fat," January says, looking down at her scrawny legs, her skinny arms dangling at her side.

"You are not," Dizzy says. Then she sighs heavily and pushes her plate away from her. "I shouldn't be eating this. I'm going to look like a cow in that suit." She glumly tosses the top back in the bag. Dizzy is hardly fat. Nevertheless, she and January continue to go back and forth about who is fatter, each claiming to be a bigger blimp than the other.

I heard these kinds of conversations before at Academy. I understand that it's a ritual, something that is supposed to make girls feel better, but it never does, because the conversation always repeats, stuck in a loop forever. I feel lucky that I have never been part of this. I've just never felt bad about my body. I've never felt too fat or particularly skinny. Melissa did something—at some point in my life—that made me feel okay about who I am. Too bad she couldn't bottle that and sell it. We'd be rich.

Jesse looks at me while Dizzy and January make pig snorting noises at each other. "So what are you two doing today?" I ask.

"Shopping," he says, pointing at a J.Crew bag he has in his hand. "One of my least favorite things to do." I immediately like that about him. I can't stand guys who like to shop. I put them in the same category with guys who use flatirons on their hair and who press their jeans.

Dizzy now has her bags open and is showing January all of her purchases. She's even showing mine.

"What'd you get?" I ask Jesse, pointing at his bag.

"Something really exciting." He pulls out a tie. "It's for work."

"Oh, yeah? What do you do?"

"Mostly show up and prove to my dad that I'm *reliable* and *trustworthy*, and that I'm *developing a sound work ethic*."

"Oh," I say. "So you're pulling yourself up by your bootstraps?"

"Something like that." He smiles.

"What does your dad's company do?"

"You heard of FauxFuel?"

Heard of it? It's practically all anyone talks about here. Melissa told me that FauxFuel is some substance made out of banana peels, dead flowers, human waste, and a bunch of other gross stuff ground up and mixed with regular unleaded fuel. It increases your gas mileage by three times while decreasing the amount of real fuel that you use. Melissa thinks it's the greatest thing ever, although she's still against driving in principle. ("All that carbon-based pollution? No way, Daph. Your feet are the most earth-friendly mode of transportation you'll ever get.")

But a lot of people in Quiet hate FauxFuel. In a town built on oil money, you don't exactly get a parade if you find a way to decrease oil use.

"Wow," I say. I think back to what one of the girls said at the lake, something about Josh's mom being so rich because she married Jesse's dad.

"What about you?" he asks.

"Just advising Dizzy. And letting her transform me into a whole new person."

He motions toward the mall corridor leading to the stores. "Bet this is a far cry from what you are used to back home. You're from Minnesota, right?"

"Saint Paul."

"That's cool. I'd love to go there sometime. I heard it's beautiful."

"It really is. I miss it," I say, but I don't feel the familiar twinge that I usually feel when I think about home.

"You look incredible," he says again. "Really, really good. Not that you didn't look good before." He stumbles over himself. "You just look...I don't know, you just look—wow."

"Thanks," I say, feeling slightly self-conscious. And kind of elated. I chastise myself silently. I don't want to be one of those girls—a girl like Brooklyn. "Whatever," I say for no reason other than to make me sound breezy in an offhanded way.

"So," Jesse says, tapping his foot against my chair. "You up for hanging out tomorrow night? That is, assuming your head is okay." He touches his own head and then smiles, his eyes wrinkling at the corners.

"Maybe," I say coyly. Without realizing it, I've lowered my volume to match his. We are practically whispering now.

"I'll call you," he says, half-mouthing the words.

That's when I realize that January and Dizzy have stopped

talking and are looking at Jesse and me. I've actually sort of forgotten they are here. Suddenly, I feel nauseous, like I'm going to hurl half-digested pizza everywhere. I must be glowing from the inside out.

"We should go," January says standing up abruptly. "I need to get home." My stomach begins to settle down.

"See you, guys," Jesse says, but he's looking at me.

"Bye." I watch them walk away.

Dizzy leans across the table and lightly slaps my arm. "You bitch!" she says gleefully. "Why didn't you say something? I knew it! You *are* into someone." She leans back and crosses her arms. "Jesse Kable. I'll admit, he seems like a decent choice, if you don't know him. Smart, great body, hardly talks to anyone, so he's got the whole mystery thing going on. I can see it. I can really see it." She rubs her fingers on her chin as if she were Dr. Freud himself. "So tell me, Daphne Wright, are you jealous of January Morrison? Because she's, like, Jesse's best friend? There's probably no reason to be jealous. Everybody thinks it's weird, but they swear they are just friends. And only friends. Personally, I think that January has, like, a secret boyfriend or something, because she's so, like, cryptic whenever she talks to me. After Jesse started going out with January at the beginning of this school year, everyone thought they were, like, the greatest couple. And then he just dumped her."

Dizzy plays with her giant hoop earrings while she thinks. "Personally," she takes a breath, "I wouldn't get too excited about him. Jesse's just sort of different. And maybe not in a good way.

You know? Before January, he dated this girl who was a couple years older than us. That's who we were talking about at the lake. They went out for, like, forever. Like six months or something. They broke up when she went to college. Texas Tech. Blech." Dizzy makes a face. "Quiet High people all want to go to the University of Oklahoma. The partying is better."

"The girl he supposedly stalked?" I remember that Dizzy was the one who cut off this conversation at the lake.

"Well, granted, that's just a rumor. But there was something weird about that whole situation. He was never quite the same after her. He's, like, so…distant sometimes. Like he's better than us or something. You probably don't want to count on this going anywhere. Even though," she admits, crinkling her eyebrows with approval, "he did seem pretty into you."

"I don't even know him," I say. "I've only talked to him a couple of times. We're practically strangers."

"Doesn't matter," Dizzy responds. "That's not how romance works. Clearly, you've never been in love." She says this a bit scornfully.

"And you have?"

"Yes. Well, sort of. A little bit. I was with Josh for a long time before we broke up. Like three months. I felt like we really had this spark, you know?"

I try to imagine Dizzy with red-haired Josh—and his biceps, Lefty and Right-Man—but my mind comes up blank.

"Romance, Daphne, happens because of a little something called chemistry—when two people are drawn together for reasons that nobody can explain. It's like putting magnets together. You can pull them apart, but they still want to be together. Nobody knows why. One of life's great mysteries."

"Actually," I correct her, "I think we *do* know why magnets are attracted to each other."

She waves her hand in front of her face. "Sometimes, two things just can't be apart."

"So do you believe the rumors? The thing about him stalking that girl?"

She drains her Diet Coke. "I only believe what I see. And I didn't see that."

We sit quietly for a minute or so until she asks, "Do you think you'll end up calling him, or what?"

"I thought you said I should forget about him."

"Daphne," she says in a very serious tone, "it's human nature or something to go for the guy who is bad for you. And you *are* human, aren't you?"

She has a point.

CHAPTER 10

Yeah, we broke up when I graduated. It just wasn't working anymore, and I didn't want to go off to college with a high school boyfriend. That's just dumb. And Jesse is so, like, deep. Intense, I guess you'd say. That got old real fast. It was like there was something inside of him that he was constantly fighting. There was good Jesse, and then there was dark Jesse. I just wanted to have fun, and dark Jesse was a real pain in the ass. And if you want to know the truth, he scared me. I was scared of him.

—Brit Gormley, in an interview with the *Quiet Daily News*

AT THE LAST MINUTE, I IMPETUOUSLY THROW A TAN CHENILLE newsboy cap on my head. I've never worn it before, because it seems cooler than I am. I nod at the mirror on my way out of the bathroom to the kitchen where Jesse is talking to Melissa.

"Did Jesse tell you he is planning to get a PhD in psychology?" Melissa asks me with excitement.

"Or go to med school," he adds.

"How could you keep this secret?" she asks me. "I could give you some tips for getting into a good grad school," she tells Jesse.

"Melissa, please. I'm sure Jesse doesn't want to talk about grad school right now."

"It's fine," he says. "Melissa is really interesting."

When he turns his back, I roll my eyes at Melissa, and she gives me a look that says, *See? He* does *want to talk to me.*

Jesse and I head for the door. "Come back without a head injury," Melissa calls to me.

"Very funny," I say.

Jesse and I aren't on a date, exactly. But I'm not sure what it is. Nevertheless, I'm so nervous that my hands are shaking—something that's totally unlike me. For a second, I fear I'm turning into one of those girls named Tiffani who dots the *i*'s in her name with hearts and writes *Mrs. Boyfriend's Last Name* all over her notebook. I try to shake it off.

"Where are you two kids off to?" Melissa asks.

"The lake?" Jesse asks me. "Unless you want to hit the game—QH is playing our big rival, the Enid Plainsmen. It's going to be a blowout."

"I hate baseball," I say.

"It's actually soccer. Weren't you paying attention at last week's pep rally?"

"Hardly. I hid in the bathroom during the pep rally so I wouldn't be swallowed up by all that cheesy school spirit stuff. The sight of pompoms makes me gag."

"It's probably genetic—the thought of cheerleading makes me break out in hives," Melissa adds.

"So you two are saying that I'm not going to win you over with my impressive ability to name every team member of the Dallas Cowboys or my all-state tennis cred?"

"Never," I say, just as Melissa says, "No," rather dramatically. Jesse laughs.

"Be home before dawn," Melissa calls as we walk out the side door. "Look for the *Viola sagittata*. They are in bloom right now! You might know them better as arrow-leaved violets," she adds confidentially to Jesse who, to his credit, nods politely and salutes her on his way out.

"We'll keep an eye out," he promises.

∎∎∎

We walk halfway around the lake until we get to one of docks on the west side. The barks from giant pickup trucks and the frequent whizz of souped-up cars off of Lakeview Road provide background noise. The sounds of Quiet traffic: boisterous, insistent, and completely unnecessary, since no one ever really has anywhere to go. Jesse suggests we sit for a while. When the wind blows, I can inhale the outdoors and him at the same time: it's a happy cross between freshly mowed lawn and the Gap. We sit next to each other with our feet hanging off the dock. I think of last Friday night, when we hung out in almost the same place, but something feels different now. My stomach is in knots—the kind you have when you're just about to stand up to give a speech that you memorized five minutes before. What is happening to me? *Get a grip*, I order myself. I've never felt this way before with a guy.

Jesse's hair is curling slightly from the humidity in the air. He smiles when he sees me looking—pushing that one rogue hunk of hair out of his eye—but his face conveys something that I can't identify. It's not the first time I've thought he is unreadable. His teeth are perfectly white, like a toothpaste advertisement. I instinctively close my mouth, wondering if maybe I should've begged Melissa for veneers. My teeth are okay, but not inhumanly white like his. He's wearing jeans and a plain, blue long-sleeved shirt. He looks put together somehow, like someone who never has a bad hair day or wrinkled pants or bad breath in the morning. He's intimidating, I decide. But when has a boy *ever* intimidated me? I recite NPR commentators' names in my head until I can calm down.

"Warm," I say offhandedly, because I always talk about weather when I can't think of anything else to say. It's a side effect of living in Minnesota.

"Yup," he says agreeably. "How's your head?"

"Functioning," I say and then inwardly cringe. What a dumb thing to say.

We sit quietly, watching the breeze blow ripples across the darkening water. The wind was out in full force earlier this evening, and it apparently scared away the joggers and dog walkers. The sky is a shiny gray, the color of monkey bars, and the air feels weird—there's a stillness in between the breezes that makes everything feel surreal.

"Tornado weather," Jesse says, holding his hands out as if to grasp the air. We watch one lone figure—a skinny girl in black spandex pants and a dark pink sports bra running sprints around the lake. She shoots down one side and then comes to a complete halt at the corner. She walks for a while with a hand on her side.

I wait until she sprints again, and I can't see her anymore as she passes through the trees on the south end of the lake. I play with my purse—an embroidered bag that Melissa got at One World— it's a free-trade product made in Guatemala. I feel stupid for having brought it, but I'm one of these people who feels naked without a purse, like I just might need an extra pen or a pack of Trident at any moment.

"Should we leave?" I ask.

"Nah, not yet. Do you feel how warm it is?" I reach out to touch the heavy air as he did. "It's going to have to turn cold first. You'll feel it."

I nod. I know about tornadoes. I remember spending summer evenings in my grandmother's basement, listening to an old radio spewing out reports about tornadoes touching down in all those small Minnesota towns: Park Rapids, Osage, Walker, Henrietta, Nevis, Akeley. Old-people names for old-people towns. It's not tornadoes in general that frighten me—it's Oklahoma tornadoes, a special brand of disaster. I remember seeing the news when the last really big one hit—people blown away were the lucky ones. It was the stories of people crushed to death, slowly, underneath cars and bathtubs and tractors that made everyone cringe. It was the people who were covered with hundreds of puncture wounds from flying nails and screws and other debris. In Minnesota, tornadoes are made of wind and air—in Oklahoma, they are made of fury.

I cautiously watch the gray sky, hopeful for the sliver of fading sunlight hanging out in the background.

"So I wanted to talk to you about something," he says. His tone is ominous—his serious-talk tone. I imagine him practicing it alone in front of the mirror. Except Jesse isn't the kind of guy who would do that.

"Okay," I say just as a car engine revs in the distance. This is also the same moment that I accidentally drop my purse into the water. I've been fidgeting with it, and I should've known that I'd eventually drop it. I'm not a clumsy person, but Jesse's presence is turning me into some kind of squirming mess. I feel like a kernel of popcorn in an air popper.

The strap of my purse gets caught on some of the weeds near the dock, so I bend over to grab it. When I do, I fall forward—in slow motion. I land on my stomach in an amazingly gentle belly flop. My face is immersed in the grimy water, and I have the urge to throw up, but I float there for a minute, wondering if I should just pretend that I've drowned. Surely that would be less embarrassing than this. But before I can float away and disappear, Jesse is in the water behind me, pulling me up with his arms around my waist. He's acting like a real lifeguard, which is probably fine if someone is actually drowning.

"I'm fine," I tell him, sputtering dirty lake water, grabbing for my hat, which is floating next to me.

The whole scene feels stupidly overdone—comical in the lamest way possible, like a Will Ferrell movie, something that my grandfather would've found hysterical. He always used to say to me, "Pull my finger, kid." That was the kind of stuff he found funny and that embarrassed me to death.

Jesse helps me get back up on the dock, even though I could've done it myself.

Probably.

This time, we sit on a park bench rather than the edge of the dock. My chances of drowning have significantly decreased. I try to avoid thinking about how I've probably contracted some sort of parasitic disease from the mucky water.

"Sorry about your shirt," I say, touching the soaking wet material, which is clinging tightly to him.

"Well," he replies, "it *was* new—to replace another shirt. Because of the blood from your head."

I want to jump off the dock again and swim away to the other side of the lake, where I can sulk in embarrassment by myself. The sprinting girl slows to a walk when she goes past our dock. She waves at us before resuming her run.

"We should go back," I say, but neither one of us makes a move to stand up. I shiver loudly, but not on purpose. My wet clothes and the drab air feel cold and clammy as they mingle together.

He puts his arms around me, even though he is damp too.

"I think I got water in my purse," I say, shaking the bag out in front of me, although I'm surprised to discover that it's held up quite well—the water seems to be rolling right off the fabric.

Guatemalan craftsmanship is everything Melissa believes it to be. She'll be thrilled.

He presses his lips tightly together, looking exactly the way he looked right after I threw up that first day in chemistry. "Do you want to be here? With me, I mean?"

"What I want is…" I'm trying to think of it, but he suddenly puts his hand on my wet hair, near the back of my head, but nowhere near my stitches, fortunately. The gesture is so spontaneous that even he seems surprised. I wince for no real reason. He moves his hand to my back.

"Yes," I say, simply and easily. The truth comes before I even consider lying. The closer he sits to me, the more I want to stay like this. Forever. What is wrong with me? Am I morphing into a girl like Brooklyn? Will I be wearing a one-piece bathing suit and talking into a fake microphone about world peace for baby chickens next?

"I suppose we should go home now," I tell him, because I sometimes say the opposite of what I feel. My stomach actually sinks when I think about leaving him. "The weather might turn." Damn my weather talk! I start to get up, but he grabs my arm. His grasp is hard, although he loosens up when I slump back down on the bench in a squishy puddle. He slides his hand down my arm, toward my hand, and holds onto it. He tugs gently, moving me closer, and I move where he's pulling me until I'm in his arms. He turns my face toward him. My awful wet hair is on full display, still dripping at the ends but already drying in odd shapes on top. Jesse pushes a wet hunk from my cheek with his free hand and then holds that hand against my cheek.

"Your hair is wet," he says. His hand is warm and smells like mints or gum. The whole thing is so absurdly romantic that I start to shiver again, and I'm afraid he'll think I'm having a seizure. He feels me shaking, and he pulls me toward his chest, my head resting on a part of his shirt that has somehow miraculously stayed dry. He puts his chin on my icky lake water hair.

"I don't know what it is about you, Daphne." He says this quietly, but I hear every word, soft and warm. His hand runs against my back, and for the first time ever, I know what it feels like to want to be with someone—really *be* with him. I can't get any closer to him, and I feel the frustration rising in my stomach. I want to feel his hands all over me. I've never thought that about anyone before.

He stands up, pulling me with him. It's the first time we've ever stood face to face, and I notice that he's very tall, taller than me, and I'm a healthy Midwestern five-foot-nine—just tall enough to feel gawky and giant. But in my water-filled, stud-covered heels, I am staring directly at his nose, the perfect height difference. He puts his hands on my shoulders, and I know he's going to kiss me.

Our lips come together like two pieces of a puzzle that you know are going to fit perfectly. We pause for one incredible moment, as if we are fighting the force of it. I hold my breath. And then suddenly, he pulls me even closer—so close that I'm not sure where he ends and I begin. He kisses me hard, and I respond without thinking. In fact, I'm so far outside myself that I can barely remember my own name anymore. It's only after we pull apart—reluctantly—that I finally understand what it's like to *want* someone. This is nothing like how I've felt with any other guy.

"Daphne," he says softly with his lips still close to mine. I have to fight the attraction. I want my lips back on his. He whispers to me, "I need to tell you something. Something about January."

I shake my head. I don't want to hear. Not now. Not right now.

He leans over and kisses me again—the first guy to *really* kiss me since Michael, one of the sort-of-boyfriends I had back at Academy. But kissing Michael was like kissing a puppy: nice, but sort of gross, because Michael always seemed to have more spit than lips. When I used to make out with him, I spent most of the time thinking about other stuff, like how people first discovered not to eat the banana peel, or an English paper coming due, or things like that. Kissing Jesse is totally amazing. It's sweet, but passionate, and I pull away before I really want to, because I am afraid of what might happen if I don't. I sigh. *This* is a moment. I feel electricity in my toenails. In my spleen. Radiating through my liver. I lean back into him, and we kiss again until my lips feel raw.

That's when the tornado sirens go off.

"Damn it!" Jesse says, looking up at the sky. "We should head back to the car." He grabs my hand, and we make a run for the car just as the sky opens up and spits out jagged pieces of hail.

When we get to the car, he pauses at the trunk and quickly pulls a blanket out, which I assume he's going to use to cover the seat of his black Mitsubishi Eclipse. I'm still pretty wet. Instead, he wraps the blanket tightly around me and gives me a warm hug. "Go ahead," he says, guiding me into the passenger seat. "You'll warm up quickly once we get the heat going."

The hail is coming down hard now, clapping loudly on the hood of his car. "I hope it doesn't leave dents," I say.

118

"Me too. This is my dad's car." He turns quickly down a tree-lined street and accelerates to well over forty, the houses on the street turning into a blur. He slows and pulls into a driveway.

"Your house?" I ask.

"Closer than my house," he says. "Mine is all the way up the hill." He points behind us. He pulls the car around back, past the three-car garage, and under the old carport next to it. "Perfect," he says. "Wanna go in the house?"

We listen to the hail hammer on the roof of the carport. "Let's wait a second," I say. Then, "Whose house it?"

"January's."

Then I definitely don't want to go inside. Yet when the wind picks up, and the lawn chairs from the deck start whipping across the yard, I know we have to make a run for the house.

"Let's go," I say with resignation.

A perfectly coiffed woman who smells like a medley of hyacinth, lemons, and money seems unsurprised to see us, as if she's used to visitors popping up during hailstorms. Probably happens all the time in Oklahoma. She efficiently shepherds us to a large closet underneath the stairs, where she insists that we stay until we know for sure that we'll be safe.

There isn't really enough room for all of us—Mrs. Morrison, Jesse, me, and Hillary, January's little sister—but we manage. Mrs. Morrison calls me Deborah and makes me put on dry clothes before joining the group—"I don't want you to get everything all wet, dear," she says while turning her nose up at me.

119

After I change into a faded T-shirt of January's and a pair of red sweatpants that are far too tight, I take a minute in the half-bathroom off the kitchen to push my hair over the bald spot. I find a barrette in my damp purse and gently clip the hair in place. Not great, but at least I don't look like the Swamp Thing's twin. I stuff my hat into my purse. In the hallway, I notice rows of family pictures taken at lakes and Disneyland and next to the fireplace at Christmas. Two smiling faces in each picture: January and Hillary. When I look closer, though, I can see that each picture has been carefully cut. An arm or a leg or some fingers belonging to a missing third person are in almost every shot.

That's the shooter, I realize with horror. It's been less than a month since his death, and he's already been excised from the Morrison household. I feel sad thinking about Mrs. Morrison bent over those photos with a razor blade, removing evidence of the shooter—her son—from her life. It's the creepiest thing I've ever seen.

There are no chairs in the space under the stairs, and even if there were, we couldn't sit on them, because the closet is basically a crawl space with about five feet of clearance at the far end. Nobody answers me when I muse out loud, wondering why people in Oklahoma don't build basements. Wouldn't that be the first thing you'd build?

We sit scrunched against the walls, Jesse and I next to each other, staring at Mrs. Morrison, who is wearing earrings the size of her head. I'm wondering how she doesn't fall over, when Hillary whips out a flashlight and a Harry Potter book to read out loud. In a strong, shrill voice, she begins, pausing only when the TV, turned up loudly in the living room, suspends programming to tell us something about the storm—the storm that is likely going to pass Quiet. "It's heading straight for Guthrie," the weatherman says gleefully, as if he were just waiting for something to take out Guthrie anyway. The smell of Mrs. Morrison's perfume makes me feel like I'm trapped in a rich old woman's lingerie drawer.

"Is your dad at Marine?" she asks when it is evident that we've listened to Hillary for as long as politeness dictates. It takes me a second, but I figure out that she means Marine Motors, the boat factory just outside of town, which is the second-largest employer in Quiet after Quiet State College.

"No," I say, not wanting to explain about my father—mostly, because I don't know anything about him. I used to ask, but Melissa never has much to say about him, except that she met him in graduate school, and he left before I was born. Even my grandmother never mentions him, and she's one of those people who will pull you aside and talk about the details of her irritable bowel syndrome. "My mom is a professor at the college."

"My dad died when I was only one year old," Hillary says haughtily, as if this is some sort of achievement. "My brother died too," she adds.

"Shush," Mrs. Morrison says, her face a tight mask. "We don't talk about that." Then she sticks her finger in her mouth, leans toward me, and wipes underneath my eyes. "Raccoon eyes," she tells me, wiping mascara on a tissue she takes out of the sleeve of her mint-green sweater set—the kind of thing you'd wear to sell southwestern jewelry at a swap meet. "A big no-no," she tells me with the wag of a finger. I'm stunned—did she actually just spit on my face? I rub at my eyes with the back of my hands and try not to puke.

"Gross," Hillary says—either about my raccoon eyes or about the spit—and returns to Harry Potter, Book 5, one that I never actually finished reading. She reads silently this time, but I can see her lips moving.

"I think we can leave now," I tell Jesse firmly.

"Let's stay a little longer," Mrs. Morrison says hopefully, "just to be on the safe side. Everybody stay put."

"It's fine," I tell her through clenched teeth.

"I'll check on the weather," Jesse says, ruffling Hillary's hair on the way out of the cramped space.

"So nice to have a man in the house," Mrs. Morrison sighs, looking longingly at Jesse's back as he walks to the living room. "A real man."

Eww. Did she just say that?

"It's fine," Jesse calls out to the rest of us.

"Let's make s'mores," Hillary says as we emerge single-file from our hiding place.

"Think of your hips," Mrs. Morrison replies.

Hillary looks like she weighs about thirteen pounds.

"Do it. Eat a bunch of them," I whisper in Hillary's ear. She just stares at me blankly.

It's lighter outside than it was when we arrived, the wind has died down, the hail has melted already, and the wind chimes are pleasantly singing in the distance. "We should do that again sometime," Hillary says, looking adoringly at Jesse.

"I don't know, Hilly. Weren't you scared?"

"No!" she says indignantly. "I'm not scared of tornadoes. Or thunderstorms. That's January."

"I assume she's safe," Mrs. Morrison says, "at the soccer game. But I bet they were rained out. I hope they went to the gym to wait out the bad weather. January just loves sporting events. She's a basketball cheerleader, you know." This last part is directed at me, and I just nod, even though I'm quite positive that January is not a cheerleader. Mrs. Morrison seems to live in a world of her own making, though, and maybe in that world January wears a QH sweater and chants "Here-we-go" from the sidelines of the basketball court. "She'd be beside herself if she was out during a storm like this." Mrs. Morrison looks to Jesse. "You know, that child has always been afraid of the tiniest bit of weather. Ever since she was a child, she's been afraid of thunder, lightning, wind—you name it. I don't know what gets into her, but I worry about her. Last time she got caught in a thunderstorm alone, I found her hiding underneath her bed, sobbing."

The color in Jesse's face seems to fade—he goes from tan to white. He looks...scared. I poke him in the shoulder. He doesn't even notice me.

"She's a big chicken," Hillary says. "It's a condition. It's called lilapsophobia—a phobia of tornadoes and other dangerous weather." Hillary then spells the word for me, like maybe I might need it for a spelling bee or something.

Jesse looks at me sideways, a strange expression on his face. "Guess we better go. Thanks for letting me keep my car protected. My dad is going to kill me if there's even the tiniest dent."

"Hail is an act of God," Hillary says solemnly, as if she is the claims adjustor from the insurance company. I remember that's what Melissa's insurance person said after she hit a deer coming home from my grandparents' house one summer.

Jesse rushes me out to the car. I barely have time to grab my wet clothes, which Mrs. Morrison has placed in a plastic bag using only the tips of her fingers, as if they were contaminated. "Nice to meet you, Deborah," she says as we leave. She smiles too widely. "I hope you'll come back again soon. I simply adore meeting January's friends." She gives me a Joker-esque smile that creeps me out.

I shiver when we get into the car. "That was surreal," I say. "Don't you think that was weird?"

"January isn't at any game. She's going to need help."

"Because of a hailstorm and a few gusts of wind?"

Jesse turns to look at me. "Trust me. I know January. This could be really serious. We don't know what she's capable of doing."

"Don't you think you're being a little dramatic?" I ask.

"You don't know January," he replies ominously.

CHAPTER 11

Jesse was always running to save January. Everybody assumed he was in love with her. But I wasn't going to tell Daphne that.

—Dizzy Lewis-Strong in an interview with the *Quiet Daily News*

JESSE TURNS HARD INTO THE MUDDY VACANT FIELD BEHIND Bear's Auto Repair, a ramshackle trailer with an old-fashioned gas pump in front. He brings the car to a jerking stop next to an old pickup, gets out of the car, and heads toward the abandoned train car before I even have my door open. But then he stops and comes back to my side of the car. "I'm sorry, Daphne. I really am. I'll just be a minute." Before I answer, he sticks his head inside, and kisses me gently on the lips. Then he shuts my door. I get the message: he wants me to stay put.

I nod my head and give him a fake smile. He seriously expects me to sit in the car and wait for him? I don't think so.

I kick off my shoes in the car and sink into the mud when I step out. It's cold and mushy, with the consistency of Melissa's oatmeal. Better than ruining my shoes. I swear under my breath. It seems like January is always on the edge of peril. It's strange the way everyone rushes to her side, as if she's a breakable vase on a high shelf, teetering at the edge during a low, rumbly earthquake. The way Jesse just knows she's in trouble signals something between them that I'm not sure I can understand. And he just knows where she is. Are people who are *just friends* that connected to each other?

I trudge through the mud about three steps before I stumble and end up elbows-first in muddy grass. "Damn it!" I say loudly.

I guess I can understand January's fear of bad weather—it sounds kind of bizarre, but in Oklahoma, being afraid of weather is, in my opinion, totally logical. Where else would swirly tornadoes appear out of nowhere and pick up things like barns and silos? But Jesse's reaction feels overly dramatic, sort of histrionic. He's been somewhat—what's the word? Ominous?—ominous all night. Especially after he said that he wanted to talk to me about January.

Against my will, my brain starts racing. I think of this stupid soap opera my grandmother watches. When I talk to her on the phone, she tells me about the lives of the people on her story. *The girlfriend is always the last to know when the man is running around with every floozy in flowered underpants*, Grandma tells me in that funny, old-fashioned way she talks. *There's another broad, but the girlfriend is just plain out to lunch, the dumb cluck.*

Are Jesse and January together, like a couple? Am I the other woman? *No*, I tell myself. *That's ridiculous. If he's in love with January, why take me along to rescue her? Prince Charming doesn't show up with a wet-haired, bald-spotted girl on the white horse behind him. But maybe he doesn't even realize he's in love with her,*

126

I think suddenly. That's even worse. Unrequited love is the worst, according to Grandma. I squeeze my eyes shut and will these thoughts away. This is why restricting relationships to hooking up every now and then—for a good make-out session—is highly underrated. I'm actually turning into one of the girls from Grandma's stories.

I'm covered in mud now, but I keep walking toward the light of the half-moon making its appearance from behind the remaining gray cloud cover. It's just bright enough for me to make out the billowy movement of a silhouette standing near the edge of the train car. I squint at the graffiti-covered side. I see weird symbols and words. *BE AWARE. I WILL HAUNT YOU.* The green letters practically glow against the night sky. Piles of garbage surround the whole area. It's so dirty and grimy that I can't imagine why anyone would ever come here, yet Jesse said on the way here that it's "January's place, where she always goes when she's trying to disappear." The moonlight illuminates Jesse, who approaches the unrecognizable dark figure, and then the two of them disappear behind the train car. The sound of cars passing on the road a few hundred feet in the distance becomes almost soothing.

I decide I'm going in. After I count to a hundred. That's all I'm giving them. One minute, forty seconds.

At eighty-two, two figures emerge in front of the train car. January is walking a bit off to the side of Jesse with her skinny, bare arms across her chest. I audibly gasp when I see her hair— she's cut off the wild, long lion's mane. Instead, she's sporting a blond Louise Brooks. The real kind. Short, short. Pixie-ish.

I instinctively touch my own head. At once, I feel conventional in comparison. My cut is just plain dull next to hers. Without the frizzy hair clouding her face, she looks almost…normal. She's stunning, actually. Not beautiful—not even pretty exactly. But dazzling somehow. Her features are perfectly contoured, her neck long and graceful. She shakes her head once, twice, and I realize with a pang of something sharp and unrecognizable that she looks like the kind of sophisticated woman—not girl—that you photograph in black and white next to the Eiffel Tower. She's the wrinkled photo you carry, because she's the girl who can't be captured any other way.

Suddenly, I feel disgustingly normal and well adjusted, too happy and unscarred to be interesting. Too boring to be someone's unrequited love. I'm just the dumb cluck. With muddy clothes.

"I told you to stay in the car," Jesse says to me.

"Excuse me? I don't take orders from you or anyone else." I stop, more because my feet are stuck again than because I'm making a point.

Jesse stops too. "Sorry," he says. "I didn't mean it like that." January tries to walk ahead of us, but Jesse grabs her arm to slow her down. She shakes him off.

From behind her appears a third person, almost like magic—an apparition in a wife beater and denim shorts. It's Nate Gormley, that kid from the lake. "What are you doing here?" I ask him. He just ignores me. "Everything okay?" I ask Jesse.

He nods at me and then reaches over and pulls January toward him, hard. She staggers in the mud and loses a flip-flop. "Let's go," he tells her.

She kicks off the other shoe and stumbles over the even ground barefoot. "I'm going with him," she says and points to Nate.

Nate shrugs. "Whatever, dude."

"She's drunk. Majorly drunk." Jesse sighs. "Come on, Jan. Come with us."

She stumbles toward the pickup, not Jesse's car. "Nah," she says. "I'm going with Nate." Nate has to help her into the old truck, giving her a big push on her skinny behind. Even so, she almost falls out twice. He doesn't even look at Jesse when he gets in the truck behind January and pulls away, spraying mud on Jesse's car—and on us. Muddy water runs down my face.

"She's drinking again. And she had a panic attack when that storm hit."

"Is she going to be okay?"

"I don't know," he says. "She's been like this ever since..." Jesse trails off mid-sentence.

"Ever since what? Since her brother? That can't be easy."

"No." He shakes his head. "It's not easy. Everyone has done their best to forget about him."

"Even his mom," I say, thinking about those pictures in Mrs. Morrison's living room.

He opens the car door for me, and I hesitate before getting in. I'm going to get mud everywhere. "Don't worry about it," Jesse says, as if reading my mind. "I'll take care of it tomorrow."

When he gets into the driver's seat, he puts his hand over mine. "I'm sorry, Daphne. I didn't mean for this to ruin our night."

"No big deal," I say, but I move my hand away from his. He

senses the change in temperature. "Can I ask you something?" Dizzy's gossip about Jesse and the phantom older girl—the girl Jesse was allegedly stalking—looms large in my mind. I've always been honest and straightforward. Why not ask him?

"Of course."

"Before me, before I moved here, were you"—I try to think of the right word—"*involved* with someone, someone who was really important to you—?"

He surprises me when he interrupts. "January and I went out a few times, but it was never anything more than that. We were never, you know, a couple or whatever. I care about her. Just as a friend."

"Before January, I mean."

He shifts in the driver's seat, a smile overtaking his face. "Daphne, are you jealous?"

"No!" I say too quickly.

"Why are you suddenly interested in my love life?" he says playfully.

"I'm not!" I yell, horrified because I feel like a fool, and double horrified because I hate the idea of being one of *those* girls. "I'm just curious," I say, trying to regain my composure.

"Well," he says, leaning toward me, "I'm telling you that I'm here with you because I like you." He kisses me on the nose before he turns the key in the ignition and shifts his car into drive.

"So there's no older girl, someone you had trouble…letting go? A former girlfriend you want to tell me about?"

"No girls anywhere," he says, suddenly cheerful—the most cheerful I've seen him. "I'm practically a social pariah."

I drop the subject, and as we drive away I twist around to look back at the abandoned railroad car. I have to blink when I see him—he's standing at the edge of the field. A flash of light from the neon sign lands on him, and I see his face clearly. He looks up at the sky and then straight at me. Josh Heller. Even in the dark and from this distance, I recognize him: a red-headed ghost. What is he doing here? And why didn't we see him before?

I blink my eyes, and he is gone. All I see are trees, rusted-out abandoned cars, old refrigerators, and mattress boxes with the springs sticking out. This is apparently everyone's dumping ground.

I face forward. "Was anyone else out there? Back there?" I ask.

"Nope. That's what worries me." Jesse's face falls, his joviality from a moment ago completely gone. "January shouldn't be out here at all, especially with that Nate kid when she's been drinking. And when it's raining. She gets so terrified."

"Oh. I thought I saw Josh Heller too."

Jesse steps on the brake, and we both slide forward in our seats a bit. He puts the car in reverse and drives back to our parking spot—my neck flopping around like a baby's.

This time, he doesn't even tell me to wait in the car, but I do anyway. Jesse stalks out of the car, walking quickly with big steps. I look behind me—there are no other cars in the parking lot. Jesse is gone for a while—more than ten minutes, according to the clock on his dashboard. Just when I start to worry, he appears at the driver's side door.

"There's nobody out here," he says.

I don't argue with him, but I do give him a *suit yourself* shrug—something I perfected around Melissa, who always thinks she's right.

We move slowly over the muddy parking lot. I twist around and look behind me again, but there's nothing there, save for the garbage.

"We used to be close when we were kids. All of us were friends—Josh, January, me, and him." I know he's referring to the shooter. "Josh is my stepbrother, you know." I nod. "So we've kind of grown up together. Our parents got married when we were eleven. And back when I lived with my mom, before she moved, I lived next door to January. They're like family to me. But Josh and I barely speak these days."

"Why?"

"A lot of reasons."

Jesse pulls the car onto a road with a sudden burst of power. We're on some winding, dark U.S. highway that I never knew led to Quiet. He speeds up until the speedometer hits seventy, and then he levels off.

He seems so serious now, his shoulders knotted up and his hands gripping the steering wheel. He's almost a different person than the one I saw just a few minutes ago—the one who was joking around, making me laugh. He steers the car left on Main. He's taking the long way—all the way around the football stadium—back to my house.

We ride in silence until Jesse flips on the satellite radio. "Want to pick a station?" he asks.

I lean over and stare at the rows of buttons and the green-lit screen telling me we are currently on Outlaw Country. I make a face. I press buttons and watch the digital screen move from gas mileage stats to a compass to a temperature reading. "What the hell?" I say under my breath, grateful that the car stereo in Melissa's car only has two buttons: up and down. Jesse snickers.

"What?"

"You look so cute trying to figure out the stereo." The kind, gentle Jesse is back with one hand on the wheel and the other on the center console. He keeps his eyes on the road while he moves his right hand to mine and gently pushes my finger on one of the pre-programmed buttons. The music immediately shifts from twangy Waylon Jennings to old-timey jazz. He moves my hand with his, and we set both of them on the center console between us.

"Daphne?" he asks when we finally pull into my driveway. "Do you know why I shouldn't be here with you?"

"I haven't the slightest idea," I say.

"Because I could see myself falling in love with you."

I jerk my head sideways to face him, but he's staring straight ahead, his eyes trained on the garage door. "I'm not sure what to say. I—"

Jesse gently reaches over and puts his hand over my mouth. "Shhh." He lets his hand fall.

"Maybe we don't need to talk," I whisper just as our lips meet, the taste of mud lingering long after we part.

CHAPTER 12

January's secrets weren't mine to tell.

—Jesse Kable, quoted in the book, *The Future of the Predicted*, publication forthcoming

JESSE CALLS ME MONDAY EVENING, JUST BEFORE MELISSA and I sit down to a dinner of frozen vegan pizza, and asks me to go to Tulsa. "I'll pick you up in an hour, okay? If you're feeling up to it. Sorry for the short notice, but this was kind of a last-minute opportunity."

I absentmindedly rub the spot on my head. The stitches should dissolve soon, but my skull is still sore. For some reason, every time it aches, I think of that day in the supply closet, stuck in that little cupboard. It's like the aching in my skull is a little physical reminder telling me, *Hey, everything is not okay, and it may never be okay again.* "What are we going to do?" I ask, shoving the dark clouds from my brain.

"It's a surprise," he says, "but I'll give you a hint: it's totally your kind of thing."

When he arrives, exactly one hour later, I'm waiting on the front steps. I contemplated doing the whole change-clothes-ten-times thing—like a movie montage—but ended up throwing on a short, white cap-sleeved dress made out of lace that Melissa bought for me at the thrift store in Quiet. I added black leggings and my favorite red ballet flats, and I threw on the jean jacket that I've had forever. In the kitchen, I pulled a white daisy from a vase on the table and stuck it gently in my hair with a bobby pin.

"We could be twins!" Melissa screamed when I walked through the living room.

"You're mortifying me," I'd responded.

"You look…different," Jesse says when I get into his car.

"Uh, thanks?" I look down at my lace dress, wondering if that was really a compliment or just a statement.

"No, I mean, you look good. I've just never seen you in a dress before. You look really good." He leans over and kisses my collarbone. Then he rubs his fingers over the area he's just touched with his lips. I get goose bumps. "You're beautiful."

"Thanks." I shift uncomfortably in my seat. I'll never get used to these kinds of compliments. Getting them is kind of a recent development—it started happening about a year ago, when I grew into my gangly body and actually got some boobs. I still feel like a gawky little girl most days. "You look good too."

And he does. He's wearing nice jeans and a baby-blue button-up shirt, which I decide must be his signature color—everything he owns is blue. The first two buttons at the top are undone, but that makes him look cool and relaxed, not like someone's creepy uncle, which is a risk guys run if they leave too many buttons undone.

"So where are we going?" I ask as he pulls onto the four-lane toll road that leads out of town and toward Tulsa.

"It's a surprise."

"No January?" I ask, half-joking.

He reaches over and takes my hand gently. "Definitely no January. She's at home, and there is absolutely no risk of thunder or rain tonight. It's just you and me—the evening will not end with us sitting underneath the stairs with her mom. As fun as that was." He grins at me.

He flips on the stereo and hits the CD player. The retro sounds of Peggy Lee soothe me. "What a lovely way to burn," she croons. My grandma had this record—an actual record. It was one of my favorites. We ride for a long time, enveloped by the sounds of the CD, pausing twice to throw quarters in the giant metal bowls at the toll stops.

"So what happened out there Saturday night? At the abandoned train?" I finally say. I'm unable to get January and our last conversation about her out of my mind, and I haven't talked to Jesse since that night. He called once, but I had Melissa tell him I wasn't home. I'm not the kind of girl who wants to look too eager.

"The usual. January drinks, and then she gets stupid. Does stupid stuff. It's become a pattern for her. Seems like she always needs someone to rescue her these days."

"Can you rescue her forever?"

He squints out the window and searches the darkening sky. Dead armadillos litter the side of the road—something I don't think I'll ever get used to. It's as if every armadillo in the state eventually ends up shriveled and rotting on the side of the roads here. "I don't know. I'd like to think people can change, but…" He trails off. "Funny how all of our conversations keep coming back to that."

"Do you believe in PROFILE?"

"Almost there," he says, more to himself than me as he turns on his right-hand signal and waits to turn toward the tall, gold building that is part of Oral Roberts University. He finally answers my question: "What do *you* think?"

"I think you are evading my question."

"Does it matter what I think?"

"Yes."

"I have a proposition," he says. "Let's not talk about PROFILE. Just for one night."

"Deal," I say reluctantly.

■ ■ ■

Jesse doesn't tell me what we are doing tonight, even after we are seated in purple-covered chairs in a large auditorium, staring at the thick, red-curtained stage. It's not until the curtain goes up and I see the lone table, the radio equipment, and Ira Glass, the host of my favorite public radio show, *This American Life*, that I figure it out.

I punch him gently in the shoulder. "How did you know that I love this show?"

"I have my ways," he whispers, holding his palms together and wiggling his fingers.

"Really, how did you know?"

"Your laptop. That day at school. You had the site book-marked, and all those NPR podcasts were on your desktop. I had to get you tickets. My dad called in a favor and got these at the very last minute."

I lean over and give him a spontaneous hug.

Watching a live radio show might be as much fun as going to my grandma's bell-ringing choir at church, but not *this* performance. We listen and watch, riveted by the whole thing. I like that I can close my eyes and still get everything. It's all about listening, which is pretty cool. The theme is criminal acts—an apt topic given our earlier discussion. The first segment is about a judge in Florida who makes shoplifters stand outside the businesses they shoplifted from, holding signs that say, *I stole from this store.* The second segment is a sad one, about an old woman who helped her husband commit suicide when he couldn't remember who she was anymore. The segment is narrated by the couple's grandson, who ends by asking his wife to help him make a similar decision when the time comes. The third segment is a funny one, about a girl who stole a pair of acid-washed jeans from her best friend at summer camp in order to wear them on a date with a guy she really liked. "This is a story about love gone wrong," Ira tells us.

"As it turned out," a frumpy woman with glasses says into the table microphone, "Donny refused to go out with me again, because he thought my pants were just that ugly. Can you imagine? Pants so ugly that nobody will date you because of them? That's how ugly these things must have been. Acid washed, pleated at the top, tapered at the bottom. *Awesome,* I thought. Fast-forward a few years. Donny ends up marrying my friend Beth—the girl who owned the pants. God, I hated her for the longest time after that."

"I bet you did," Ira says.

"But you want to know what? Here's the big twist: twenty years later, Donny cheated on Beth with a college student. He took off and left Beth with three kids and half a million dollars of debt."

"Well, there you have it," Ira Glass says, in his nasal-y voice. "Crime doesn't pay…unless it does."

The applause is deafening. Among all these public radio nerds, I feel at home.

"Thank you," I tell Jesse when we walk outside the big double doors of the theater. "I know it's kind of dorky."

Jesse reaches for my hand. His is warm and soft, big enough to engulf my palm and fingers. "*Dorky* is a good thing," he says. "I like that about you."

The car is parked far away, down a dark side street where we found meters to feed when we first arrived. On the way into the theater, the streets were crowded: lots of people were going in and out of restaurants and stores, business people were locking office doors, heading home with briefcases and laptops. Now, it's almost deserted, save for the few people who come and go from the dingy little bars scattered haphazardly along the street.

"So," Jesse says as we walk quickly, with me trying to keep my ballet flats on my feet, "does crime pay?

"I guess it does. Sometimes. But you never answered my question from before." So much for our deal not to talk about PROFILE. How could we *not* talk about it? "Do you think people can change? Does being predicted mean your life is predetermined? That everything you do will ultimately lead you back to something—whatever it is—that PROFILE says you'll do?"

We walk past a huddle of homeless men who are sharing a bottle of something in a paper bag. "You got any change you can spare, friend?" one of them asks Jesse. He drops my hand and reaches into his pocket, pulling out a crumpled bill. "Bless you," the man says.

Jesse puts his arm around my shoulders and leads me toward the car, parked another half-block down the street. "I think everybody does the best they can."

■■■

I—the girl who prides herself on having no body image issues—suddenly come down with a case of *oh-my-god-do-my-calves-look-fat-in-this-swimsuit?* So I do something I've never done before: I go for a run. It's after nine on Tuesday night, the first day I feel absolutely one hundred percent healed. My head doesn't even hurt anymore. The run is part of my plan to get in shape for Josh's birthday pool party that Dizzy can't stop talking about, even though it's still a month away. "You'll totally have to get a killer suit," she told me in school today.

It's after dark. Melissa has warned me not to run after dark. "I know Quiet is a small town, but you can't be too safe." She's in the garage, working late again. Lacing up my shoes, I decide that

I can sneak out and be back before she even notices. I grab her key chain—the one with the tiny flashlight on the end of it.

The air is warm and thick. For the last week, everyone had been saying that spring was definitely here to stay. And just like that, in a matter of a day or so, summer trampled over spring and blanketed everything with humidity, so even when it's not that hot, it feels sticky.

I turn left on Monroe Street and jog toward the small pond on campus. I find my stride after a while, near the Coleman Center, the college gym, feeling nothing but the hard slap of pavement against my Nikes.

When I trip over something, I have exactly a tenth of a millisecond to realize that I'm flying through the air before I land on my knees, skidding across the sidewalk with my palms downward.

"What the heck?" someone says.

"Sam?" I peer up at the hulking Sam Cameron as I struggle to get up. "Where did you come from?"

"Hey," he says. "Hey, Daphne." He smiles at me and holds out his fist for a fist-bump. I give him a little pound just to be polite, even though I feel like a jackass doing it, even though my knees are killing me.

"I tripped," I announce, as if it were not patently obvious.

"I know." He points behind me at the strong cord across the sidewalk, where construction crews poured fresh cement earlier in the day. It's hardened now—a fact that becomes clear as the stinging of my knees works its way up my legs. "Looks like a trip rope," he says. "Doesn't seem all that safe."

"No kidding. I didn't even see the rope."

"Yeah, well, I think there are supposed to be cones here." He looks around and then points at the two bright orange cones sitting on top of someone's car. "A joke." I notice that he's wearing a bright yellow sweatband over his floppy blond curls.

"Ha, ha," I say sarcastically as I stand up and brush the dust off my knees. "Damn it." I wonder if I'm cursed or something, destined to injure myself on a weekly basis.

He bends over to peer at my knees and then notices that one is bleeding. A lot. "Gross." He stumbles backward and looks away. I bend over and try to brush the bits of gravel out of the cut. "I hate blood," he says.

"I remember," I mutter, thinking of that night at the diner.

He stands with his back to me, his hands on his hips. By the dim light of approaching headlights, I see that he has pit stains. Still, he is kind of cute. I guess I can maybe see why Brooklyn and all the other girls are gaga over him.

The sound of a bouncing basketball causes me to turn around. We both look. I'm surprised to see that it's Jesse. "Hey," Sam calls, "I got a patient for you."

Jesse quickens his pace. "What's up? You okay, Daphne? What are you doing here? What happened?"

I hold my knee up at the same time he bends down to look at it. "Another injury. I feel like I'm always wounded and bleeding lately."

"Then I guess it's a good thing I'm not a vampire," he says cheerfully.

143

"And if I'm not wounded, I'm drowning," I say.

"It's a good thing for you that I have a hero complex. And it's a good thing that I happened to be here. Small world."

"Phew." I wipe imaginary sweat from my brow.

"What are you doing out here anyway?"

"Besides sprawling out face-first on the pavement? Jogging."

"I didn't know you jogged."

"I don't, obviously. And apparently, you just hang around and wait for me to have accidents." I feel like a girl in a Gothic novel. Frankly, I feel a tiny bit like January. I recoil a bit in horror.

"Okay, kids," Sam says, "enough of this. Let's play b-ball, Kable. Isn't that what you came here to do?" He grabs the ball from under Jesse's arm, dribbles out a few feet, and then turns suddenly and throws it hard at Jesse's chest. Jesse catches it, but not before it knocks the breath out of him. He doubles over slightly.

"Hey! What's your problem, Cameron?" he says, throwing the ball back.

"What's yours?" Sam says in a tone I haven't heard since second grade. "I'm going inside," he says, heading toward the entrance of the gym, pausing briefly to look at me. I look down at the fresh cement.

"What's his deal?" I ask.

Jesse sighs. "Long, long story."

"He's being an ass," I say.

"A little bit. He's not used to meeting a girl who doesn't want him."

"I don't even know him."

"Doesn't matter," Jesse says. "You're the new girl. And he wants you to notice him. He wants you to fall all over him."

"I'm not used to being such a hot commodity," I say, wincing when I touch my knee. That's mostly true. I've never had trouble finding guys to date, but I'm also not exactly a supermodel.

"Daphne, you have no idea." Jesse's voice turns serious. He moves toward me.

"We're like magnets," I say cheesily, thinking of what Dizzy said that day at the mall. I'm softening, feeling the pull toward him.

"No," Jesse says firmly. "Definitely not. The attraction is more like gravity." He puts his hands on either side of my face.

"Gravity?"

"Yeah, inevitable."

"Unstoppable. Invisible. And totally necessary," I add, mildly repulsed by my own sincerity.

My knee stops stinging as soon as our lips meet.

When we pull apart, Jesse speaks first. "I had a great time Monday night."

"Me too," I say. "Thanks for taking me."

Before Jesse can answer, Sam returns to us, bouncing a basketball with each step.

"I thought you were playing basketball inside," I say.

"Nobody showed. Big date on Monday, huh?"

"Sam," I say, "didn't your mother ever tell you that eavesdropping is rude?"

"Honestly, it's no big deal. I'm spoken for. I'm with Brooklyn. So it's not like I'm jealous of you, Kable." So what Jesse says is true. He *is* jealous. Sam then says to me, "You must like guys who aren't available."

"What is that supposed to mean?"

"You ever wonder why Jesse spends so much time with January Morrison?"

"What are you trying to say?"

"He's not saying anything," Jesse answers. He shifts his weight from one foot to the other and then crosses his arms in front of his chest. "He's just being an asshole." He shoots Sam a look that I'm not meant to see.

Sam holds the basketball at his chest and moves a few steps backward. "Yeah, I'm just being a jerk. Forget about it." He walks toward the parking lot, bouncing the ball hard against the pavement.

"He's acting like an idiot," Jesse says after Sam is gone.

"Yeah," I say, but I realize as soon as the word is out of my mouth that I wouldn't know. I hardly know any of these people. Is Sam a jerk? Or is he telling the truth that I just don't want to hear? Because the truth is, I don't want to be *just* Jesse's friend. I want something more. The shock of it makes me feel almost sick to my stomach. Is this what it feels like to want to be with someone? Nauseated and riddled with jealousy?

When I finally fall asleep that night, I dream of Jesse and January walking on a wide suspension bridge spanning a sparkling river. As soon as I yell, "Hey! Look! Over here!" January turns to me with a smirk on her face.

"We're leaving," she says as she grabs Jesse's hand, and they run across the bridge side by side, leaving me abandoned.

"Wait for me!" I call.

Even my dreams have turned melodramatic. I guess this is what happens when you fall deeply and totally in lust.

I'm officially a cliché.

CHAPTER 13

People didn't really know me. They thought I was just some dumb jock. I wasn't. I'm not now either. They all way underestimated me. Especially Daphne; she thought I was just some idiot. She didn't know me at all.

—Sam Cameron, quoted in the book *The Future of the Predicted*, publication forthcoming

"COME ON. IT'LL BE FUN," DIZZY SAYS AS WE WALK UP THE front steps of the school this morning.

"I don't know. It's not really my thing. Frat parties are kind of Neanderthal, aren't they?"

"What else do you have planned?" she asks, as if she can't imagine I'd have anything else to do, ever.

I yawn. "I don't know, Dizz. It's only Wednesday morning."

"True," she says. "I don't even know what I'm going to do in five minutes."

"Go to class?" I ask.

"Maybe. We'll see how I feel when the bell rings." She stops in her tracks. "Oh. My. God. Have you seen her?" She's pointing at January, who is digging through her locker. "Nice hair," she says sarcastically. "Looks an awful lot like yours. Only not as hot," she quickly adds.

We watch January run her hand through the front of her hair and leave it standing on end in an appealing mess. "Actually, she does look really cool."

Dizzy loudly says to me, "Dude, she's single-white-femaling you. Weeeird. Have you seen that movie, *Single White Female*? It's classic. We should Netflix it."

I don't even respond. I'm distracted, because today is the day that Jesse and I *go public*. Whatever that means. After the incident with Sam last night, Jesse called me.

"So you up for lunch together tomorrow? In the cafeteria at school?" he'd asked.

"Fine dining? Of course, I'm always up for that. I'm hoping they'll be serving the lobster thermidor and braised spring vegetables."

"Would you settle for a Sloppy Joe?"

"Sure," I say. And with that, it was settled. Up until now, we'd been avoiding each other at school, mostly because we hadn't wanted to talk about *us* too much, ruin whatever good thing we have going. But today, we will sit next to each other in the cafeteria and try to avoid sharing smoldering looks over our milk cartons. We will not pretend we are perfect strangers, which is what we have been doing.

For the first time ever, I lament that there is no millennial equivalent to *going steady*. I have no words to describe what's happening with Jesse or the feelings that I'm having. I wish for the zillionth time that I hadn't spent the bulk of my teenage years in private schools. At Academy, relationships revolved around two things: sex or a mutual interest in SAT prep guides. Anything that wasn't a hookup was just a stepping stone for getting into a good college. I don't even know what to call Jesse. *Friend* doesn't do us justice. *Boyfriend* makes me feel like I'm thirty-five. What's left? I lament the paucity of the English language. Oh, god. I'm channeling Melissa again. I laugh out loud.

"What are you cackling about?" Dizzy asks me now. We are headed for New QH: English for Dizzy, chemistry for me.

"Nothing," I say.

"You've got a secret," Dizzy singsongs, her face just inches from my ear. "She's got a secret," she chants. Today, Dizzy is wearing a micro-mini plaid skirt with suspenders, and her hair is braided with a red ribbon through it. She tugs on the ribbon.

"*Maybe* I have a secret," I tell Dizzy, checking my watch to see how much time I have before the late bell. The hallways have already started to clear out, and we're walking at a snail's pace now, stopped back near the row that contains January's locker. Brooklyn and Lexus join us.

"Daphne and Jesse are the flavor-of-the month," Brooklyn spits out. "Sam told me all about it." Well, so much for secrets.

"Thanks for sharing that, Brook," I say.

In the distance, January's neck stiffens, and her shoulders become rigid. She's listening. Brooklyn follows my gaze. "Look who's here," she says to all of us. "Somebody forgot to take the trash out. After what her brother did…well, I can't believe they let her back in the school." January hears it. I can tell by the

151

way she almost shrinks, standing there in her green-striped tights with a long white T-shirt hanging sloppily past her thighs. "You must hate her more than all the rest of us do," Brooklyn says to me in a fake confidential tone. "Not just because she's trying to steal Jesse, but because of what her brother did to you. Making you hide out in that cupboard. I'd be a basket case if I were you. I can't believe you can even face school." Things have been weird between Brooklyn and me ever since the diner incident. She never officially apologized, but I get the sense that she's trying not be a total bitch. She gives me a pageant smile.

"I'm fine," I reassure her.

"No!" Dizzy yells suddenly—a delayed reaction—while she playfully swats my shoulder. "You and Jesse! I knew it! And I love it! I mean, I hate your guts, but I still love it!" She gives me a wink. She's changing the subject away from the shooting—something that I still can't think about for very long or I start to feel queasy. "Why didn't you tell me this was serious, ya whore?" I still haven't gotten used to being called *slut*, *bitch*, *skank*, or *whore* as a term of endearment, especially because everyone is just as likely to use those same words to mean something bad. Melissa would go into immediate cardiac arrest if she heard the way girls talk to each other here.

"What?" Lexus screams. "Jesse? And this girl?" She points at me. "High five!" she yells.

"Oh, yeah," Dizzy says. She grabs my arm and stops me from moving forward. "Daphne and Jesse are hot like fire." She squeals, "This is so sexy!" She hits me on my shoulder again, harder this time. "Why didn't you tell me? I thought it was just some kind of crush. I didn't realize you two were going all Brad and Angie on me."

"Well," I say carefully, "we were kinda keeping it quiet. And it hasn't been that long. It's not like we're getting married or anything. We're just, you know, getting to know each other."

January slams her locker shut, no books in her hands, and heads toward the library.

"Keeping it on the chill," Dizzy says, nodding her head as if she were a part of the whole plan from the very beginning. She leans over and hugs me. "This is very cool."

"Yeah," Brooklyn says stonily. "Very cool. We're all very happy for the great Daphne Wright." She walks—book-on-the-head-style—in the direction of the library, following January.

"What?" Dizzy says mock-innocently. "What'd I say? Well, whatever. Forget her. Listen, Daph," she flips her braid over her shoulder, "I have to run. I can't be late today. Last week, I walked into English ten minutes late, and Mr. Boren made me spell everything I said for the rest of the class period. And I can't spell worth shit. Ugh." She shudders. "I'm retro-cringing just thinking about it." She grimaces and then takes off, skipping down the hallway until she trips over one of her heels.

Cafeteria lunch is revolting: cold pancakes with sticky cinnamon and sugar rice on the side. Who thinks up these combinations? Jesse and I sit at a table in the corner in the cafeteria. Dizzy, Lexus, Cuteny, and a few other people from the lake join us. It's

153

my first lunch in the cafeteria—I usually run home and grab a quick sandwich or hide out at the picnic tables at the back of the school where nobody but the druggies and nicotine addicts hang.

"So you guys are, like, doing it now?" Cuteny asks me when Jesse begins talking to a guy at the table about tennis—some foreign exchange student from Germany.

"Nice," she says. Cuteny raises a plastic forkful of pancakes to her nose and then drops the whole thing on her tray and pushes it away from herself. "Ugh," she says. "I'm definitely going on a starvation diet. It won't even be hard now." She gags for a while and then applies a coat of lipstick. "I'm glad you aren't like these two over here." She nods at Dizzy on her other side. Josh is standing over her, rubbing her shoulders and kissing her neck while she eats. I make a face at my plate.

"So, Daph," Cuteny says, "have you heard anything about when they are going to release the predicted lists?" Her eyes shine with the prospect of gossip.

I don't know. Neither does Melissa. But it's only a matter of time, she says. "No idea," I tell Cuteny.

"Oh," she says sadly. Then she pulls her tray back toward her and picks up the fork to nibble on the edge of the hunk of pancakes. "I thought you'd know." She perks up then. "Hey! We're all going to a frat party on Saturday. You coming? I can promise debauchery." She giggles. Her eyes scan the room and land on a table in the far corner. She drops her fork and grabs my arm. "Ugh," she says, holding her stomach.

"What?" I watch her pale eyes go wide and then narrow again.

Her eyeliner is kohl black and applied in little swoops at the corners of her eyes, so she looks like a fair-haired Cleopatra.

"There's January," she says, "with that Nate Gormley kid. I can't believe they have the nerve to show up here." She says this as though we are at a private party they've crashed. "Ever since that day, do you just find yourself feeling nervous? Like every time you walk past somebody in the hall, you're like, *Are you going to shoot me?* You know?"

The truth is that I *do* know. In geometry today, I practically jumped out of my skin when someone blew a bubble and popped it with a sonic-boom of a smack. I wasn't the only one who recoiled. Everyone looked around sheepishly afterward. We *expect* people to walk into classrooms and shoot at us. Somehow, that's almost sadder than the fact that it happened.

"You never know what she might do." Cuteny's high-pitched squeak of a voice almost sounds menacing. "Do you want to know who else is predicted, I think?"

"No," I say, "it's really none of my business."

Cuteny spits the chewed pancake into a napkin. "I shouldn't be eating this," she tells me. "Pancakes are so fattening. Like eating lard patties." She looks around the cafeteria. "Kelly Payne," she says. "She's predicted. I'm sure of it."

I glance over at Kelly Payne, who is sitting alone at a table with her earbuds in her ears and a paper lunch bag in front of her. She looks normal to me—shoulder-length brown hair pulled into a ponytail, jeans, pale gray sweatshirt, big hoop earrings dangling almost to her shoulders.

"She told you?" I ask.

Cuteny rolls her eyes. "No, but everybody knows. Kelly Payne's dad is in prison for arson. He burned down his girlfriend's trailer. Isn't that so trashy? And all three of her brothers are in prison. They got busted for having a meth lab. People like them give Okies a bad name. She lives with her grandma or something. How could she not be predicted with a family like that?"

"But you don't know for sure that she's going to follow in her family's footsteps. Genes don't quite work that way." By now, I notice that Jesse is listening to our conversation. He leans into me and rubs his arm against mine. He puts his hand above my knee and gently squeezes. He wants me to stop talking. I ignore him.

Cuteny shrugs. "What's there to know? That's just who she is." She says this last part with cold finality.

"Maybe she wants to sit with us. She must be lonely." I say it because I know it will make Cuteny livid. It does.

"Are you serious?" Cuteny's eyes go wide. Her pupils dart around in her eyes like little blue pinballs. "We don't sit with her. Not now. Not ever. You can't trust people like that. Take my word for it, Daphne."

"Come on," Jesse says quietly, pulling on my arm to leave or to shut up.

It only takes me a second to decide. I pull my arm away, slide off the bench, take my almost-full tray to the row of garbage cans lined up in front of the stage, and dump the contents on top of a heap of other pancakes and rice globs. Clearly, nobody was a fan of this menu. Instead of returning to our table, I make a beeline for the corner, the table where Kelly Payne is still sitting by herself, bopping her head in time to music piped into her ears. "Excuse me," I say loudly. She looks up. Her skin is mottled on one side, as if she has deep acne scars. Clumps of heavy makeup cover the tiny little pits. She pulls her headphones from her ears.

"I'm Daphne Wright," I say, sticking my hand out to her. The room seems to grow quieter. I glance to my side again, and I see that Dizzy and Cuteny are watching me.

"What do you want?" she asks suspiciously.

"Do you want to sit with us?" I ask. I point in the direction of our table. Dizzy's mouth is wide open, her surprise unmistakable.

"What is this?" Kelly asks me. "Are you making fun of me? Why do you want me over there?" She points at Dizzy and Cuteny, who are whispering to each other now. Jesse wears an expression of utter surprise.

"No, of course not. I just thought you might want to join us."

Kelly looks down at her lunch bag. "Oh," she says to the bag. "That's cool. But I'm fine here. Really." She puts her earbuds back in.

"Well, if you change your mind…" I say. Kelly nods at the paper bag.

When I get back to the table, Dizzy lets me know just how scandalized she is by my behavior. "Daphne Wright! Do you know who you were talking to?"

"I *told* her," Cuteny insists.

"Do you want to commit social suicide?" Dizzy demands. "Pity is fine. That's one thing. But you can't just be talking to them like that, being friendly! You don't know how dangerous these people can be."

"Not to mention," Cuteny adds, "the danger you put yourself in just by associating with someone like that." We all turn to look at Kelly Payne, who is sitting with her shoulders slumped and her elbows on the long, empty table.

"You need to be careful, Daphne," says Dizzy. "You can't trust these predicted people, right, Jesse?"

Josh laughs uproariously, like he's in the front row of a comedy show.

Jesse doesn't respond. In fact, he looks like he's on another planet. He's staring at some point off in the distance, but when I follow his gaze, I see nothing but kids holding trays of pancakes and lunch ladies with mustaches. I nudge him with my shoulder. "Jesse?"

"Jesse," Dizzy says impatiently, "I'm talking to you."

Jesse stands up, all six feet or so of him towering over Dizzy. His eyes are flashing. "Dizzy, why can't you ever just shut the hell up? For once, just close that goddamn mouth of yours! Nobody wants to hear your inane babbling! Nobody!"

We all sit in shock as he storms out the side door.

■■■

"Hey," I say, climbing up on the aluminum table. I've found Jesse out back, sitting on top of one of the picnic tables, staring out toward the grade school playground. In the distance, there are happy little kids running around, climbing monkey bars, totally unaware of just how shitty life can get once you grow up. I never realized how lucky I was when I was eight.

He runs his hand through his hair—that one piece is out of place, as usual—but he says nothing.

"Dizzy is like that sometimes. She talks a lot, doesn't she?" Jesse still doesn't answer. I sit quietly until I start feeling annoyed. My grandfather used to do this to my grandma; he'd just ignore her until he was ready to talk. Meanwhile, she had to sit around and look like a fool just waiting for him to get tired of not speaking.

"It's not that big of a deal," I say. "Dizzy was just talking. I'm sure she didn't know that you would—"

"Stop it!" Jesse yells. He's so loud that the smokers standing off in the distance puffing on their cigarettes look over at us. "Shut up!" he yells into the distance. "Shut up!" Now I can't tell if he's talking to me or the little kids who are running around like maniacs, playing some kind of hyperactive game of tag.

I stand on the seat of the table and then jump to the cement. My wedge sandal heels make a satisfying *thwack!* on the pavement. "I'll just leave you alone," I say coldly.

"No," Jesse says, standing and grabbing my arm. "No, don't go."

I hesitate, but then move back to the table. We both sit on the bench, me with my arms crossed, Jesse with his hands tightly clasped together, looking like someone deep in prayer.

"It's not you," he tells me. "It's me. It's them. It's January. It's everything. It's—"

I interrupt him. "January is fine, right? I mean, I just saw her this morning. Sure, it must suck to be predicted, but that doesn't mean that everybody has to get all melodramatic about—"

It's his turn to interrupt me: "You don't get it, Daphne. This is so much bigger than you. You have no clue what's going on. You just walked in here, what, like a month ago? You don't know the first thing about January. About any of us." He waves his hands in front of him. "Do you have any idea what it's like to know the things that January knows about herself?"

"Of course," I say, offended a bit that Jesse seems to think I'm so dim. "Of course I get it. We've already talked about this. I just think—"

His look stops me mid-sentence, and his eyes narrow slowly. "Don't you get why I'm mad? Why I can't stand all those ignorant snobs in there who think they can judge people—that they can judge January—because of some stupid test? It's not right. It's not fair. Daphne, how can I *not* be mad?" He rests his chin on his knuckles. He's pensive now, watching a garbage truck trying to back into an alley across the street.

"Oh," I say, realizing for the first time how passionate Jesse is. About January. Because when it comes down to it, Jesse's interest in January—his outrage at the injustice being heaped upon her— seems overdone. It's like he's in love with her or something. A series of flashbacks light up in my mind: Jesse and January at the mall, at the diner together, everywhere together. Jesse running to rescue January at the train tracks. Jesse and January together while I rolled around beside them like a third wheel—a really dense third wheel, come to think of it. Do I need a neon sign to spell it out for me? Wait! I practically had that. Isn't that what Sam was saying that night by the Coleman Center? Maybe he should've taken out a full-page ad in the newspaper or rented a skywriting plane. Then maybe I could've figured it out. "Oh," I say, the realization hitting me straight in the gut. The few bites of pancakes that I managed to choke down at lunch have turned to paste, threatening to shoot up my throat and all over the picnic table. I swallow hard. "I get it," I say quietly.

I stand up, the pancake globs settling down, my anger rising. Why didn't he tell me? Why drag me into this mess? Why make me feel—whatever it is I feel—about him? The anger reaches my lips. "Look, I came out here to help you, not to be your punching bag. If you want to act like an ass, be my guest, but I'm not going to stand out here and listen to you." I wipe the seat of my pants with my sweaty palms and stalk off.

"Daphne," Jesse calls. I hear his voice—sad, firm…pleading, maybe—rise above the little kids who are lining up to go inside.

I pretend I don't hear him. I just keep walking. Dignity demands it.

CHAPTER 14

Jesse is my stepbrother, but that doesn't mean I like the guy. Honestly, I can't stand him. Everybody always thought he was perfect. Even my mom liked him better than she liked me. But he's nothing but a loser. I tried to tell Daphne that.

—Josh Heller, quoted in the book *The Future of the Predicted*, publication forthcoming

I AM NOT AGAINST PARTIES IN PRINCIPLE. IT'S JUST THAT I'VE always hated big groups of people who are just standing around with nothing to do except comment on how much fun they are having standing around. That's pretty much the dictionary definition of a frat party, if you add beer and random hookups.

On Saturday night, Dizzy and I are walking down a dark street, peering at the houses, trying to figure out which one is Delta House. "Are you sure we'll get in?" I ask.

"Of course," Dizzy says. "We're girls. They always let girls in."

Dizzy and I are wearing tank tops and tight jeans with flip-flops, outfits that Dizzy assures me will camouflage the fact that we are not in college. I yank my tank top up high. Dizzy does the opposite and lets her attributes get plenty of air.

Eventually, we give up squinting at signs and painted frat names on the sides of ivy-covered houses and just follow the crowd of people in front of us. Dizzy pokes me in the ribs with her index finger. "I like these odds," she says nodding her head toward the swarm of guys.

"I thought Josh wanted to get back together with you," I say.

"So?" she shrugs. "That doesn't mean I don't want to make him jealous. He's gotta work for it." She beams.

I feel strangely relieved to be back in her good graces. We've had an uneasy truce since Wednesday, the day at the cafeteria when Jesse blew up at her. In Dizzy's mind, Jesse's outburst warrants an eternal cold shoulder—from her, me, and everyone else in the universe. The fact that I had the nerve to go after Jesse that day in the cafeteria is, to Dizzy, tantamount to an outright betrayal of her. This is in spite of the fact that I've been avoiding Jesse myself since Tuesday.

He called me that night: "It's not you, Daphne," he'd insisted. "Tell Dizzy I'm sorry. That was completely out of line. I need to learn to control my temper better." I'd simply said, "Okay," and hung up. He didn't come to school for the rest of the week. Somebody told me he had the flu. Jesse was avoiding me. Or avoiding everyone. I'm not even sure anymore. I pretended not to care, but it must have been obvious to everyone that I cared a lot. Even Melissa has noticed that I can't sleep and I can't eat, and this is a woman who once failed to notice that I didn't take a bath for two weeks. (I was seven at the time.)

The inside of the fraternity house is a disaster zone. The kitchen countertops are filthy and covered with empty plastic cups. People are standing around wherever they can find space. One girl is sitting with her butt in the sink.

"Money?" says a guy wearing a sideways baseball cap. He's sitting at a card table in the middle of the room.

"Excuse me?" I say.

"Money. Three bucks apiece to drink." He holds red plastic cups toward us. Dizzy grabs them, and pulls a twenty out of her pocket. "I'm not going to drink," I tell her.

"Still costs you," Sideways Cap says. "And it's five bucks for guys. Three bucks a cup for girls. You girls don't drink as much," he tells us. "Keg's downstairs." We carry our cups toward an open door that leads to some steps.

"Hey," Sideways Cap suddenly yells, "you girls underage?" Dizzy and I freeze. "Yeah, you are," he says. "You run if the cops show up."

"We will," Dizzy assures him.

"Cops?" I say. "Dizzy, maybe we should leave."

"Oh, don't be such a bore," she says and flits down the steps.

At the bottom of the stairs, we see a basement rec room that's been converted to a dance floor. Some people are dancing in the middle of the floor where strobe lights are shooting off bright, flashing rays that make my head hurt. The kegs are in the far corner of the room, next to the bathroom. The line stretches around in circles, and I realize that a lot of the people who appear to just be standing around are actually waiting to refill their cups.

"Dizzy," I yell. She leans over until her ear is practically touching my lips. "I don't want to drink."

She nods at me and yells back, "I know. Me neither. Let's just get some to hold. We'll look dumb without cups."

"I don't want one," I protest, but she's already talking to the guys in front of us.

When we finally reach the front of the line, Dizzy hands over her plastic cup to the guy who is filling cups from the keg. She grabs mine and hands it to him as well. "Fill them up," she says.

He takes one look at her—her hair twisted into a complicated French knot, a hairdo that was last seen on my grandmother, circa World War II—and he smiles widely. "Hello," he says.

"Hi," I answer. He only looks at me briefly before he turns back to Dizzy.

"Y'all ready to party?" he asks, but it's clear he's only talking to Dizzy, who shakes her hips and waves her hands over her head in answer.

"Let's mingle," Dizzy says after we get our beer, and I try to follow her through the crowd of people, but there are just too many people. After trying to move around for awhile, I accept that the best we can do is stand in one place and let the crowd carry us around the room with it. After an hour, my beer cup is still full. I haven't even tasted it, because it smells vile.

Dizzy starts to dance, beer sloshing out of the sides of her cup. The guy standing next to her is trying to dance with her. "Hey," he says and grabs her around the waist. They slow dance to a fast song, and the next thing I know, I'm left alone in a sea of people, close to the stairs. While people with red cups are still entering the basement area, others are fighting their way up the stairs, an epic traffic jam. I follow the crowd up to the kitchen, which is packed with people. I make my way through the living room, stepping over entwined couples on the floor.

I find another staircase leading up—this one is narrow and not carpeted. It's so narrow that I have to squeeze flat against the wall when a thundering herd of beefy guys comes running toward me. I think I feel the staircase shake. At the top of the stairs, closed doors line the hallway. Each door sports either a poster of a partially nude girl, a sports-themed poster, or a handmade sign with something rude scrawled across it.

The door of the room across the hall opens, and a muscled guy steps out. He's not wearing a shirt, and his jeans are unbuttoned at the top. "Hey," he says to me. "Can you come here?" I step closer to him. "Do you know anything about girls who can't stop throwing up?"

I don't, but I follow him into the room, where I see a skinny girl covered with a blanket huddled at the edge of a bunk bed, her face stuck in a small 49ers garbage can. The smell is awful, and I almost gag when her vomit hits the can. "She's been doing this for like a half hour now," Shirtless tells me.

"Cody," she moans, and it echoes dully in the half-full metal garbage can. She lowers the can, revealing her face. It's January. Her short hair is wet, probably from sweat, and slicked back into a smooth cap covering her head. She looks pitiful. "I'm dying," she says.

"How much beer have you had?"

"We had vodka," she says, pointing to the bottle, which has rolled under the bed.

Cody holds up his hands. "I didn't know she'd drink so much so fast!" He picks up a shirt that has been draped over a desk chair and says to me, "Can you stay with her? I better get back to the party."

I want to tell him no, but I feel sorry for January, whose head is lolling in circles, her eyes not focusing on anything in particular. Shirted Cody leaves, but he doesn't close the door all the way. I hear other guys in the hallway, and he says to them, "Hey, drunk slut in that room."

"Cool!" the others say.

"No, don't go in there," Cody tells them. Such a gentleman.

I can't leave January now—it would be like leaving a corpse to vultures. I sit down next to her and try not to inhale through my nose. "January?" I say. "Do you need to go to the doctor?" I try to remember what the signs of alcohol poisoning are. We learned about it in health class, but I can't remember anything except pale skin. I peer now at January's face, trying to tell if she's unusually pale or blue-tinged underneath her makeup. She reaches out, grabs my hand, and squeezes tight. "Stay with me?"

"I'll stay with you," I tell her.

"I didn't let him do it," she tells me. "Cody, I mean. I didn't let him do anything to me."

"It's okay," I say. "He's gone now." I see a small fridge in the corner. I open it and find it stocked with beer. There's one Coke in the very back. No water in sight. I grab the Coke and open it. "Drink something," I tell her.

"It's not like I am a virgin," she tells me, "but I've never had so much vodka before. I just met him tonight. I didn't want to do anything with him. I wouldn't do that kind of thing." She gags slightly, but she doesn't throw up.

"You'll be okay," I reassure her, not knowing if this is true or not. Could this really be the girl Jesse loves? Pale and shivering, she looks so pitiful. I put my arm around her in a fit of sympathy. Maybe this is what Jesse sees in her. He wants to protect her.

"Yeah," she agrees, and then she puts her head on my shoulder. "Do you hate me?" she asks after a while.

I answer honestly: "No."

"Even after what my brother did?"

"You aren't your brother," I say firmly. "You weren't the one with the gun."

"I could've been. We share the same genes. What's to say I won't be standing at school with a gun pointed at you on Monday, Daphne?"

My hand trembles on her shoulder. I have no response to what she's just said. "I'm so drunk," she says, her head lolling against my shoulder blade.

I suddenly begin to worry about Dizzy, who is also drinking, also downstairs with all these fraternity guys who are waiting for girls to get drunk. "January," I say. "Do you think you could wait here while I go downstairs for a minute?"

"No," she says, looking frightened. So I sit with her for a long time until her head drops back and she begins to snore loudly. I try to position a pillow behind her head, but she's sitting at such an awkward angle that I can't do it.

I get up quietly, leaving the trash can next to her. I open the door and look around. At the far end of the hallway, on the opposite end of the staircase, two guys are standing by the radiator. Both of them are wearing Sigma Delta Tau shirts. Dizzy informed me tonight that Delta is the coolest frat on campus. I worry that if I lock the door, January won't be able to get up to let me back in. I consider shutting it and leaving it unlocked, until I hear one of the voices from down the hall say, "Some of these whores are so wasted. It's not even funny. Scoring isn't even work. It's just like tackling midgets or sneaking up on deaf people."

"Yeah," says the other voice. I wonder if these guys have been tested by PROFILE. Could we make them wear giant P's so we'd know?

I go back in the room, quietly close the door, and lock it. January is half-awake again, rolling her head around. I look around the room for a phone, but there isn't one. It drives me nuts that I don't have a cell phone. Recently, I saw someone on TV say that the pope has an iPhone. I'm truly behind the times. The pope is probably updating his blog from some remote village right now, and I'm holding a puke bucket.

"January," I say. "I need to use your cell phone." It takes her a while, but eventually she wakes up enough to point to her purse—an odd-looking satin pouch—which is thrown halfway under the bed. I have to get on my stomach and extend my arm to get it.

I search January's contact list, looking for familiar names, trying to decide who to call.

"I have to throw up again." January interrupts my search. She says *fro up*, like a little girl. I know I should help her, but instead I get up and move to the other side of the room. She retches so violently that I wonder how she doesn't regurgitate an organ or something.

"Ohhh," she moans. "Take me home, please."

I flip through the contact list and find one number I recognize: Jesse. I hesitate for only a second. And then I flip the phone shut. I can't call him.

I could drive her home myself, but I don't know if I could even get her to stand up, let alone walk out of the frat house all the way to the parking lot. And what about Dizzy? I can't just leave her. I think briefly of calling Melissa, who would help me. And she wouldn't lecture me about it either—she would just come and take care of things. But I don't want her to see me at a frat party. Even though I haven't been drinking, I'm sort of embarrassed for even being here in the first place. Melissa thinks parties are for people who have no goals in life.

I close the phone, and then open it again and search the contact list again. I have no choice.

"I need to ask you a favor," I say without even saying hello.

"Daphne?" he asks. "What's wrong?"

"It's January. Can you come and get us?"

He doesn't ask why. He simply says, "Where?"

I tell him Delta House and give him directions to the room

upstairs. "And bring five bucks," I say, remembering that they won't let him in otherwise.

I'm almost asleep when I hear footsteps outside the door. "Jesse," I call.

"Shhh," January says. "My ears."

"Jesse," I call again, louder.

The footsteps stop outside the door, and I hear it open. I gently push January's head off my lap harder than I intended, and then I have to reach to catch it before it cracks on the hard, uncarpeted floor. I try to stand up, but I fall back on the bottom bunk as soon as I do because my leg is so numb. A million pins cut through it, and I'm in so much pain, I hardly notice that the person standing in the doorway isn't Jesse.

"Hey," he says. I look over from my odd position—one leg on the floor, one leg out as I shake it all about, just like that old song from kindergarten. It's Josh Heller, wearing the same plaid shorts from that night at the diner. His red hair is expertly gelled into a perfect polygon. "Is Jan still alive?"

"How'd you know she was here?"

"Just ran into her new boyfriend. Cody. Looks like she's had a rough night." We both glance at January lying on the floor, looking sick and miserable.

"I got it from here," Josh says, a smirk on his lips. "You can go."

Even though January is not really my friend, I don't want to leave her with anyone who won't make sure she gets home safely. It's the right thing to do. "I'll just wait here," I say. "Someone is coming for her."

"Seriously," Josh says. "I got it." He sits down on the ratty armchair that's positioned about three inches from a TV. "Jan's practically family."

The thought still makes me uneasy. I'm trying to figure out what to do when January's cell rings. Josh is closer and snags it before I can. He looks at the display and hangs up, then turns off the phone and pockets it.

By this time, my leg is coming back to life, so I stand up. "Let's just get January out of here and back to her house so she can go to bed."

"Aw, she's fine," he says. "She's a pro at this. In fact, I bet she'll be just like this next weekend too. Right, Jan?" He gently pokes her in the side with the toe of his shoe.

"Screw you," she whispers.

Josh abruptly turns his attention back to me. "Listen, there's something I wanted to talk to you about anyway."

I raise an eyebrow. "Really?"

"Yeah. I think what you did to me was totally shitty."

His blunt tone catches me by surprise. What is he even talking about? "Me? What did I do to you?"

"Someone told my parents I pushed you into that diner window. They took away my car for a week!"

"Maybe someone was right. But how could I know? I was too busy having my head shoved through glass to see."

"I told you—it was an accident."

"Either way," I said, "it's over now. Whatever." He looked desperate for me to believe him, and even though I wasn't quite sure he was totally innocent, he also seemed genuinely upset that I'd been so hurt.

"I'd really appreciate if you didn't mention anything to Dizzy about last Friday night."

So he *was* there when Jesse had to rescue January in the middle of the thunderstorm. "Why were you hiding?"

"I don't think it's necessary for Dizzy to know that I was with January, do you?"

I do that thing again, that thing where I think about what to say, which I can see makes Josh nervous.

"Did you tell her already?" he asks with just a hint of desperation in his voice. "Is that why she's being such a bitch?"

I take advantage of my position. "I'm sure she has plenty of things to be mad at you about. January might even be the least of them. But who knows?" The idea of Josh and January together seems almost…comical. Without warning, I accidentally conjure up a picture of her skinny arms wrapped around his freckly shoulders. Ew. Then my mind shifts to her arms around Jesse. I erase the picture quickly. "Do you really think I'm not going to tell Dizzy that you're playing her?"

He cracks his knuckles and then looks at me imploringly with his big green eyes. "I would never hurt Dizzy. I promise you. Mistakes happen, but I swear to you that I love Dizzy. I don't want to hurt her."

There's nothing I hate more than being wrong, but I'm starting to think it's possible that I've misjudged Josh. I watch him fiddle with his broken shoelace. He reminds me of J. R., a dog that

Melissa and I dog-sat for two weeks over winter break one year. I thought Melissa was going to explode when he ate her flash drive. J. R. just sat there looking penitent, like he deserved every newspaper whack she threatened him with. I have the sudden urge to scratch behind Josh's ears.

"Let me tell you how it's going to be. Whatever is going on between you and January is over," I state. "It will not happen again. Or I *will* tell Dizzy."

Josh holds out his hand for me to shake. "I swear, it's over. And I hope we can manage to be friends?"

"I think I can manage to avoid throttling you or tampering with your brakes," I say.

"I'll take it," he says. He heads for the door. I watch him clomp down the narrow stairs.

I'm still standing in front of the open door when the two vultures emerge from the end of the hallway. "Can we come in?" one of them asks.

"Ah, no. Absolutely not." I stand with my back blocking the door.

We hear January moaning again from inside the room. "I think I'm going to die," she says.

"Aw, come on," the taller one says. "We just want to hang out with y'all."

I cross my arms and stand with my feet apart, as if I'm a military guard. "No chance," I tell them. "This room is off limits."

"Pretty please?" the shorter one says, and he leans forward until his elbow is resting on the door frame.

"Just for a minute?" the other says, and then he leans in on the other side of the frame. I feel trapped with both of them breathing on me. They smell like beer and cigarette smoke.

"Come in," January says weakly from behind the door.

I turn around and yell, "No!" at her.

"Hey," a voice from the stairway calls. "Daphne!" We all turn to see Jesse standing there. "I tried to call you back," he tells me, "but I got Jan's voice mail. Where is she? Why do you have her phone?" He walks toward the three of us and between the two guys, who are both smaller than he is. They move away from me. "The guy downstairs wouldn't let me in. He said the kegs are dry. No more guys allowed. I had to sneak in."

The Sigma guys are still standing there dumbly, so Jesse turns to them, "Don't you all have someplace to be?" They nod and move toward the stairs. "Jerks," Jesse murmurs. "I hate frat boys."

Jesse is wearing dark jeans with a tight black shirt. Over that, he's wrapped in a roomy leather jacket, even though it's pretty warm outside. He looks different—older, sadder, less Oklahoma. Sexier. A little bit scary.

"I thought you were sick," I say to him. He touches my cheek, but I move away. I haven't forgotten about the cafeteria debacle. "We've got to get her home."

January has managed to sit up on the bottom bunk, and she looks miserable. "I look like hell," she mumbles glumly and only somewhat coherently. Maybe she really said something else. But *I look like hell* would have been appropriate.

"What happened?" Jesse asks me.

"I found her here drunk, halfway unconscious, and pretty

much a sitting duck with those frat boy Neanderthals looking for someone to take advantage of."

Jesse turns to January. "Janny," he says sadly, "Why do you do this to yourself?"

"Y'all know why," she says. "PROFILE." They look at me as if it's my fault that Melissa's stupid scientific advancement is ruining people's lives. She'll probably win a Nobel Prize, and I'll spend prom night organizing my sock drawer. I hang my head.

Jesse helps January off the bed. She leans over like a rag doll, and he practically has to carry her under his arm. "Come on, Jan. I'll take you home."

I reach the end of the narrow stairs first. Jesse descends awkwardly behind me with January attached to him, and I immediately catch sight of Dizzy. She is standing near the banister, dancing by herself, a weird little disco/riverdance that makes her look a tiny bit spastic. When she sees me, she yells, "There you are! I've been looking all over for you. Let's go. I'm starving. Let's get pizza or something."

Josh is standing near her. He moves closer and puts his arm on her shoulders. She purses her lips and says in a baby voice to him, "I just might let you come along, Mister." When she sees Jesse, her tone changes. "Oh, who invited him?"

Jesse is still slowly hauling January down the stairs. He stops and looks at Dizzy. "I'm sorry about that day in the cafeteria. I shouldn't have said that to you."

Dizzy turns her nose up in the air. "Whatever," she says. "I don't care."

"And," Jesse says, turning to me, "I owe you an apology too. For everything." His forehead wrinkles as he looks at my foot. "I don't know what to say."

"We're cool," I say calmly, although I feel something else. I feel…sad. Like I've lost something I never quite had.

"I got this," Jesse tells us all, pointing at January. "Y'all go. Have a good time."

"Sure," Dizzy says brightly. She looks at me. "You better drive."

"Go on," Jesse says to me, as if I'm waiting for his permission. Now I'm really annoyed.

I ignore him and look at January, who smiles weakly at me. "I owe you," she says. Her eyes focus for just a second, and in them, I see something calculating, a glinting glow that tells me she's plotting. And then, in just a millisecond, her eyes glaze over again. She droops into Jesse's arms, a pile of bones and skin and alcohol-curdled blood.

"Thank you for doing this for her," I say coldly and formally to Jesse. I nod in January's direction. He moves her away from him gently, and she grabs hold of Dizzy like she's a drowning woman.

Dizzy staggers backward. Jesse leans into my ear and whispers, "I did this for you too." His lips brush my cheek, and I feel a shiver run through me.

I shake it off quickly. "Please," I say loudly. "How dumb do you think I am?"

Even Dizzy looks surprised. "Whoa, Daph," she says. Josh moves closer—he doesn't want to miss this. He smacks his fists together.

"Come off it, Jesse. I'm not an idiot. It's pretty clear that you don't have much time for anyone but January."

January tries to speak, but Dizzy tells her to shut it.

"Daphne," Jesse says softly, looking around him. He wants Josh and Dizzy gone. "Can we talk about this later? Alone?"

"I really can't see that there's anything to talk about."

Josh laughs obnoxiously, enjoying every second. "Shut up," I say without even looking at him. "Nobody wants to hear from you, Josh. Come on, Dizz," I say. "You must be hungry."

Dizzy grabs my hand. "We don't need them," she says, nodding at Jesse and January.

"Of course not," I respond with enthusiasm that sounds false even to me, but I forge ahead. "Hope you and January have a great night." I wave at Jesse with two bitchy fingers. "And please don't call me," I add.

"Yes, don't call us," Dizzy says as if she is an extension of me.

"Ladies," Josh says, putting one gross arm around me and the other on Dizzy. "I think we have a threesome."

I manage simultaneously to not vomit and walk out the side door without a backward glance at Jesse.

I remember Melissa's first rule of science: Always go with your gut. Unless your gut is wrong. Not a very helpful maxim, actually.

And what happens when your guts are a twisted heap of anger and indecision and confusion and false hope?

And maybe even love?

179

PART III
one of them

CHAPTER 15

Each student will receive his or her PROFILE report in the mail prior to the public announcement. We ask that individuals refrain from sharing their status until we have time to adequately prepare everyone for the news.

—Mrs. LeAnn Temple, principal of Quiet High

He is a person of interest. That is true. But let me be clear: he has not been charged with anything. At this time.

—David Witt, chief of Quiet City Police

I WAKE UP BEFORE DAWN WITH THE KIND OF HEADACHE THAT starts within your skull and radiates throughout your entire body. Little electrical pulses of pain shoot from my cranium to the bones in my toes. I lie awake for a long time curled up with my head under the blanket. I must eventually drift back to sleep, because the next thing I know, I'm back there. Back at school. I am right back in that cupboard again, folded away, hidden from the dark shadow pointing a gun at me. When I wake up, I feel like I'm suffocating. My heart is racing, my ears stinging from someone screaming loudly.

"What?" Melissa comes running into the room. "What in the world is wrong?" She pulls the covers down from over my head. I blink my eyes. It takes me a second to realize that I'm the one screaming.

Melissa is smoothing my hair down now. "What's wrong, Daph? Are you sick?"

I'm embarrassed. "Just a bad a dream," I say, shrugging it off. "No big deal." I lift the edge of my bedroom blinds and peer out at the street. It's long past sunrise, but the day is so gray and soupy that the streetlights are still on. Rain drools from the ominous clouds. "Ick," I say.

When the phone rings, both Melissa and I jump. I pick up the handset next to my bed.

"They found her." It's Dizzy.

"Found who?" I ask. Melissa is still sitting with me. I motion for her to go, but she doesn't move.

"January."

"She was lost?" I shoo Melissa again, and this time, she gets up and leaves—reluctantly.

"There's bad news."

"Dizzy, what's going on?"

"I don't know if I should tell you."

"Then why did you call?" I say impatiently.

"Daphne, listen to me. I have to tell you something."

I rub my head, squint my eyes, and sigh heavily. I just want to take a long shower, eat some breakfast, and then go back to bed. "What?"

"Someone attacked her last night. When she didn't come home, they called the police. The cops found her early this morning."

"Oh, my gosh," I say, sounding like my grandmother. I don't know what else to say. "Is she all right? What happened?" I ask quietly, but Melissa's radar hearing hones in anyway.

"What's wrong?" she says, coming back to my bedroom.

I mouth, *January.*

"Who?" Melissa says. I ignore her.

Dizzy is so excited, she can barely form words. It takes a minute until she can pull herself together enough to talk. "She's alive. But she was beaten pretty badly. She's in the hospital."

"What happened?" I ask, sitting at the edge of the bed.

Melissa crouches next to me, pushing her ear into the receiver. "What?" she whispers to me. I shake my head but move closer to let her hear.

"They don't know who attacked her."

"She was attacked? What does that mean?"

"Yes. Attacked. Beaten half to death."

"But Jesse took her home."

"She didn't *get* home." And then Dizzy erupts into dramatic sobs, which only sound about one percent genuine.

Melissa takes the phone from me. "Dizzy?" she says kindly and patiently. "Dizzy, what's going on?" She sounds far more tolerant than she ever does with me.

Melissa listens a long time, nodding her head periodically. Then she turns to me. "January is sedated now. There's nothing we can do except wait."

"Dizzy, let me talk to your mom." Melissa stands up and moves to my desk chair.

I stay sitting on the edge of my bed, my face in my hands, trying to take it all in. January? Attacked? I think of those scummy frat boys, hanging around outside of the room. *Drunk slut in that room,* they'd said, as if they'd found an old sofa in someone's garbage heap—free for the taking. You can have it if you can carry it. She was beaten badly, Dizzy said. What else happened to her? I wonder. And then I think about Jesse. Was he hurt too? He was with her when she left.

I hear the soothing hum of Melissa's voice on the phone, talking to Dizzy's mother. She lets out an endless string of *um-hum*s and *eh-heh*s, until she thanks Dizzy's mom and I hear this: "No, I have never been to a home candle party. Sounds fun." She makes a face at me. "I'll be sure to do that. Thank you...No, thank *you*...Okay, now...Take care of Dizzy. Bye." She hangs up.

"I think we should go to the hospital," I say.

∎∎∎

"I didn't realize that you were so close to January," Melissa says in the car.

I'm not, I want to reply, but I don't, because I can't even explain to myself what I am feeling and why. Sure, it's normal to feel bad and scared when someone has been attacked and beaten badly enough to be in the hospital. But there's something else— something else nagging at me that I'm not ready to name or even admit. The terror I feel radiating to the ends of all my limbs is intensifying, and all I know is that something is terribly wrong. All I want to do is see January.

Melissa drops me off at the double doors while she finds parking. I'm too distracted to appreciate the fact that she agreed to drive rather than walk the three miles to Quiet Regional Medical Center. The person at the front desk won't tell me which room January is in, but I must look pitiful, because she reaches across her desk to pat my forearm and tells me that I can find family and friends in the third-floor waiting room. I take the stairs instead of waiting for the elevator, feeling more worried as I climb each step.

Jesse is in the waiting room, sitting alone in a chair, staring at a blank television screen. He looks up and sees me, motioning for me to sit next to him. "I'm glad you're here." He grabs both of my hands. I let him, though my initial urge is to move away from him. "This is all just so surreal," he says.

"What happened?"

He swallows hard and shakes his head back and forth, his eyes fixed on a point just to the right of my head. It feels like he is signaling, *No, no, no, no* to a phantom person standing behind me. "You guys left the party," he finally says. I nod. We had. We'd all left together—Dizzy and me and Josh. We'd walked to my car, and I'd driven us all to Pizza Hut, where we split a large pepperoni—a greasy lump that I can still feel in the bottom of my stomach.

"I left her in the kitchen. She was sitting in a chair, drinking a glass of water. And she looked better. She looked alert, and she was talking. And I asked this girl to keep an eye on her while I ran to get my car." I nod again. Parking is impossible in that neighborhood, with all the narrow one-way streets and college kids who leave their old junkers in any available space. Jesse would've had to park in the library lot, blocks away, just like we did. "I got the car, pulled up front, and ran inside—not five minutes after I left her—and she was gone. The girl—the girl who was watching her—was still there, and she said January went to the bathroom. I looked all over that house, but she was gone. I drove around looking for her. I couldn't find her."

"Maybe she was in someone's room." I'm thinking of shirtless Cody. "Has anyone talked to that snake Cody? Did you go upstairs?"

"No, I didn't."

"Why didn't you tell anyone she was missing?"

"I should have," he says, dropping my hands and punching his palm with his fist. "I should have, but after I drove all over town half the night, I just figured, you know, that she'd turn up. That she was probably off with some guy she met."

"And you're sick of being her babysitter?"

He doesn't answer. He just leans back heavily in his chair, pushing it away from me. "I just decided, you know, to let her be. Let her take care of herself for once. But I should've done something." He lowers his head. I get up and lean over him, toying with the idea of putting my arms around him. "I didn't dare call the house and risk getting her mom. Her mom freaks out over everything."

"Did anybody see her leave? At the party, while you were getting your car?"

"By the time I got back, the kitchen was pretty much empty. Everybody was probably in the hot tub or something. I don't know. I checked rooms upstairs."

"I thought you said you didn't check rooms."

"No, I *did* check," he says sharply. I drop the subject. He's probably confused. Why would he lie about something like that?

"Do they know what happened? Do you know?"

"Nobody knows," he says. "They found her out by the abandoned train car. Somebody beat her with a baseball bat or a piece of wood or something. They just left her there."

I gasp in spite of myself. I just can't fathom someone attacking another human being like that, no matter how many times I hear that it actually happens. "Was she...?" I don't know how to say the word *raped*. It's too awful to even say.

Jesse shakes his head. "No."

"Is she going to be okay? Did she see who did it?"

Jesse shakes his head. "That's the thing. She doesn't remember anything at all. The last thing she remembers is the frat party. She's going to be okay, but it's going to take a while. She has a lot of bruises and a couple broken bones, but nothing that won't heal. Fortunately, the bastard who did this was either really weak, or he lost his nerve. It could've been worse. She's going to be fine. *Physically* fine."

"Good," I say, but it doesn't feel so good. "It had to be someone who was predicted," I add hopefully. "That's how they'll find the guy. They just need to look at the predicteds." My voice rises. "That's what they'll do, I bet. Don't worry," I tell Jesse, "this will be over as soon as they look at that list, right? It could very well be someone who has been PROFILEd. Melissa says they have a lot of names on file. They'll get the guy, right?"

He nods at me, giving me a weak smile. "Right," he says.

He wraps his arms around me, holding me tight. I let him. I squeeze my eyes shut against his shoulder, the cotton of his red T-shirt rubbing soft on my cheek. I inhale spring-rain scented fabric softener.

"I'm going to get a coffee," Melissa says loudly, to no one in particular. She apparently came into the waiting room after parking the car.

When we can no longer hear her footsteps, Jesse pulls away and looks me in the eyes. "There's something more I need to tell you—something I need to explain. Before you hear it from someone else."

"You don't have to explain anything to me," I say quickly. But he does. Once and for all, I want to know what's going between him and January. I reach up and touch his face, his cool, smooth skin sending electric shocks through my fingertips. But I don't want to know right now. "Don't talk," I tell him, moving my lips to his.

He sighs intensely as soon as we touch. We kiss deeply and tenderly for what seems like a long time. I forget that we are in the middle of a hospital waiting room until he speaks and I come crashing back to reality. "Daphne," he says, his lips fluttering against mine, "I can't." He pulls away from me and raises his hands to either side of my head, smoothing my undoubtedly un-smooth hair. "You're going to hear things about me."

"No," I say, trying to shake my head, but Jesse holds his hands firmly.

"Listen to me," he says quietly. "By tomorrow, everyone will know. Everyone will be talking about me. And about—about what happened to…" He's stuttering and stopping, completely stripped of the cool confidence that he usually has. "…about what…happened to January."

I know with sudden certainty—a certainty I've never felt about anything before—what he is telling me. It explains why he acted that way in the cafeteria. He wasn't reacting to Dizzy's rant about January. He's not in love with January. He meant it when he said that nothing happened between them. Why didn't I see this before? This isn't about how he feels about her. It's about how he feels about himself. I raise my hand to my mouth, my fingers touching my raw lips, all the lip gloss long kissed off.

Jesse is predicted.

"I got the letter in the mail last week."

"No," I reply, because I don't know what else to say.

Jesse casts his eyes downward. "It's true. I wish it weren't." He meets my gaze, his dark eyes glazing over as if he is retreating far into himself. "Daphne, you have to be ready for what people are going to be saying about me.

I say nothing, but I must look stricken. "Honey," a passing nurse says to me, part concerned mother, part nosy health care professional, "are you okay?" she asks, her drawn-on eyebrows, red like clay, making an alarmed arch on her forehead. She rubs my back. "What's going on?"

What am I supposed to say ? *Sorry, I've just found out that this guy right here has a negative PROFILE, which means he may have brutally attacked someone, this utter mess of a girl who I was honestly jealous of. Because, you see, I thought I was in love with him.*

I say none of that. Instead, I say to the nurse, in a voice that sounds foreign to me, "I'm totally fine, thanks." I say it brightly and cheerfully, a friendly answer better suited to a different question. *Do you want a coffee? I'm totally fine, thanks. Do you need a tissue, dear? I'm totally fine, thanks.*

For a second, I think I'm going to cry while six eyes watch: Jesse's, the concerned nurse's, and another nurse's—the younger one, with moles all down her neck. She stands off to the side, stage right, watching me with her head cocked in curiosity. I rub at my eyes experimentally. Nothing happens. There are no tears. A tidal wave runs through my stomach, the aftershocks worse than the initial disaster. I want to scream—to freak out—but I'm strangely frozen, a version of myself I didn't know existed. "Good-bye," says the voice of this other Daphne. "Good luck," she says without a trace of emotion.

"I'm sorry," Jesse whispers. "I'm so sorry."

CHAPTER 16

Jesse wouldn't hurt anyone. I'm sure of it. I'd bet my life on it.

—January Morrison, police interview

THINGS ARE CRAZY AT SCHOOL. IT FEELS LIKE THE AFTER-math following the shooting. Only worse. At least after the shooting, we were out of classes for a whole week—enough time for everyone to realize that thinking about it doesn't make it go away. *Not* thinking about it does that. So everyone talked about the next lake party and who won the baseball tournament and whether or not someone was hooking up with someone else's boyfriend. And little by little, it faded, disappearing like the bullet holes in the walls. A little plaster of Paris in our minds and everything was peachy.

But today, after January's attack, the general feeling is almost gleeful. It's far less terrifying than after the shooting. This time, there's pity for January, but it's tempered with smugness—a sure feeling that this would never happen to someone who didn't deserve it. Dizzy even said that out loud. Practically. This is a story that has a plot everyone can understand: bad girl behaves badly, gets what she deserves. The shooter was random in his aim. But whoever attacked January chose her. And the fact that January is genetically flawed gives the story a nice moral: everybody gets what she deserves. Sad but true. Or is it?

Dizzy is the first person I see in the hallway. Her face is flushed, and her eyes are glinting with excitement. "This is crazy!" she exclaims. And then she says, "Gee, Daph—are you, like, sick? You look awful."

Between the news cameras and the hysterical parents who want to pull their kids out of school, I can hardly hear her. "Thanks," I say, reaching out to touch my swollen eyes. I sniff stridently. Melissa forced me to pull myself together and go to school in spite of spending most of the night awake worrying. Early this morning, all the tears I'd been holding in started to slip out of my eyes. The first one landed with a heavy plop on the ugly quilt my grandma made me when I was a baby. The second and third landed on my chest, just below my neck. The rest came shooting out in all directions until I felt like I was going to drown myself. Melissa came and sat with me and then helped me wash my face and apply a vat of cover-up before school.

"They're going to arrest Jesse," Dizzy tells me now, completely oblivious to how wrecked I am. "He's predicted. It had to be him. He was the last one to see her. And his whole story about looking all over the house—total lie. Nobody saw him do that. Cuteny's dad told us everything." I remember that Cuteny's dad is a detective with the Quiet Police Department—he's on the news all the time. He's fat and has a scraggly mustache that hangs over his lips. I hate him, even though I've never met him. I fight the leftover tears back. Dizzy doesn't seem to notice that I'm upset. "Gosh, Daph, I feel kind of guilty. We left her with him. The police are probably going to be contacting you too, you know. And Jesse's stepmom and dad said he didn't come home until well after three, which is after the time that the doctors think January was attacked."

"What are they doing here?" I ask, pointing at a cameraman who is moving closer and closer to us.

"Can you girls stop moving so much?" he asks.

"This," Dizzy says, waving her hand around, "is just the biggest news story to ever hit Quiet High. Outside of the shooting."

"Where's Jesse?" I ask.

"Not here, if he's smart. Josh wants to kill him. He's extremely chivalrous. Poor January," Dizzy says, sniffling into her hand.

"I thought you didn't like her," I say sharply, hoping that being mean will make me feel better.

"Well, I don't. But of course I feel sorry for her. And it just proves what I suspected about Jesse all along." She spits out Jesse's name like a rotten piece of broccoli. "I knew he was a bad penny, what with stalking that girl. Someone should've stopped him before he really did something bad. Like this."

"Dizzy, you said yourself that the stalking thing was just a rumor. Besides, you were psyched when we first started going out."

She ignores this fact. "We all should've known better. It was hotness hypnosis." She shakes her head. "We were blinded by his ridiculous body."

Before I can answer, Sam and Brooklyn appear. Josh is

hovering behind them. He's wearing his gym shirt with the sleeves rolled up, and I wonder if he's trying to get his biceps on the evening news.

Dizzy throws her arms around Josh. When she lets him go, Josh puts his arm protectively around her. "How is she?" I ask. "Does anyone know?"

Sam takes over. He's one of those guys who has to take charge, who has to know all about what's happening. "Everything is under control," he says. His hair is wet—fresh from a shower—hanging in lank pieces across his forehead. He looks different, small somehow, like one of those dogs that ends up being the size of a squirrel after it has a bath.

"And Jesse?" I ask.

"Fuck him," Sam says. The words are toxic. He catches himself, though, and puts on the Boy-Next-Door persona. "Gee," he says. "Oh, my gosh, I'm sorry! I'm just so…darn mad!" He lightly kicks the wall in front of him. "I hate when women are mistreated. It just gets to me."

"We should've known he'd do something like this," Josh says. He balls his fist and punches the wall hard. "I'm just glad it wasn't you, baby." He squeezes Dizzy tightly. What's this? Is Josh actually being nice?

Not to be outdone, Brooklyn pats Sam's arm. "Just think if it had been me, honey."

"I just hate to see people taken advantage of," Sam says.

"It wasn't Jesse." It's the first time I've said these words out loud, and I suddenly feel like a huge weight has been lifted from me.

I say it again. "It wasn't him." If I say it a few more times, it will be true.

Josh turns around. "Don't you get it? Jesse is predicted to be a violent criminal. You can't act like that's no big deal. He needs to be stopped. Daphne, he can't be allowed to hurt someone else." He sounds calm. And reasonable. And sincere. This has to be Bizarro World.

Dizzy speaks next. "Listen, Daph: Jesse is predicted."

Josh steps in. "We all should've suspected. We are stupid if we pretend that it doesn't matter, that somehow those stupid tests are wrong. The tests *aren't* wrong. Jesse was predicted for violent crime. Jesse will never be anything but a lousy criminal. That's what he always has been, and it's what he'll always be. He's a loser, a felon, lower than dirt. And the sooner we all accept that, the better."

"You said it," Brooklyn chimes in. And then she laughs. Like this is all a big joke.

I'm too angry to stick around.

CHAPTER 17

The girl was discovered in the early hours of Sunday, April 24. The victim is a female, 16 years old. Found in a field near an abandoned car at the train tracks. It appears she was beaten with a baseball bat.

—Quiet Police Chief David Witt

CRIMINAL JUSTICE WAS THE ONLY ELECTIVE WITH OPENINGS when I started at QH. Now I'm stuck in a class taught by a former prison guard who has a bad habit of calling everyone by some abbreviation of their last name. Mr. Victor ("Call me Vic!") spends most of our class periods showing recorded episodes of *Dateline* about really sickeningly twisted murders. He notices me today, because I walk in late after having spent a ton of time in the bathroom with Dizzy, who insisted on redoing my makeup. She's put so much eye makeup on me that I'm probably *mascary*. I don't even care. "Hey, Wri," Call-Me-Vic says as I step through the door. "I need your help." Everyone turns to look at me.

"What?" I ask warily, sitting down in a chair in the back row.

"I'm in major trouble with the higher-ups." Everyone groans in sympathy. "Apparently, I'm not giving enough 'exams.'" He puts *exams* in quotation marks to underscore his belief that exams are actually flimsily costumed versions of something else—something sinister. "We gotta do a test next week. I need everyone to get above a seventy percent. And it's gotta be a book test. Nothing from *Dateline*." People groan again.

"I can handle it," I say, knowing that if I don't think about school, I'll just obsess about Jesse. I pull a frayed textbook from my backpack. I'm probably the only person in the room who has read it. The book is kind of interesting, actually. I never knew that one out of ten men is a psychopath. That explains a lot.

Call-Me-Vic laughs an obnoxious bray, his seemingly seven-foot body bending oddly as he manages his convulsive laughter. "I know *you'll* ace it." He rolls his eyes, and everyone giggles. "I need you to tutor some of your classmates who aren't as, ah, bookish as you are." More snickers. "So today, while I run one of my favorite episodes, 'The Cannibals Next Door,' I'm going to need you to do some hard-core tutoring." Call-Me-Vic points at Nate Gormley, the tiny, rat-like boy that I first saw at the lake smoking with January. Today, he wears an old windbreaker with the sleeves rolled up and sweatbands on his wrists. "Gorm, dude, you're never going to make it. Go with Wri right now. Chop-chop." Call-Me-Vic claps loudly. I mutter under my breath and stuff my book in my bag as Nate Gormley makes his way toward me. "Library," Call-Me-Vic yells after us. "Go to the library."

"I'm not a retard," he tells me in the hallway.

"I never said you were. And you shouldn't use that word."

"I got suspended last week, and then I kinda got behind."

"Huh," I say, still thinking about Jesse, the tears pooling in my eyes again. I swipe at my face. We walk past the few reporters who are still milling about in the hallways. They're obviously convinced that there's some story here, something to air on a program that Call-Me-Vic will probably show in class tomorrow.

"You hear about Jesse Kable?" Nate asks me.

I don't answer, but I do hold the library door open for Nate, who punches the library metal detectors on his way in, as if they'd offended him in some way. I look over at the empty chairs by the paperbacks, where January was sitting that day. It seems so long ago.

"Jesse Kable," he repeats. "He's one of them predicted. Which is no big surprise."

"Let's get started," I say sharply, slamming my backpack hard against a table.

"Chill," Nate says. "Nothing to get worked up about." He sits on a chair and leans way back on it, his freakishly long arms almost dragging on the nasty library carpet.

"Why is Jesse being predicted no big surprise?"

Nate shrugs. I pull the arm of his chair forward and bring the legs smashing down on the floor. "Come on," I say.

"Why you so interested?"

"It might be on Vic's test," I say sarcastically. "Tell me."

"Jesse stalked a girl—his ex. Her name is Brit. Totally freaked her out. She wouldn't even answer her phone after a while. She had to move to get away from him." I think about what Dizzy told me at the mall a couple of weeks ago, about Jesse having an older girlfriend who went away to college in Texas.

"Yeah, right," I say, calling his bluff. "You're just making this up. That's all a big rumor."

Nate leans on his chair again. "Suit yourself."

I throw a notebook on the table and then toss a pencil at Nate's face. He doesn't even try to catch it.

"Let's get started," I say, flipping the book open to the chapter on mass murderers of the twentieth century.

"You wanna know how I know about Mr. Perfect?"

"Not really."

"'Cause Brit's my sister."

"That's not exactly Jesse's version of the story." That night in the car, he told me there was no older girl. Dizzy's story was just a rumor.

"And you believe what that guy says?"

"Why wouldn't I?"

"Well, for one thing, he's lying to you. He went out with Brit for a long time. They were a Quiet High item." He makes a face at the word *item*, like he's above that kind of thing. Nate flips his hat around backward and scratches underneath. His hair is kind of mangy. I wrinkle my nose. "And I suppose he also didn't tell you about her face."

"What about her face?"

"The two black eyes and a split lip. I'll give you three guesses, genius—who do you think done that to her?"

I tap my pencil on my notebook faster and louder. "How do I know *you* aren't lying?"

He rolls his shoulders. "Mmmaoh," he says without opening his lips. The lazy person's way of saying *I don't know*. Melissa would sooner have her fingernails pulled out than listen to me butcher the English language that way. "Maybe I am lying. But your boyfriend just happens to be around a lot of girls who end up with their heads bashed in. Don't cha think?"

Melissa goes to bed at 10:23, just before the sportscast on the local news show. I stay up in the covered porch off my room, pretending to read, even though I can't concentrate on individual letters long enough to let them form words. I keep thinking of Jesse's lips on mine Sunday night at the hospital. I can't concentrate on anything else.

Before Melissa retreated to her bedroom, we watched the ten o'clock news together, but there was nothing new about January. It was all the same information we'd read earlier online. *A Quiet High junior—no name being released yet—was found severely beaten near Perry. She is in good condition at the local hospital. Police are pursuing leads but have not yet named a suspect.* I had to turn off the TV.

I am sitting in the dark when I hear a car in the driveway. Turning off the lights, I peer around the curtains. Then I take stock of myself. I am wearing my flannel PJ's with pictures of vegetables on them.

Not cute.

Hideous, actually. I've had these pajamas since I was twelve, back when I didn't realize that vegetables should never adorn clothing. I make a mental note to put them in the thrift store donation pile. With my luck, Melissa will buy them back for me.

He's sitting in the car with his headlights off while I contemplate whether or not I have time to run and put on jeans. Ultimately, I opt against changing clothes because I don't want him to knock on the door and wake Melissa. I check through the curtains again—he's still just sitting there, although now he's gripping the steering wheel with both hands as if he's about to drive away.

I quietly open the front door and step onto the front steps—the cement is grimy underneath my bare feet. Jesse opens his door and starts to get out, but I wave him back into the car and tiptoe across the cold grass to the passenger's side door. I open it and slide into the seat next to him.

"Hi," he says, closing his driver's side door so gently that it barely makes a click. "Hope I didn't wake you." I pull my door even more gently. He's in his dad's car again, the black Eclipse. It smells like breath mints.

I shake my head. "It's okay." I pull down the visor out of habit—it's something I always do when I get into a car. I flip it back up right away.

"Are those eggplants?"

I look at him. "What?"

He points to my PJ's. "Eggplants. Corn cobs. And are those tomatoes?"

"Radishes."

He raises his eyebrows and smiles.

"Stupid, I know." I pull my legs up to my chest. My knees almost touch the dashboard.

He reaches across to the bar under the seat and moves me back a bit. "No," he says. "They look very…healthy."

He turns the key forward until the radio goes on. It's on the Hair Nation satellite station. I reach across and turn it up. He turns it down after a minute.

"I needed to see you."

"How's January?" I ask.

"I can't see Jan anymore. Her mom won't let me in…" He trails off. "January is a pretty strong girl. Actually, the doctor says she looks worse than she really is because of all the swelling. There could be brain damage. Nobody knows for sure yet, but I—"

"Jesse." I put my hand on his wrist. He's clutching the wheel so tightly that I can feel his muscles and tendons straining. He's wearing cargo shorts, a QH T-shirt, and a baseball hat. He looks younger tonight than he did at the frat party.

He turns his body sideways to look at me. "I didn't do it, you know."

"I never thought that you—I mean, I assumed that you would never—" I can't quite figure out what to say. I don't sound convincing at all. I *want* to believe that he wouldn't do it, that he couldn't be capable of beating a girl with a baseball bat, leaving her all alone, bloody and broken, behind an abandoned train car covered in graffiti and littered with empty beer bottles and cigarette butts. "I wouldn't be here if I thought that you could… do something…like that." Nate's sister had to move out of state to get away from him. I think about that now. Maybe that's a lie. Maybe it isn't. But why would Nate lie to me?

"I know about Brit Gormley," I say.

He nods, tapping his fingers in time to the music that I can barely hear. He says nothing.

"Quiet is so small," I say. A vision of the phantom girl—Nate's sister, a rat-esque girl with a faint mustache like Nate's—pops into my mind. If he would stalk her, maybe even hit her, then...I can't take it past there.

"Why didn't you tell me about her? You said there was no older girl. But there was. I know there was. Why hide her? Are you still with her?"

It takes him a long time to answer, and I'm tempted to just leave. Why spend time with someone who lies to me? But then he speaks. "I thought you would think less of me."

"I don't buy it. Besides, if that's true, I *do* think less of you. Do you love her?"

"No. We hung out for a while. But things didn't work out. Then all the rumors started about me stalking her or whatever. That's all false, but I didn't want to bring it up. I didn't want you to know that. I was afraid you might not believe me."

"And I'm supposed to believe that now you are telling me the truth?"

He doesn't answer.

I try again. "Where did you go that night? Where were you looking for her? You can only drive around for so long, right? And how come nobody at that party saw January leave by herself? Why are they saying she left with you? Nobody saw you searching for her around the house. How could anyone *not* see that? " It dawns on both of us at the same time what I am truly saying: I doubt him. I am asking him to defend himself, which can only mean one thing: I believe that maybe he is capable of doing this. I need him to deny it. To answer every question I've asked.

"You don't believe me," Jesse says. He isn't mad. He is resigned. "I've answered all of the questions the police have asked me. I'm telling the truth, Daphne, I swear. I'm sorry I didn't tell you about Brit. That whole relationship was a mistake. There was nothing to talk about."

"We're talking about January now. People at the party saw you leave with her."

"No, they saw me *with* January. Nobody saw her leave. Nobody. And almost everyone there was drunk. Of course they can't answer any questions about me. Some of them hardly know where *they* there that night."

I nod. I am not supposed to ask any more questions. This should be enough to convince me. But I am too quiet. Jesse moves closer to the driver door, as if he's trying to get as far away from me as possible. "I think I understand, Daphne. You don't trust me."

I don't know what to say. Because the answer is that I *don't* trust him. People don't lie unless they have something to hide, right? It occurs to me for a millisecond that I'm making a bigger deal out of the Brit thing than is absolutely necessary. Isn't it possible he didn't want to talk about her? It's not like I was jumping out of my seat to tell him about the time I was madly in love for three minutes with a guy named Donald who had halitosis and an unhealthy obsession with model airplanes. There are things we do that we don't necessarily want to be judged for later. But in light of everything with January, my saner side argues, isn't it right to be suspicious of someone who is just so damn hard to figure out? And then there are the PROFILE results...

"I just need you to know that I would never, ever hurt anyone. You know that, right?"

I don't answer because I can't.

"Right?" he demands. "Daphne, are you listening? You know, right?"

I feel like my lips are glued together. I cannot speak.

"You better go in," he finally tells me.

I take a long time getting out of the car—plenty of time for him to stop me, plenty of time for me to say something.

But he doesn't stop me. And I don't say anything.

CHAPTER 18

Dear Mark,

Glad to know you miss me at the lab, but frankly, it's kind of a relief not dealing with the PROFILE results. My heart dropped to my knees every time I saw the data on another kid sentenced to life as a predicted.

You know my position on this, but let me repeat it: it's not that I think PROFILE is wrong, as in factually wrong—I think it's morally wrong. I don't care if the results are accurate. It's wrong to do this. They're just kids, Mark. Doesn't that bother you?

Hoping you come to your senses,

Melissa

—Email from Dr. Melissa Wright to Mark Miliken, senior researcher at Utopia Laboratories

I LEAN OVER TO HANNAH CRAMER, THIS GIRL WHOSE HAIR ALWAYS looks wet even when it's dry. She's pretty much the only person in the room who is listening to Madame Ada, our French teacher. I stick my foot out in the aisle and gently nudge the side of her shoe. I note that she is wearing pink socks that perfectly match her pale pink T-shirt—she *always* matches her socks to her shirts. I imagine for a minute what it would be like to sneak into her sock drawer and mismatch all of those cute pairs. After a few nudges, she half-turns and looks at me out of the corner of her eye. Hannah Wet/Dry hates to be interrupted when she's learning. "*Quoi?*" she says in a hiss loud enough that Madame Ada pauses.

"Not in French," I hiss back. Madame Ada has selective hearing: French words always get her attention, but as soon as she hears the obnoxious sounds of English, she moves right along in her lecture. Right now, it's something about Pierre and a *cadeau*. At Academy, I was taking Russian, a language they don't offer at QH. I jumped into French II without any prior knowledge. Whenever I hear French words now, my brain doubles over in pain and resists—and not just because Madame Ada's Oklahoma pronunciation would be enough to make anyone cringe. You don't have to know French to know that *oui* doesn't sound like "wee-ah."

"What's going on?" I ask Hannah Wet/Dry.

She turns from me and tears a sheet of paper from her spiral notebook before flipping back to her class notes. She carefully writes on the free page, pausing periodically to etch French words in her notebook. I wait patiently for her to pass me the note, but first, she pauses to rip all the rough edges from the paper where it was attached to the spiral binding. She carefully stacks up the little pieces of paper on the corner of her desk. Finally, she hands the note across to me. I unfold it.

Mrs. Temple announced that we will have an assembly during third period. Didn't you see the reporters outside? They are here because Mrs. Temple has something really big to announce. Did you do your French homework? We had a quiz this morning. You missed it.

I smack my hand on my forehead. I'd forgotten about the quiz. And, no, I didn't do my French homework, although I had carried the book home with me and cracked it open once last night before I decided that I really didn't feel like doing French homework. A brief stab of panic infiltrates my chest. I may be looking at my first grade lower than an A since I began my education in preschool. Melissa forced me to get out of bed today, but I still missed chemistry for the second time this week—and it's only Tuesday. And now a French quiz. I put my head on my desk and zone out. Why bother trying?

I find Dizzy after class, and we head to the bathroom so she can touch up her makeup—just in case one of the reporters wants to interview her. By the time we get to the gym, it's full. The reporters have been cordoned off into the space behind the basketball hoop near the east doors. Their cameras are scanning the crowds, and we all stare back at them from the rows of hard bleachers. I feel like I'm in a zoo.

"Shhh," Hannah Wet/Dry says to everyone behind her as Mr. A.—the gym teacher, who has never worn anything but shorts in his life, as far as I can tell—tries to get everyone to quiet down. "Mr. A. is trying to start the assembly, and I can't hear anything." Hannah Wet/Dry puts her finger to her lips.

Dizzy rolls her eyes and makes a face with her tongue sticking out of her mouth like a thirsty dog. Dizzy thinks Hannah Wet/ Dry is the most annoying person on earth. Or one of them, anyway. Dizzy gets annoyed fairly easily.

Mr. A. stands at the microphone in the middle of the gym. "Students," he calls, "settle down!" After a few seconds, everyone gets tired of talking, and that's when Mr. A. hands the microphone to Mrs. Temple, who has managed to find an entire suit— skirt, jacket, shell—made of sweater material for the occasion. I wonder if she's been searching for sweater shoes. Those would really complete the ensemble.

"People," she begins, in the way she begins every speech to the school, "I have some serious news to present today, and I trust that you will all be able to handle it with grace and maturity."

Someone in the crowd makes fart noises.

"You might be wondering why we have news crews with us today." She stretches her palm toward the group of cameras in the corner, turning to offer a posed half-smile/half-grimace. Very principal-like. "I'd like to turn the floor over to someone who can tell you." She hands the microphone to a man in a black suit wearing a brown tie decorated with brightly colored fish.

"Who's this clown?" Josh asks.

"The superintendent," Hannah Wet/Dry says, like she has school board trading cards and can identify any of them on command. She leans over and adjusts her pink socks, carefully comparing each foot—the folded-over tops may have been an eighth of a centimeter off.

The superintendent takes the microphone and covers it with

one hand while he whispers something in Mrs. Temple's ear. She nods twice and then points at all of us. Then they nod together.

"Christ," Josh says, "can we get this show on the road already?"

"What I have in my hands," Fish Tie says, rattling a piece of paper, "is an extremely important document. I cannot emphasize enough the gravity of what I'm about to say. Your principal, Mrs. Temple, and I have discussed the matter, and we feel that you boys and girls are mature enough to handle the information I am about to share with all of you." He goes on in this vein for a while longer until he can't ignore our restlessness anymore. "Boys and girls, I have here a very significant list. As you are well aware, Quiet High has been the site of some very advanced and complex trials for a program called PROFILE."

"Oh, hell," Josh says. "This is old news. Does he think we're dumb? Who hasn't heard about the whole PROFILE debacle?" He pronounces *debacle* like *dee-BACK-el*.

"As you are all no doubt aware, one of our Quiet High students was a victim of a ruthless attack recently." This is news to nobody. Fish Tie continues, "Many of you know that January Morrison suffered severe injuries as a result of a brutal physical attack. We have reason to believe that she knew her attacker, although she does not remember what happened. We also do not believe that this attack is in any way connected to her brother, recently deceased. Detectives are investigating the situation. I want to reassure you, boys and girls, that you are safe here in the halls of our school."

"Phew." Josh breathes a fake sigh of relief.

"I know this has been a trying time for all of us. I'd like to offer up a moment of silence for the members of the Morrison family, who have endured so much."

The gym falls silent. Someone sniffles. Josh tries to reach up Dizzy's shirt, but she swats him away. "Be respectful, Josh," she tells him. I think of little Hillary with her Harry Potter book. I wonder if she thinks about her future. Is it ruined, just like January's and her brother's?

"Now," Fish Tie says after a few seconds, "police believe that they have a suspect." Dizzy and I look at each other. The sound of talking goes on instead of dissipating, as Fish Tie probably hoped it would. You can tell that he wants to deliver his big news and hear a collective gasp. The fact is, we all watch the news, we all have Internet access, for crying out loud. We know that he is going to talk about Jesse.

Because I am prepared for it, I don't cry when Fish Tie announces that the suspect is a Quiet High student. He doesn't have to say Jesse's name. And I don't cry when he announces that PROFILE predicted the suspect for violent crime—a fact that could be used as evidence against Jesse in a trial. I simply zone out for a minute, thinking about what that means. It's possible that Jesse will go to jail for a very long time. Hannah Wet/Dry gasps when Fish Tie says this. I give the side of her head a dirty look for no real reason.

"We have decided that for the safety of all students, we will publicly release the scores of the predicted." He waits for a response, but nobody gives him one. "With this information—the predicted list—we can better serve the needs of our at-risk students. We do not bring these names to your attention in order to promote any kind of cruel or discriminatory behavior against these particular individuals. We have made this decision because we believe that this is the right choice for our school, especially in light of the January Morrison situation. We do not need more young people to get hurt. Individuals predicted to commit violent crimes and to have antisocial and persistent problematic behavior will be immediately moved into separate classes, away from the other individuals. Those of you who are not predicted to be violent criminals can rest assured that you will be safe."

Josh begins applauding. Fish Tie, who has no sense of irony, nods in our direction, as if thanking Josh for the recognition.

"These alternative educational arrangements will be made for our predicted students with the aid of our guidance counselor, Dr. Tufte, and the students' parents or legal guardians. I must stress again that these students will be kept in Old QH classrooms; they will have a separate cafeteria, gymnasium, and facilities. All relevant classes housed in Old QH will be shifted to New QH. We ask that nonpredicted individuals refrain from visiting Old QH at any time. Our fine school security guards will enforce these rules stringently." Fish Tie smiles at a fat guy in a uniform standing next to Temple. Everybody calls him Porkchop.

I look around the crowded gym. Everyone else is doing the same thing. We're all trying to figure out who these predicted individuals are—who among us will be relegated to Old QH?

"Our top priority is to separate these individuals out for safety purposes," Fish Tie says. "If you have questions or comments, I welcome you to submit those in writing, either on paper or through an electronic medium."

"Seriously?" Josh says to no one in particular. "He wants me to send him an email telling him he's a douche bag?" People around us snicker, including Dizzy.

"One final comment: I want to congratulate those of you who are not predicted. You are a team comprised of our finest students. You are Quiet High's most outstanding individuals, and we will strive to create an educational environment that will best help you reach your fullest potential." Fish Tie applauds himself, but nobody joins in except for Mrs. Temple.

"Hannah, you're going to be awfully lonely," somebody behind us says.

Nobody seems particularly alarmed, although we've just been told that we are going to be divided up like cattle, treated differently based on a number assigned to us by a computer. I think about what school will be like once we are divided. "This is just like summer camp," someone says.

"Yeah," her friend answers. "It's like color wars."

Fish Tie senses that he's losing us, so he moves closer to the microphone and begins talking faster. "Please stay with me, boys and girls. Before we go back to our regularly scheduled classes, I want to reiterate the reasons for our decision to handle matters thusly. I'd like to stress that this measure is designed solely for the purposes of improving our fine institution. The initial implementation of our new track program, however, may be difficult.

As a result, we are asking that you leave the building immediately following this presentation. We will reopen the school tomorrow with classroom assignments rearranged. Mrs. Temple and I ask that you strive to treat each other—no matter what your placement— in a respectful fashion. We also ask that you remain ever-vigilant for any criminal activity on school property and in our greater community. Individuals who have been predicted will not be excused for their behavior. Instead, they should be aware that we are watching them..." He pauses and then adds, almost as an afterthought, "In order to help them."

Someone in front raises her hand. "Shouldn't we, like, put these predicted people in jail or something?" She's met with a small chorus of support.

"No," Fish Tie says, "these individuals will not be charged with any crime until they actually commit it. Our job is to simply remove them from the mainstream population. We hope that further training and isolation from the general population will help them to reform."

You can tell Fish Tie is done answering questions, but the girl keeps pushing him. "But you said that being predicted means they *will* commit a crime. How can they reform? If they weren't going to commit a crime, they wouldn't be predicted in the first place, right?"

Fish Tie clears his throat for about an hour until Mrs. Temple joins him at the microphone and takes over. "Excellent question, Ashley," she says. "PROFILE is very complicated, and I urge all of you to read more about it and how it works. Utopia Research

Laboratories has generously provided this literature"—she points to a tall stack of glossy booklets on a table by the door—"that can answer many of your questions. This situation is new to us too, and we're just going to have to work together to figure out how it will operate. I will tell you that PROFILE tests will be given across the country, starting next fall, so we here in Quiet will not be alone for long. Still, the rest of the country is looking toward us to see how we handle this situation. Let's set an example."

Mrs. Temple hands the mike back to Fish Tie, and I'm pretty sure that it's not lost on anyone—except for maybe Josh, who is updating his Facebook page from his phone now—that she never answered the original question: *Can a predicted person change?* I get the eerie feeling that they don't know.

"Now," Fish Tie resumes, "as you file out of here today, you will be given a copy of the predicted lists. That way, you will be aware of which students are in which category. Your fine teachers are stationed at the doors with printouts." He waves at the teachers, who are standing at each set of double doors leading out of them gym. He flashes us a brilliant smile and closes with a friendly, "Have a productive rest of the year!"

"Oh, this is sooo going to work," Josh says sarcastically.

We file out together, and while some people are talking, it is mostly quiet. The mood is somber, and we all stand in line patiently and politely to receive our copies of the predicted lists. Dizzy begins to read it aloud, but I slip away and find a vacant classroom just off the gym. I absorb the numbers before I get to the names.

PROFILE Results for Quiet High
Total number of students at Quiet High: 341
Sophomore Class: 123 students
Junior Class: 115 students
Senior Class: 103 students

Total number of students predicted for violent crime: 7
Sophomore Class: 2 students
Junior Class: 2 students
Senior Class: 3 students

Total number of students predicted for antisocial and persistent problematic behavior: 68
Sophomore Class: 23 students
Junior Class: 26 students
Senior Class: 19 students

I stare at that piece of paper until the black ink turns into swirls that make no sense to my watery eyes.

So there we are—reduced to numbers. We are eighty-seven juniors against twenty-eight others who are no longer one of us. I read the list of names, scanning for ones I recognize. Jesse's name pops out at me first. The other junior predicted to commit violent crime is Nate Gormley, my tutoring project. No big surprise there.

I move to the antisocial/problematic behavior list. I remember my grandmother telling me about how she went to the Vietnam War Memorial in Washington, D.C., years after the war, and she scanned the black granite, looking for the names of the men she knew. Maybe this is how she felt. Kelly Payne is on the list. And January, of course. I'm surprised when I see Lexus. Next to Dizzy, she is probably the most popular girl in the whole school. Sam, Dizzy, Cuteny, Josh, Hannah Wet/Dry—almost everyone I know—is on the "good" list. Report to New QH, the paper tells me. I am one of the impressive students, the pride of Quiet High that Fish Tie was talking about.

Dizzy finds me in the deserted classroom. "There you are. What are you doing?" I don't have to answer, because she keeps talking. "Josh and I are going to The Mall. You have to come. I'm dying to show you this dress I absolutely have to have. It's eighty dollars, but it'll be worth every penny once you see how much cleavage it gives me. Wowza!" she exclaims.

"Dizzy?" I ask her, without getting up from the desk I'm sitting at. "Aren't you scared?"

"Scared of what?"

"What's happening here?"

She smiles, her teeth as white as the picture on a box of tooth-whitening strips. "What's happening here is what's *meant* to happen. Roll with it, Daph."

CHAPTER 19

Let's just divide them into two groups: those who are worthy and those who are worthless. Seems pretty simple to me.

—Joanna Heller, mother of Josh Heller

MELISSA AND I EAT BOWLS OF TOMATO SOUP AND GRILLED cheese sandwiches before walking back to school for a seven o'clock meeting. The PTA called an emergency evening meeting with parents and students to *address ongoing concerns about school safety.* That's what they told us all this afternoon, our first day in our new classrooms. It was weird knowing that just on the other side of the building, the predicteds were in class. I wonder what it feels like to be them. Jesse is temporarily suspended, but he hasn't been arrested. It's all anyone can talk about. The general atmosphere at school is weird, like everyone is waiting for something terrible to happen but pretending that everything is fine. It's like when you watch a horror movie, and you know that the helpless babysitter is going to eventually bite it, but you hold out hope for her anyway.

The PTA meeting is in the choir room—the largest classroom in the school. Regardless, we are wedged together in extra chairs brought from other rooms. The music stands are lined up neatly in the dark corners of the room. I note that most of my classmates have brought larger, older versions of themselves who turn out, naturally, to be their parents. Brooklyn Bass is sitting with a short, squat mother who looks exactly as I imagine Brooklyn will look ten years and thirty pounds from now. Her dad wears a short-sleeved dress shirt and an old burgundy tie. His hair is slicked back on his head and he breathes with his mouth wide open. Hannah Wet/Dry sits next to her mother, who has a short pixie haircut, presumably to take care of the wet/dry problem.

I feel bad momentarily that Melissa and I look absolutely nothing alike. Maybe looking like your parents provides some kind of psychological comfort. I read once that if people are told other people have the same birthday as them, they are more likely to like each other. Maybe it's the same with parents—it's easier to understand each other if you have the same pug nose or the same out-of-control eyebrows.

We sit next to Hannah and her mom, who Melissa apparently knows. "Can you believe this, Marsha?" Melissa says to Hannah's mom. "It doesn't take much to whip a mob into a frenzy, does it?" Hannah's mom nods in agreement.

Sam Cameron's mom, a varnished-looking woman, enters from the side door and goes to stand in front of the room at the choir director's music stand. Sam sits down behind her, looking bored, next to a man who has a full beard so fair that I have to squint to see that it's a beard and not just bad skin. This must be his dad. Mrs. Cameron is wearing a red suit so bright that she looks like a radish in heels. Her hair is a shellacked bob swinging in one big piece when she moves her head. "Good evening," she says quietly, leaning forward as if she is speaking into a microphone. "I'm glad that so many of you were able to attend this informal discussion on such short notice. Thank you."

Brooklyn's mom says, "You are so welcome," very loudly. Mrs. Cameron looks over her tortoise-shell glasses with a disapproving expression.

"Some of you know my son, Sam Cameron," she continues, pointing at Sam, who waves halfheartedly. "And my husband, Dan Cameron." The man smiles and then scratches his beard. His teeth are tiny, which make his gums seem huge. "And I'm Jillian Cameron, president of the Quiet High PTA." She pauses as if she expects applause. "Undoubtedly, most of you have heard about what happened to your children's classmate, January Morrison." She sniffles and reaches for a tissue out of her suit sleeve. "I'm sure the family would want to thank all of you for your good wishes and prayers. January is still in the hospital, but I am happy to report that she will be able to come home soon. With the help of her dedicated care team, doctors are positive that she will make a full recovery."

Brooklyn's mom claps now, but it takes awhile until anyone else joins in. "Thank you," Jillian Cameron says. "I'm sure Mrs. Morrison finds it gratifying to know that we are all such supportive friends, family, and neighbors. We are the reason that Quiet is such a wonderful community, and I can't tell you proud I am to live here and raise my children in this fine town." It feels like she's getting ready to announce her candidacy for mayor. Melissa must feel that too, because she sighs while crossing and uncrossing her legs three times in a row, a sure sign that she's getting bored.

"A lot of you are wondering what's going on with the investigation of Miss Morrison's attacker." She says *attacker* with a low grunt, as if the word almost sticks in her throat. "The police do have leads, and they are questioning various individuals. I don't want to alarm you tonight. That's not why we're here."

I watch Brooklyn's mom nodding vigorously, hanging on every word coming from Mrs. Cameron's mouth. Brooklyn's dad holds his hand in front of his face and tries to surreptitiously pick his nose. "We are here tonight because of PROFILE. Every one of you here has a child who was PROFILEd in his or her sophomore year. As controversial as those tests might be, we cannot overlook the possibility that certain terrible and tragic events could be prevented if we have the appropriate information. An ounce of prevention, as you all will agree, I'm sure, is worth a pound of…" She trails off here, seemingly unable to find the right word.

"Cure," Melissa whispers to me. She can't help herself.

"That boy attacked my Brit," a rat-faced woman says. Nate's mom. "She was darn lucky it wasn't worse." Then she hacks with a smoker's cough and clears her throat of the world's thickest phlegm.

"Excuse me," Melissa says loudly now, raising her hand. "I'm very sorry about what happened to January, and we all want to keep our children safe, but what exactly are you proposing here tonight?"

"Well, Mrs.—?" Mrs. Cameron waits for Melissa to fill in the blank.

"*Doctor*," Melissa says. "It's Dr. Wright, but you can call me Melissa."

There's quiet murmuring throughout the room. Everybody knows who Melissa is now because the paper mentioned that she's the original inventor of PROFILE. They crane their necks to get a good look at her, this woman who brought PROFILE to little old Quiet High.

"Well, Melissa," Mrs. Cameron replies, "I wouldn't say that I'm proposing something. Rather, I'm presenting options for us to consider. In the interest of keeping the children safe, of course."

"Of course," Melissa says, and I elbow her because it sounds like she is mocking Sam's mom. Which she probably is.

"I do understand a parent's urge to keep those results private," Mrs. Cameron says. "Our first instinct is to believe that the results must be wrong in cases where we find out something we don't want to know. But in addition to isolating those people who may be dangerous and who may be putting our children at risk, we need to know exactly what each predicted child is capable of doing."

Brooklyn's mom erupts in applause again. A handful of people join in.

Melissa talks over the clapping. "And what exactly do you want to do? Should we lock up the violent predicteds and throw away the key? Should we put a list of future teen mothers on Facebook so nobody asks them to prom? How can you in good conscience do that?" I slink down in my chair. Melissa is right, but I never stop being embarrassed by how blunt she is.

"Mrs. Wright," Mrs. Cameron says, "I do think that you of all people would understand the importance of taking PROFILE scores seriously." She surveys the crowd with a smug look on her face. "Many of you probably know that Mrs. Wright used to work for Utopia Laboratories, the company who developed and executed the PROFILE tests in our community." Everyone turns to look at Melissa. Of course they know her.

"It's *Doctor*," Melissa says amiably. "And I do have a connection to Utopia Labs. I was part of the team of scientists who read and interpreted the PROFILE scores we collected at Quiet High for the past few years. I am not, however, prepared to support any initiative that would in any way ostracize or detain any student based on a PROFILE prediction. I'm against these classroom separations. It's simply a violation of an individual's rights. And I don't want my daughter making decisions about people based on what a test said they might do at some future point."

Brooklyn's mom raises her hand. "I completely disagree with what that woman is saying." She points at Melissa. "These PROFILE tests can help us sort out the bad kids—even better than we already have. We have the information right at our fingertips. If the attacker was a student at QH, and if the student was a sophomore or older, we can find him. We just need to find out who was predicted for attacking a girl with a bat, right? I think we all know who that is." She looks around her, searching for some kind of validation.

"I'm sorry," Melissa says. "I have to correct you here. PROFILE doesn't exactly work that way. The test can't reveal what *exact* crime someone may commit. It can only tell you the predisposition someone has toward violent personal crimes. Determining the actual crime is part of Phase II of the research."

I look at her searchingly. There's a Phase II of research?

Hannah's mom jumps in. "I'm Marsha Cramer," she says in the same weepy voice Hannah has. "I'm a psychologist at Quiet State College, and I happen to be familiar with Melissa's work." They smile at each other. "Melissa is trying to explain that while PROFILE does provide data about a person's possible future actions, that data should not necessarily be used to make important decisions about our children." Melissa nods in agreement.

"Well, I disagree," Brooklyn's mom says.

"A lot of scientists have said—"

Brooklyn's mom cuts off Hannah's mom. "I don't care what scientists say. My opinion is equally valid, and I think the results should be public. I just feel it's the right thing to do. I feel it in my heart."

Melissa snorts loudly.

Sam's dad stands up and moves to the podium, putting his arm around Mrs. Cameron's shoulders. He is shorter than she is. "Can I say something here, honey?" She steps aside and gives him the podium. "I may not be a 'scientist.'" He uses air quotes. "I may just be a guy who can give you a hell of a deal on some great import cars." He flashes a grin, but nobody laughs.

He forges on. "I may be just a simple guy who still believes in family, church, and country, but I know one thing for sure: an innocent girl is in the hospital because some animal beat the crap out of her. And not too long ago, our kids were held hostage in this school by a crazed shooter. That shooter could've killed my boy." Mrs. Cameron looks adoringly at Sam. "Well, that girl is in the hospital, and I want to find the bastard who did it. If that means violating the rights of some criminal, well, so be it."

Brooklyn's mom begins clapping, but this time, most of the room joins with her. Sam's dad stands a little taller, talks a little louder. "What good are these tests if we can't use them? It's time to put a label on these kids who aren't going to be good, productive citizens. Let's prevent another Columbine. Hell, let's prevent another Quiet High shooting. Let's prevent another girl being viciously attacked. Let's not take the side of the criminals."

The crowd roars—it feels like a football game. I half-expect the room to begin a round of the wave. Melissa stands up and waves her tiny hand in the air, calling for attention. "I'm not saying we should take the side of the criminals. I'm just saying we need to think about this." She practically has to yell to be heard over the noise in the echoing room.

Mrs. Cameron pushes her husband to the side and moves back to the podium. "I think we've all thought about this. We've all prayed about it. We all love our children. It's time to smoke out the rotten apples. The time is long overdue." Melissa is too angry to even snicker at the ridiculous expression—how do you smoke out apples?

She and I leave before the meeting officially ends.

CHAPTER 20

Buses: Predicted individuals shall not ride on public school buses. Such individuals should make alternative arrangements for transportation to and from school.

Education: Classes for predicted individuals and nonpredicted individuals shall be conducted separately.

Dating: Mixed-status dating and general fraternization shall be strictly prohibited.

—*Rules to Live By,* an underground pamphlet circulated at Quiet High

"SAY SOMETHING WORTHWHILE," MS. KAPLAN WARNS US. "THE point is to gain a richer understanding of the text and the social milieu in which it was written. This should not be a prodigious task, people, if you've been paying attention."

This is how Ms. Kaplan talks, calling books *texts* and using words like *prodigious* and *milieu*—words that have zero linguistic value in a high school classroom. Nobody thinks she's brilliant. We just think she's wound too tightly. Ms. Kaplan is young, but she seems old—and not the good kind of old, but the bad kind that smells musty and yells at kids to get off the lawn. She has a Master's degree in British literature from a very important college, and you can tell that she's pretty bent out of shape about being stuck at QH, so she compensates by teaching a college-level class. "Work with your partners, people," she tells us now. "I expect you to use your time wisely. You should have already read your assigned novel. Work on analyzing the book and preparing a presentation for the class based on critical theory. Remember your central question: Should your novel be included or not included in the American literary canon?"

I look over at my partner, who is making exploding sounds meant to sound like cannons—the kind with two *n*'s. Great. Fate got pissed off and paired me with Josh Heller. He tried to trade partners, but Kaplan wouldn't bend, noting that he needed to learn how to work with people, *even if they are difficult*. Yeah, *I'm* the difficult one.

Josh and I were assigned *An American Tragedy*, which I've already read. It's very long, and he's been trying to plow through it in class while I wait impatiently and stare into the hallway through the open door. I can't help but notice that he's only a few pages into the book—a fact that drives me nuts.

He puts the cannon away, reads for a minute—his lips moving as he goes—and then sets the book down, not even bothering to mark his page. He moves his desk closer to dopey Sam Cameron, who is inexplicably also in our AP class. Since coming to QH, I've figured out that AP means absolutely nothing—everybody takes the AP classes, leaving the "regular" classes open for only the absolute dumbest or laziest students.

"Dude, I'm so glad those losers are gone," he says now to Sam. He's referring to the predicteds.

"Yeah," Sam says.

It's the second day of school we've had with the predicteds out of sight. It's almost like they have just disappeared. Nobody talks about them—not even about Lexus, who used to be in our class, and who was Brooklyn's best friend. Now Brooklyn calls her That Stupid Skank, Lexus Flores, as if that is her full legal name. But I detect a certain amount of regret in her voice. Brooklyn misses her.

Sam holds his phone up high for Josh to see the picture he just took. The two of them are flexing their forearms and taking close-up pictures of themselves with their phone cameras. The latest result is a photo that looks a lot like a bare butt. They've probably taken at least ten arm-butt photos already, but they never seem to grow bored. Josh laughs so hard that he snorts.

"Don't you dare bend that book open!" Ms. Kaplan yells at someone in the back of the room. Watching us strain the bindings of paperback books is her own personal hell; she can hear it from a mile away.

I doodle and wonder how many hours it's going to take me to single-handedly prepare and write our presentation in the next two days. I watch Brooklyn step out from the classroom across the hall to take a phone call. She leans against the lockers. "I know," she's saying, "I can't wear yellow. Not now. Not after what happened at last year's prom." She sounds disgusted. I try to imagine what might have happened that would keep her from wearing yellow. A swarm of angry yellow jackets were released in the school gym and ended up roosting on her yellow dress? The red stripes painted on the gym floor marking the four-square courts clashed with the dress? She takes out a compact and squints at her teeth in the mirror. The fact that she's worried about gunk in her teeth makes me despise her a tiny bit less. Insecurity is a real bitch.

With quick jerking movements, I slide my desk closer to the open door, bizarrely interested in the yellow conversation. That's when I see Jesse walking down the hallway. He doesn't see me—he walks with his eyes straight ahead. I sit up straight. He's back in school. The suspension is over, and the school can't do much else right now. So far, he has not been arrested for January's attack, but he is guilty, according to everyone at Quiet High. And he isn't supposed to be in New QH. All of the predicteds are kept in one small area of Old QH. But he walks like he belongs here.

Josh, done with arm-butts for the moment, follows my eyes to Jesse. "I feel kind of sorry for the guy," he says matter-of-factly. "His dad is probably going to kick him out. My mom wants him to. It's gotta be rough."

"Shut up," I say.

"What? I'm trying to be nice."

I look at him suspiciously. "*Can* you be nice? Do you have that capacity?"

"Come on, Daphne, don't you think you're awfully hard on people? Not everybody is as perfect as you are."

"I never said I was perfect," I say huffily. What he said rankles me, though. Melissa is the type of person who makes everyone else feel inferior. Am I a mini-version of her?

"I'm just saying that Jesse is predicted. And it's better for him—and everybody else—if he's not around anyone he can hurt. Believe it or not, I don't want him to hurt you, Daphne. I respect you. I like you." There's a strange look to him—an eerie shining in his eyes. Is he actually being nice again?

"I really don't want to talk about this."

"Are you still defending him?"

I don't answer.

"You know he's guilty."

"Then how come he's not in jail?" I answer.

"What's going on?" Sam asks.

"Daphne is awfully cranky. Must be that time of month." They both laugh hysterically, like this is some original joke.

I cross my legs one way, uncross them, and then cross them the other way—a gesture unconsciously borrowed from Melissa. I flip my book open, bending the binding until I hear a satisfying snap.

■■■

"What's wrong?" Dizzy asks me. "You're thinking about Jesse, aren't you?"

We are at Whataburger, an impromptu lunch decision made at exactly the moment we saw the cafeteria's beef stroganoff, a lumpy mess of paste-like substance over chunks of sawdust.

"You've been acting weird lately." She stuffs a fry in her mouth. "What's your deal?"

"Weird things are happening. For one, I'm working with your

boyfriend on this English project," I say, instead of answering her question about Jesse.

"Lucky you," she says without irony.

"Even Sam Cameron would be more help, and I'm not entirely convinced he's even literate."

"Sam has a crush on you, you know. He has ever since he saw you on your first day."

"If I'm supposed to be flattered, I'm not. Besides, what about Brooklyn?"

"Eh," she says, "they hook up. It's not a love match." Dizzy shakes her head at me, first a slight up and down nod, followed by a vigorous shake back and forth. It's a very Dizzy-esque gesture—it illustrates how many contradictory thoughts she is having at once. She reaches for my fries, even though she still has half of hers left. She chews while she pulls out a mirror from her backpack and opens it. She blinks her eyes rapidly at her reflection, making that long-O mascara face at herself.

Dizzy wears heavy blue eye shadow today that matches her low-cut tank top. She looks like she's twenty, at least. I like that Dizzy is not ashamed to be partially manufactured—so different from Melissa. She snaps the mirror shut and skims it across the table, where it lands at the edge near me. Is this a hint? I pick it up and open it. I find lettuce in my teeth.

"I'll be honest. Sam Cameron is cute, I'll grant him that. But he is dull. D-U—" She drops the end of the sentence and adds a series of obnoxious snores. "Not my type. But I thought you two would be good together."

"Thanks," I say. "You really know how to increase my self-confidence." I slide the mirror back, running my tongue over my teeth for good measure.

"I didn't mean it that way. I just meant that you are…good. A good girl. And Sam is good. Two good kids. You kids make us proud," she says in her best little-old-lady voice. "You don't drink, you don't smoke, you don't sleep around, you hardly have any fun at all. Josh has some really hot friends that I could introduce you to. We could—"

"And Jesse?" I interrupt.

Dizzy pushes both our trays to the edge of the table, taking my fries away. She puts her hand on her stomach to indicate she is full. I reach out and pull my tray back toward me. "Jesse is very manipulative," she says with authority. "Take this thing with Brit Gormley. Now, that's interesting. I knew something was weird about the two of them together. Brit looks like a dumpy version of Lexus. What did Jesse see in her? And then to stalk her? Jeez, I could see if she was like stripper-hot, but you wouldn't ever think that, like, Brit would do much for a guy. Whatever. But I knew something was wrong because—hello! Girls that aren't very cute don't leave guys who are as hot as Jesse. This explains everything. She broke up with him because he was probably, like, beating her daily or something."

She expects me to respond, but I don't. Instead, I watch Kelly Payne walk in through the front door of the restaurant. She's with Nate Gormley.

"Oh, man," Dizzy says. "Look at those two. Speaking of predicted romance." She makes gagging noises.

Kelly walks up to the counter while Nate grabs a handful of ketchup packets and heads to a table near us. He immediately sees Dizzy and me staring at him. "Hey," he says to me, raising an index finger in greeting. I give him a half-smile. My tutoring work is over now that Nate is in classes with the other predicteds. Naturally, Temple forbade them all from watching Call-Me-Vic's gory videos. They're taking typing instead. Nate shakes his leg and taps his fingers on the tabletop as he waits for Kelly, who is clearly going to bring him food.

"Let's go," Dizzy hisses at me.

"I'm not done eating," I respond.

Her eyes widen in alarm, and she whispers, "Daphne, come on. I don't want to be here. Not with him. We don't know what he'll do."

"You're being silly," I whisper back.

"No, I'm not being silly. Look what happened to January. We don't know what these"—she searches for the right word— "people," she finally spits out, "are capable of."

Nate stops tapping and shaking. "Hey, are you talking about me?" He has a smirk on his face. "Because I can take it. Anything you want to say about me, you can say to my face."

"No, we have nothing to say," Dizzy says primly, sliding out of the booth and then grabbing my arm. "We're leaving." In the process of pulling me, she runs smack-dab into Kelly, who is carrying a tray of food. The food lands down the front of Kelly's pale sweatshirt and white capris. "Watch it," Dizzy says coldly.

We're almost out the door—our trays of half-eaten food still

238

sitting at our table—when I hear Nate call out, "Hey, hey! Come back here! You owe her an apology! You owe me a burger!" We keep moving, Dizzy dragging me by the wrist.

By the time we get to Dizzy's cute little yellow Volkswagen bug, which she calls Bug-a-boo, she's in tears. "I've never been so scared in my life," she weeps. "Think about what could've happened to us! We were in danger!"

"Dizzy," I say calmly, "I don't think we were in danger. This is kind of ridiculous, don't you think? I mean, you weren't scared of them before all this predicted stuff, were you? How is it any different?"

"Because now I know enough to be scared. And you should be scared too, Daph. They take advantage of people like us, people who are trusting and decent human beings!"

Her hands are still shaking, but she's pulled out of the parking lot, and we are going back to school. The sun shines brightly, and I've forgotten my sunglasses, so I pull down the visor. "I don't know, Dizz. I think maybe this whole thing has been blown out of proportion."

"So, what, you want to hang out with them or something?"

"No. I don't know. I'm just saying that I don't think that freaking out around them is necessarily the—"

"Think whatever you want, Daphne. But I'm warning you— you'll be sorry if you don't take this predicted thing more seriously. Not to mention that you're going to be the social outcast of the century if you now want to, like, be all chummy with that loser Nate and skeevy Kelly Payne."

"Come on, Dizz. He's not that bad. Besides—"

"Listen." She holds up her hand. "I'm saying that unless you want to end up like January, you better decide who you're going to hang around with, and you better decide quickly."

CHAPTER 21

Love the predicted, hate the prediction.

—Sign outside of Quiet Main Street Baptist Church

I SPEND MY TIME DURING MY MORNING CLASSES TWEAKING MY presentation notes and messing around with my PowerPoint slides. By the time fourth period rolls around, I'm completely exhausted, but Josh looks refreshed, like he's just had a nap. When I come into English class and sit down next to him, he says seriously, "You look like death, Daph. You should really get more sleep."

It took me until four in the morning to finish the presentation for English—without Josh's help. I crashed until Melissa poked her head in my room at seven and asked me if I was planning to go to school. I tamed my hair and put on under-eye concealer, mascara, and a coat of pale pink lip gloss. My goal was modest: to try not to look like a cadaver with clothes on.

I ignore Josh, turning my back on him, and wait for Ms. Kaplan to walk in and give her disappointed sigh before we begin. She opens by telling everyone, "Remember, sounding recondite doesn't make you smart—it just shows how much you *don't* know." Too bad nobody taught *her* that.

Josh and I are first. He stands next to me at the front of the room with his hands in his pockets, head up, shoulders back, as if he's been waiting his whole life to talk to Ms. Kaplan's fourth period English class about Theodore Dreiser's magnum opus. While I talk, Josh looks at the printout that I gave him. Then he picks at a freckle on his forehead. Talk about dead weight.

My first slide is a picture of the author, Theodore Dreiser. I talk about his background as a journalist and his desire to use fiction to talk about social problems, just as a journalist chronicles human events. The novelist, however, seeks to explain *why* people act as they do, rather than merely reporting events. Then I start talking about the book, about how it was based on a true story of a man who killed his pregnant girlfriend, and Dreiser used that true incident as the basis of his novel because he believed it typified the kind of crime that could *only* happen in America—a crime fueled by greed, desire, sex, and the American dream.

Brock Martin—the guy who everyone calls B. M., because he has diarrhea of the mouth—raises his hand. "So what is this book actually about? Can you provide more detail?"

I sigh and go over what I just said. Nobody seems at all disturbed by the fact that I'm merely repeating myself, only using simpler language. "It's the story of a boy with no money who meets a girl with no money who he gets pregnant. Then he meets a rich girl and falls in love. But in order to marry this rich girl, he has to get rid of the other girl. So he murders his pregnant girlfriend by pushing her out of a boat. Naturally, he gets caught." It's about as much as I can simplify an eight-hundred-page book.

"Makes sense," Josh says, suddenly coming alive as if I've just explained how cold fronts move rather than told a chilling story about a man who murders his pregnant girlfriend.

"It's just like that one guy," Brooklyn says.

"Yeah," a few others say, apparently knowing exactly who she is talking about. She clarifies for me. "That guy in California who murdered his wife. Same exact thing."

"Yes," Ms. Kaplan interrupts, "but I think the important thing about the book isn't so much the plot but the themes Dreiser is presenting. Right, Daphne?"

"Yes," I say, glancing at my notes and then looking at Sam, who is now perched on the edge of the front table, drumming his fingers against the top of it.

B. M. raises his hand again. "B. M.," I say, knowing that I'm being mean.

The name doesn't seem to bother him, but everyone else snickers. "So you think this guy's behavior was justified—killing the pregnant girl so he could be with the rich girl, the one that he truly loved?"

"Yeah, money is super-important," Brooklyn notes.

"Well," I start, realizing that my notes aren't really going to be any help. I drop them on the podium. "It's obviously wrong to murder someone, and I think everybody agrees with that, but in the context of the book and what the author was trying to illustrate, Clyde's actions are somewhat understandable. To end up with Roberta, the pregnant girl, is to end any hope he ever had of living the kind of life he'd dreamed of. He dreamed he would

243

have money, power, and prestige. That's what he thought the American dream was. That's what everybody thinks. And then if you don't get that stuff—the money and the power—what do you do? Maybe our culture kind of sets us up for disappointment."

Josh picks this time to actually participate. "So you're saying this chick traps this dude by getting pregnant and forces him into staying with her because of that? 'Cause that seems pretty messed up to me."

"I don't think that's exactly what happened. She just got pregnant, and in those days, she didn't have a lot of other options. She needed Clyde in order to survive. Literally."

"I don't know," Josh says. "She sounds like a whore." Everyone laughs. Ms. Kaplan rolls her eyes but doesn't say anything. It's patently obvious that Josh hasn't read the book, but Kaplan probably doesn't even notice.

Brooklyn raises her hand again. I look to Ms. Kaplan for help. Am I going to get to give my presentation or what? Monday's presentation on *The Great Gatsby* ended in ten minutes without a single question. "Brooklyn," Ms. Kaplan says. "What would you like to add?"

"So," Brooklyn says from the back, throwing her hair back in pageant pose, "what would you have done if you were Roberta?" Ms. Kaplan is looking at me like I am supposed to answer the question. I really just want to get back to the presentation. I look to Josh, who has now lost interest in the discussion and wandered over to the windows, where he is staring longingly outside at one of the custodians who is making wide loops on the riding mower. "I don't know. This isn't exactly part of my presentation." Ms. Kaplan waves her hand at me, a gesture to go on. I sigh. "I guess I probably wouldn't wind up pregnant like Roberta, and I certainly wouldn't trust somebody like Clyde, who seems pretty shifty throughout the book. The novel just proves why women need to be responsible for their own futures. Roberta never should have been with somebody like him. She should've believed in herself and demanded a guy who would treat her with respect."

Brooklyn smiles at me, a wide, lipsticked smile. Ever since that night at the diner, when she tried to hit me with her purse, she's been very cold to me, a blocky gust of wind at waist level. She clears her throat. "Kinda like a girl who's going out with a guy who is predicted?" She winks at me then.

I blink once. Then twice. "Excuse me?"

"Well, everybody here knows, right?" She looks around her.

Ms. Kaplan looks interested—an unusual look for her. "Brooklyn," she says, "I'm intrigued. Are you finding parallels between real life and the novel? Class, this is called a *mimetic reading*." She hurries to the board and scrawls the words in yellow chalk, forming big, bubbly letters. "Go on, Brooklyn." She seems to forget that I'm supposed to be giving a presentation.

Brooklyn smiles, because all eyes are on her. "Everybody knows what happened to January." A couple of girls in the corner begin whispering to each other. "And everybody knows that Jesse is a suspect, and he's predicted. So this is pretty much a closed case."

"I don't think this has anything to do my presentation," I tell Ms. Kaplan.

"Mimetic readings can be multi-layered," Ms. Kaplan tells me and turns back to Brooklyn. It becomes clear that she's enjoying being part of the gossip. I bet she has a Facebook profile and tries to friend all of the cool students.

"And everybody knows that January and Jesse were *together*." Brooklyn emphasizes the word *together*, making it feel like more than just an adverb. "And January was pregnant—some of us knew that. You do the math."

The room goes silent. Even the lawn mower outside comes to a grinding halt. I get that nervous feeling—the feeling that comes over you right before you puke all over the floor in gym class or get a horrible gas pain as soon as you're alone in a room with a guy.

"Well, Brooklyn," Ms. Kaplan says, walking to the board, "this may not be the most appropriate time to have this conversation." *Finally.* "Daphne, why don't you finish your presentation." It's not a question. Brooklyn doesn't meet my eyes. She looks guilty, because even she knows she's gone too far.

I can hardly find the words to talk. They all stick in the very back of my brain, where I've been storing all my fears about Jesse.

It doesn't take long to gather gossip and figure out what Brooklyn was talking about in class. According to Cuteny's dad, Dizzy's constant source of information, January *was* pregnant. As in, she is not currently pregnant. She had a miscarriage a couple of months before the attack; Dizzy doesn't think she told anyone.

It's impossible not to speculate about who the father was, which is exactly why Brooklyn decided to throw January under a bus and announce this "secret" to me in front of everyone.

Dizzy shows up at my house the night after the presentation. She hands me a mint chocolate chip ice cream sandwich. "Let's not fight," she says, plopping down on the steps off the sun porch.

"We aren't," I say.

"I know, but yesterday, after we left Whataburger, I just felt like you were mad at me. Because of what I said."

I take the ice cream. I don't have the energy to argue with Dizzy. Besides, she's probably right—if I want to be accepted at QH, I need to accept that predicteds and nonpredicteds are not going to be best friends with the rest of us. We sit on the porch, listening to the crickets chirp. Dizzy's wild hair is wound up in a tight bun on the top of her head—she has two brightly colored chopsticks (or maybe pencils—I can't quite tell) stuck through the curls. She's wearing some kind of a denim jumpsuit—the kind of thing that a famous person would wear to a private club at three a.m. Dizzy somehow manages to pull it off. "I've got a date tonight," she finally says.

"Josh?" I ask.

"Josh," she repeats. "I think I've made him wait for me long enough. He's dying to officially get back together with me." Any other girl would sound arrogant saying this, but Dizzy sounds as if she's just reporting the facts, like a disinterested ten o'clock news anchor.

I debate telling her what a complete jerk Josh is and decide against it. One time, when I was in sixth grade, I desperately wanted Melissa to buy me this red dress with white buttons down the front. I coveted that dress, but Melissa wouldn't hear of buying it. It was eighty-three dollars, which Melissa announced was exactly four times—plus three dollars—more than what any reasonable person should pay for a dress.

I begged for that dress, promising to do extra chores, to babysit, to forego Christmas and birthday gifts forever, if necessary. The thing was, I could *see* myself in that dress, and the more she told me how wrong it was—how cheap the material, how unflattering the style, how overpriced—the more I couldn't be dissuaded.

Eventually, she caved and bought it for me, and not for Christmas or my birthday or any other special occasion. She just put it in my closet one day, and it was mine. Naturally, I wore it once and realized the white buttons were tacky, the red a funny tomato color, the hem too short for my long legs. I never wore it again. In fact, I felt guilty for years every time I saw it in my closet. I only got rid of it when we moved to Quiet, and when I threw it in the donation pile, I said to Melissa, "Why didn't you try harder to talk me out of that dress?"

And she said, "I did. And that just made you want it more. It was an eighty-three-dollar lesson for me: Never try to talk someone out of something that's bad for them."

I imagine that Josh is Dizzy's tomato-red dress with obnoxiously large white buttons.

"What do you have planned?"

She shrugs. "We're going to hang out at the tracks, I guess." She says this as though it's perfectly obvious that's what they will do. I think of the night I saw Josh there, the night of the thunderstorm, when Jesse rushed to find January.

"It's not a surprise, you know," Dizzy says, adjusting one of her chopsticks. "January is predicted for alcoholism and out-of-wedlock teenage birth." The words come out like names for conditions: measles, smallpox, the mumps. "Getting pregnant and all was obviously, like, destiny or something. Just one of those things you can't stop."

"Like an oncoming bus," I say.

She leans over and links her arm through mine. "I'm sorry. I know you really liked Jesse."

The mention of his name makes my stomach lurch—it's fear and grief rolling around inside of there, mixing up a toxic cocktail for me to carry around in my duodenum.

Dizzy touches my back. "How do you feel?"

I stare glassily across the street, watching a fluffy white dog scratching at a tree. "Harold!" a woman in too-short shorts screams at him. "Not on the magnolia!"

"I don't know." I can't put how I feel into words.

Dizzy pats my hand, her fingers just a tiny bit sticky from her ice cream sandwich. "Don't be so hard on yourself. You're just a trusting person, Daphne. Anybody could've been fooled by a sociopath like him. I mean, it seemed like he had it all—rich, smart, super-hot. I'm not surprised you fell for him," she says soberly. "The best thing you can do now is just forget about him. He's a loser. He was stringing you along, making you look like an idiot while he was plotting to kill January. That's so messed up! What you need to do now is..."

She keeps talking, but I stop listening.

CHAPTER 22

What surprised me the most is the way those kids accepted the predicted results without even a second's worth of hesitation. Not a single one of them, not one, publicly protested what was happening. Here they were, being rounded up like common criminals, segregated in their own school, and they said nothing. And their classmates watched it happen. They accepted it all.

—Melissa Wright, quoted in the book, *The Future of the Predicted*, publication forthcoming

THE CHEERY VOICE OF THE NEWSCASTER HITS ME IN THE face: "Jesse Kable, son of Richard Kable, CEO of FauxFuel, is the prime suspect in a local high school girl's brutal attack. Police expect to make an arrest later today. This is the first criminal case in history where police are using controversial PROFILE results as primary evidence. Mr. Kable's lawyer expects that his client, if arrested, will be released immediately. He states, 'There's no precedent for using a person's predicted status as viable evidence. In this case, the police have absolutely nothing to link my client to the crime.'" I turn off the television.

"Daphne," he yells, loud enough to rise above the clatter of lockers opening and closing and voices shouting through the hallways. I am on my way to geometry class when I see him, wearing a baseball cap and dark glasses. He's coming in the main doors, heading right for me.

I take off, walking in the other direction, toward the circular hallway that leads to the metal shop, wood shop, and music rooms. I look at the clock: I have two minutes to get to class on the other side of the building. I continue walking through the dark hallway, which rings the gym, peeking into rooms I've never seen before. It's beyond my reasoning abilities to figure out why shop classes are so popular. Who could possibly want to make a bird feeder or a wind chime? Isn't that what Home Depot is for?

I run into him when I pass the third classroom—he's entered the hallway from the other side. The bell rings, and doors shut. The hallway grows quiet, save for the distant sounds of violins playing in the larger music rooms further down the hall.

"I saw the news this morning," I tell him.

"I know you're scared, and you have every right to be." He takes off his glasses and holds my hand gently, his other hand placed over it. He looks harmless, so I have to remind myself that he may be a liar. And worse.

"I can't talk to you, Jesse. I'm really sorry. I'm just really confused."

"You have a right to be confused," he says.

"Don't patronize me." I raise my voice. I know that I have to be strong.

252

Melissa warned me that he would probably come looking for me. "Be careful," she whispered to me, even though we were alone in our living room. "He's going to want talk to you again. He's going to need you. And you have to remember that people are far more complex than science can ever predict." Hearing Melissa suggest that science has shortcomings was a lot like seeing my grandmother, a devout Catholic, stomp on rosary beads while wearing combat boots.

"Don't patronize me," I say to Jesse again, but quieter now, almost a whisper. "I know I have the right to be afraid and confused and everything else. And I am." I realize that I am clutching his hand.

"Right," he agrees, and he drops my hand, which suddenly feels very cold. Then he puts his hands in his jeans pockets, and we stand there facing each other for a few seconds before he finally says, "Will you get out of here with me? Just for a little while? I want to talk to you, but I have to leave. I'm not even supposed to be here at school. But there are things I want to tell you. Things I have to say."

He reaches out, as if to touch my face, and I look down. His hand hovers near my cheek for a second before I feel his skin against mine, his smooth palm cupped against my hot cheek. I move away quickly, but we both know I am coming with him.

■■■■

In his car, on the way to the lake, I worry that maybe he's taking me someplace to do something…bad. And everyone will think I am an idiot for trusting him.

But he doesn't seem to be dangerous. He turns on the stereo and sings along to an old Nickelback song. He messes up the words but forges on anyway. Do killers listen to Nickelback on the way to a crime site? It seems unlikely.

When we get there, we walk to the end of the dock. Jesse takes off his sweatshirt, puts it down on the weather-worn wooden slats, and pats it before I sit down. We let our feet dangle for a minute, and I lean over to roll my pant legs up higher. As I'm bent over, I feel Jesse's hand on my back, and for a second, I think he's going to push me. I think of Roberta and Clyde in *An American Tragedy*. I immediately sit up. "What are you doing?" As soon as the words are out of my mouth, I realize that he is simply holding onto the back of my shirt.

"You look so precarious," he tells me. "I didn't want you to fall over." I think about the last time we sat on the dock, when I dropped my purse into the water.

"Oh, sorry," I say, an apology for snapping at him.

With pant legs rolled up, sunglasses perched on my nose, both of us leaning back on the dock, watching the ducks cluster around a dropped hamburger bun, things feel almost normal.

I am the first to break the silence. "Jesse, I already know."

"Let me say it. I have to say it to you myself, Daphne." He takes a deep breath. "January was a friend. A close friend. I never lied to you about that. I know I wasn't honest with you about Brit Gormley. But I am being honest about January." I pull my legs up, hugging them close to my chest. "January started seeing someone. Hooking up with someone who was bad for her. What you might not know is that she was pregnant. And she—"

"I know," I interrupt. "Dizzy told me."

"Dizzy?" he says. "How does she know?" Then he bangs his hand against his forehead. "I forgot. Dizzy knows everything."

"Cuteny is feeding her information. Josh too."

He turns to me and says with an urgency I haven't heard from him before, "What else did Josh say?" The sentence rings familiarly in my head. It takes me a second to sort through the data. And then there it is. Josh in that frat boy's room, the night of January's attack. *What has she told you?* he had demanded of me.

"I don't—"

"What else did he say?" Jesse insists, and for the second time ever, I feel uneasy with him.

"Nothing," I say.

"Daphne, they say I'm predicted, but there has to be a mistake. That's not who I am."

"I'm hearing *a lot* about who you are."

"And you're saying that you believe it all?"

"Jesse, I don't know." I throw my hands up as I say this, almost losing my balance, which would have meant toppling sideways into the water. Jesse looks angry and confused. I stand up, wiping the seat of my jeans with my hands. "I want to go back," I tell him and turn to walk back to the parking lot. Jesse grabs my ankle hard—hard enough to hurt. I stumble and fall face first on the wooden dock. Fortunately, I land on my hands, rather than my face, so I'm left with scraped palms—palms that had just healed from my jogging fall—rather than a broken nose.

Jesse scrambles to a standing position and runs toward me. "Daph! Daph! Are you okay? I didn't mean to make you fall."

"I want to go back to school," I tell him, getting up and holding my scraped palms toward my chest. I turn to walk away.

Jesse paces quickly in front of me and blocks my path.

"I'm leaving Quiet," he says.

I pause. "You can't. They police said that—"

"They'll never be able to hold me. My lawyer is sure of it. They don't have any real evidence."

"Where are you going?"

"Somewhere else. Someplace that's not Quiet. Maybe to live with my mom out West. I don't know."

I say nothing, although I want to scream, *Don't go!* Something holds me back—maybe it's the way he blinks nervously, those eyelashes batting so quickly. He looks…guilty. I gasp when I think it.

"What?" Jesse says worriedly.

"Nothing." I squeeze the tears back into my eyes. "I just want to go." Suddenly, I feel the urge to be away from him, while another part of me can't bear to see him go. "I'll walk back," I announce.

I take off walking, but somewhere along the way I break into a run. The wind is so strong that I feel like I'm pushing against a heavy wall. Still, I keep running. I can hear Jesse in the distance. "Wait!" he's yelling. I stop when I feel like I can't breathe anymore. I put my scraped hands on my knees and bend over, dry heaving. I look at my palms, which are oozing blood and sand.

Then there is Jesse. He reaches for my hands, but I flinch—against my own will—and he drops his hands to his sides.

"Did you do it?" I ask him. I'm so confused—my mind running back and forth, like a tennis match against itself. One side is *he did it*, the other side is *he would never*.

"If you are actually asking me if I had anything to do with January's attack, I have nothing left to say to you, Daphne."

Once, years ago, Melissa slapped me when we'd had a fight about something. The skin on my cheek stung for long after her hand connected. This feels the same. I begin to explain. "I just mean—"

He interrupts me. "I know what you mean."

I want to say something, but words can't escape from my mouth. The tennis ball in my head moves from one side of the court to the other. The ball lingers on one side. January's prediction was right on. And all of those people at the school seem so sure that the tests are our best hope for preventing bad things. Even Melissa never came out and said the tests are wrong—she just said it's dangerous to tell everyone what the test results are. *But isn't it just as risky to not tell people?* I ask myself. *Don't we have the right to know who's a threat to our safety?*

"Jesse," I say, holding back tears and clutching my arms with both hands. "I'm just not sure what to say." All I know is that I feel like I need to get away—get away from him and all of this. I want to go home. Back to Saint Paul. Back to a time before I knew anything about PROFILE.

I walk away, and he lets me go.

CHAPTER 23

I'm charming. That's how I got away with it. Girls like me. They fall in love with me. Have you noticed a pattern? It's easy to get them to do exactly what I want them to do.

—Quote from a suspect in a police report

WHEN I FALL ASLEEP, I DREAM OF HIM HITTING JANUARY, beating her until she is almost unconscious, and then leaving her alone in that abandoned train car. But in the dream, it's not Jesse after all. It's someone else—someone I can't see through the shadows.

I wake up with my heart beating a thousand beats per second.

I skip school for the rest of the week. Melissa doesn't make me go—instead, she brings me bowls of Lucky Charms in bed every morning, and at night she brings me McDonalds. If I didn't know better, I would think the apocalypse was upon us. I spend most of my time in bed, pretending to be sick. I amaze myself at my ability to sleep for so long. Even when I'm not tired, I can drift into deep sleep that lasts for hour after blissful hour.

I haul myself out of bed and slouch to the living room every night at ten to watch the evening news. I don't like the anchor, a woman with a varnished hairdo. Next to her is a man with white hair whose droopy eyelids twitch when he's feeling sympathetic. Friday night's lead story is about a two-year-old who went missing during a game of hide-and-seek. She fell asleep in the dryer, and a police dog had to sniff her out. The next story is about foreign arms dealers. Then a man named Consumer Detective Dick interviews a woman about her washing machine. It doesn't spin right, but the company won't give her a new one or fix the one she has. Detective Dick recommends that we avoid that brand of washer.

After a commercial, but before the weather QuickCast, they talk about Jesse. I turn the volume up as loud as my head will allow. "Jesse Kable," Droopy Eyelids says, "the local teen accused of savagely attacking a teen girl last week, is no longer the prime suspect in the case. Kable was under suspicion because he was the last person to see the girl at a Quiet State College fraternity party before the incident. He has also been identified by the controversial test PROFILE as a future violent criminal." His droopy eyelids remain steady, as if propped up by invisible toothpicks. He goes on to say that Jesse's fingerprints didn't match the ones found at the crime scene. I breathe a sigh of relief. I feel like I've been holding my breath for an eternity.

■ ■ ■

Dizzy calls at least fifteen times from Tuesday to Saturday. Melissa tells her I am sleeping, which is hardly ever a lie. On Sunday, Dizzy rests.

Late Sunday night, I get an email from Jesse: *I'm leaving town for awhile. Please don't call me or contact me. I wish you the best.*

On Monday morning, Melissa turns on my lights at six a.m. She opens my closet and throws jeans, a pink short-sleeved shirt that I hate, and flip-flops at me. "You're going," she says. There is no room for argument, so I don't bother.

◼◼◼

"Everybody up," Mrs. McClain says. "Orderly lines."

Hannah Wet/Dry clutches her test paper in her hand as she makes her way to the door. I leave mine on my desk. Let it burn.

We were in the middle of chemistry lab when the fire alarm went off, the bleating beep rousing all of us from our silence. I am not the only who jumped. Even though we are in our new classroom—and Mrs. McClain is back with a full prescription of antianxiety meds—any loud noise or sudden disturbance reminds us all of that day. We jumped, and then we all pretended that we didn't. Nobody wants to talk about that anymore. It's *so* one month ago.

We are supposed to be taking a test, but I get the feeling that most everyone is just pretending to be conscious. The beep of the alarm has made me draw a jagged line across my paper—the first mark on it. I'm going to fail this exam—another failure.

Mrs. McClain waits for us to line up, patting her tightly permed gray hair. It doesn't move at all. I worry about how flammable she is right now. She waits for everyone to go completely silent before she leads us out the door, reminding us to mind our manners. I feel like a kindergartner.

We leave New QH by the library doors. That means we don't have to go anywhere near Old QH—or what everyone now calls *the Zoo*, because that's where all the predicteds are locked up, like animals in cages. Dizzy knows people who have been over there to observe the animals. "The predicteds are like a sideshow," she told me plainly this morning, no hint of disapproval in her voice. And the predicted themselves are known as *Lifers*, as in lifelong convicts, imprisoned in their own biology. Already, the halls echo with discussions of Lifers, and a couple of nights ago, the school was tagged—*Lifers for Life* drips across the gym door in spray paint. Obviously the Lifers themselves did it, everyone is saying, because we—the good guys, the normal people—would never deface public property.

Once outside, in the already blistering heat of a mid-May day, Dizzy leaves her group and finds me. Mrs. McClain is standing next to me, having a coughing fit—one of those old-lady coughs that starts in her feet and rattles her whole body. "Did you hear?" Dizzy whispers, her eyes gleaming. I squint at her through the sunlight. "It's not a fire. We're being evacuated. There's a predicted in the Zoo with a gun."

"Oh, dear lord," Mrs. McClain croaks. It's not clear if she has overheard Dizzy or if she is choking to death. We ignore her. The police and fire trucks have arrived, and they are pushing everyone to the farthest ends of the parking lot. Dizzy and I move to the bleachers by the baseball diamonds.

"Now, what's going on?" I ask her.

She juts her chin out proudly. Dizzy loves having information before anyone else does. "I just saw Josh. He was at the Zoo this morning."

"Why?"

"I don't know," she says. "Slumming, I guess." She laughs and then gets serious. "That's when it happened. Nate Gormley—you know that kid, right?"

"Yeah, the kid from Whataburger. My tutoring project."

She whips around to face me. "You were in a room alone with that kid? You're lucky he didn't try something."

"He's harmless, Dizzy." I try to sound less annoyed than I am. Lately, everything that comes out of Dizzy's mouth makes me want to slap her and tell her to grow up. Melissa tells me I'm projecting my anger.

"Nate pulled a gun on Josh. He wouldn't let Josh go."

"Shut up!" I say. "But that doesn't make sense. How'd you talk to Josh if Nate held him?"

"Well, he *eventually* let Josh go, I guess."

"So how'd Nate get into the Zoo with a gun?" Even before the predicted list, the school had metal detectors. The only difference now is that nobody at New QH has to go through them. We have our name badges instead.

"I don't *know*," Dizzy says with exasperation.

"Dizzy, did Josh actually see a gun?"

"Well, yeah. I mean, I'm pretty sure he did. I'm almost positive. Josh told Mrs. Temple. Temple called the cops. That's why they're all here." She waves her hand at the fire trucks and police cars in the parking lot—all of Quiet's force, probably.

"So Nate is still in there?"

"Oh, no. Temple pulled him out right away. The first cop car left with him."

"Then why are the cops here?"

"To find the gun!" Dizzy is just plain huffy now.

"So let me get this straight," I say. "Josh was in the Zoo this morning. He saw Nate. He thought Nate had a gun. He told Temple. Temple called the cops. The cops are now looking for a gun that may or may not exist." It's not like I think Nate is a pillar of society. I just don't think Josh is the world's most reliable person.

"Well, when you put it that way, it's not much of a story, is it? I'm just telling you what Josh told me." She pulls a lock of hair over her lower lip, a habit I've noticed that she seems to have recently acquired. It makes her look like she has a black mustache. "I'm just glad Josh is okay."

I exhale loudly.

"God, Daphne. At least *try* to pretend you like my boyfriend."

The bleating alarm is off now, and if the parking lot weren't full of cops with guns, it might feel like a normal day—back when we all went to the same school, with no Zoo, no Lifers. I take a deep breath. "There's something you should know, Dizzy. I'm not sure that Josh is necessarily the most honest person in the world."

"Are you saying that he lies? Because he doesn't. He's not predicted."

"Well, you should know that Josh and January, um—" I try to think how to phrase it. What do I really know? That three weeks ago, Jesse and I went to pick up January at the train car, and I saw Josh there? And he doesn't want her to know about it? As Dizzy would say, when you put it that way, it doesn't make a very good story. But she has a right to know. "Josh was with January one night. I saw them."

"So?" Dizzy drops her lock of hair and puts her hands on her hips. "You and I are together right now. Does that mean we're sleeping together?" She says the last words in a heavy, breathy way.

"I'm not saying anything bad about Josh except that I saw him with January one night, and he really didn't want you to know. He told me not to tell you. That's all. That's all I wanted to tell you, and I'm sorry I didn't tell you before."

"Well, so what if he was with January? She's a slut. Everybody knows that. She's, um—biologically predicted to be a whore. Of course she was probably after my boyfriend. That's who she is. It's not like I get mad at my dog when he pees on a tree. It's kinda what dogs do." She smiles a half-smile, but I feel like we are on the verge of a fight. I want to back down, to agree with her, but something inside me feels out of control. I think it's guilt—this big, blocky weight sitting on top of my chest. It feels like heartburn. Or maybe heartbreak.

"Do you really think that? Do you really think people are so simple?" I feel the weight shifting around, waiting to break into a million pieces and disappear. "I don't think January, or Nate, or Kelly Payne, or even Lexus, who used to be your friend, are any different than they were before these stupid predicted lists came out. They're just people. And if you are going to treat them like"—I can't even think of the right word—"subhumans, like dogs, then I'm not sure you and I have much in common, Dizzy. January needs help. She doesn't need you or anybody else calling her a whore—for something that she's done in the past *or* may do in the future. Furthermore," I go on after pausing, "I'm really sick of listening to you talk about how wonderful Josh is. Can't you see he's an asshole? Do you need a PROFILE test to tell you that?"

Dizzy is silent for a few seconds. Finally, she arches her eyebrows and then squints against the sun to look me directly in my eyes. "Are you saying it was Josh?"

"What?" Did she even hear what I said?

"Are you saying Josh attacked January? Because I can refresh your memory about that. It was Jesse who did that. It was your boyfriend, not mine." She says this softly, an attempt to diminish the blow.

I hold up my hand, but she doesn't stop talking. She just gets louder. "And another thing—what's your sudden interest in the predicted. Are you, like, their little spokesperson now? I don't know if you want to be a complete outcast here at QH, but if I were you, I'd knock it off. You need to remember that there are people like us, and then there are people like them. If you want to be a Lifer lover, that's your business. But I don't want to have anything to do with that. We are not Lifers."

"That doesn't make us better," I protest.

"Of course it does! We *are* better than the predicteds. They deserve to be in the Zoo, and if you can't see that, then I'm not so sure you're as smart as you think you are." She walks away, but I see her a few minutes later, near her car, laughing with Brooklyn, who is holding a pageant crown out for Dizzy to examine. It all overwhelms me: the incident with Nate and Josh, and the Zoo and the Lifers relegated to the crappiest part of the school, and the police wandering the school grounds while we blister in the sun.

Just another day in a segregated school.

I long to be back at Academy, back in Saint Paul, where everything was simpler.

They announce it at school on Tuesday: there was no gun. But that doesn't mean much—the illusion of a gun at QH is almost as bad as a real one. "Be aware, students," Mrs. Temple fire-breathes through the intercom speakers, as if we're all holding semiautomatic pistols in our hands, "we will not tolerate violence at Quiet High. Not now, not ever."

"I still think he did it," Dizzy announces in geometry.

"Well, kids, when there's no evidence, there's no evidence. If it doesn't fit, we must acquit," Mr. Oakes, our dorky geometry teacher says, almost apologetically. "I'm referencing the O.J. Simpson trial," he tells us, apparently not willing to take full credit for the aphorism.

"Being predicted is the only evidence we need," Dizzy says, and Brooklyn seconds that sentiment. "Nate is a dirty, rotten maggot. He should be shot. And tortured," Dizzy adds as an afterthought. Brooklyn claps.

I roll my eyes. Whatever happened to innocent until proven guilty? If left up to Dizzy—and everyone else at Quiet High—this whole predicted thing is going to be the beginning of the end of the constitution.

"Lay off Nate," I say from my position scrunched up against the wall in my regular seat. The chairs that used to belong to predicteds—Jesse's desk, Lexus's—remain empty. It reminds me a little bit of the place Melissa took me to visit when we first moved to Quiet: the Oklahoma City bombing memorial, the empty chairs a chilling reminder that people who were once here no longer are.

"Sorry," Brooklyn says snidely, "I didn't realize you two were the best of friends. But it figures, Daphne, what with you being the biggest Lifer lover here."

Lifer lover. It's a phrase I keep hearing at QH. It's not even clever, really. But people love to say it, even if it's not true. Anyone who does anything that could be considered dumb, lame, silly, or even just mundane is a Lifer lover. And anyone who goes near the Zoo—for any reason except to gawk at the predicteds—is a Lifer lover too.

"Are we going to have to go to school with Lifers next year?" Ruth wants to know, her eager eyes peering out from under her baseball cap.

"That remains to be seen, dude," Mr. Oakes replies.

"I think we should put them in their own schools," says Dizzy. We haven't spoken to each other since yesterday at the baseball diamonds. She sits with Brooklyn now, passing notes and pausing occasionally to listen to Mr. Oakes.

"The school board is considering options," Mr. Oakes tells us.

"Well, personally," Brooklyn announces in her pageant voice, "I think we should lock all of the predicteds away someplace and let them kill each other." She flips her hair over her shoulder and smiles at Mr. Oakes like he's a guest pageant judge. "But remember, we need to hate the sin, not the sinner. Let's all remember that."

I surprise even myself when I feel my vocal cords begin to vibrate. It takes me a second to realize that the words I'm hearing are coming from my mouth. "You're so fake. You don't care about anybody. You just want to gossip." I raise my voice, until my own head hurts from the screech that appears to be emanating directly from me. Mr. Oakes takes a step backward and perches on the edge of his desk, as if he might slide behind it and hide at a moment's notice. I go on, "You don't know the first thing about how it feels to love someone who everyone else has turned against. You don't know. All you know about is yourself and your pageants." I turn to the rest of the class. "PROFILE obviously doesn't work, or it would know that Brooklyn here is a stupid, conceited, selfish little bitch."

The room is dead silent. When even Mr. Oakes can't decide what to say, I grab my backpack and leave. I can hear the flip-flop of my shoes all the way to the door. I look at Dizzy before I leave. She just shakes her head, as if to say, *Now you've done it.*

Melissa has been in bed for hours already, but I haven't come even close to falling asleep. I grab the phone after only half a ring.

"Hello?"

"Hello," he says formally, grimly.

"Hi," I reply, my voice cracking on the single syllable. I'm surprised to hear Jesse's voice.

We are silent for twenty-three seconds. I count the ticks coming from my watch on the bedside table. "You're still mad at me," I finally say.

"No," he says. "I'm just—" No words adequately finish the sentence, apparently, so he just stops. "I'm sorry about sending you that email message."

"I understand. But, please, Jesse, listen. I had to ask you those questions. I have to know—"

He cuts me off. "Let's not start this conversation again." He's right. There's nothing more I can say. "I'm calling because I need to ask you a favor," he says.

"Of course."

"I'm not coming back to Quiet. Maybe not ever. I don't know. I'm with my mom right now in Utah. The thing is, I'm worried about January."

"Oh," I say. Of course he's worried about January.

"With all this crazy predicted stuff going on, January is going to have an even harder time. I need to know someone is looking out for her."

"Of course," I repeat.

"Daphne, I need you to promise that you'll make sure nothing bad happens to her. She needs a friend, and I don't know of anyone else who I can trust to be there for her. Can you do that?"

"One guardian angel coming right up." I laugh awkwardly. Jesse doesn't laugh. "Yes," I say seriously, "I'll look out for her, but not because of you. I'll do it because she needs a friend."

"Thank you," he says.

I hold the phone to my ear long after the line is dead.

CHAPTER 24

It bothers me that they can use public restrooms. We don't feel safe anymore. If we can't get rid of them, can't we make the predicteds use separate public toilets? It's a matter of public health.

—Marianna Bass, mother of Brooklyn Bass, in a letter to the editor of the *Quiet Daily News*

MELISSA AND I ARRIVE AT THE THEME PARK, FRONTIER City, in Oklahoma City just as it opens. I refused to take the bus with everyone else.

It's our class trip, an annual tradition at Quiet High for the junior class to celebrate the end of the year at a stinky amusement park—a day complete with bagged lunches from the cafeteria and parent chaperones. "Surprise!" Melissa had said with real glee when she told me last night that she had volunteered to chaperone the trip.

"But I'm not going," I told her. We'd argued for about ten minutes, and then I just gave up. Melissa always wins.

This morning in the car, she'd used her disappointed voice to say, "You've always wanted me to get involved at your school, right?"

Yeah, when I was *eight*. I don't have the heart to tell her this.

Riding roller coasters with your mom while she tells Bucky Roy not to spit at the top seems kind of mortifying now. And pointless.

"Yes," I had said to her with forced enthusiasm. "This is great, Melissa. Thank you." If she wasn't listening closely, I might actually have sounded sincere.

I step into the park with trepidation. It's hard to think about roller coasters and fried cheese curds when all I can focus on is Jesse. And about the fact that I'm now a total outcast at school. After the geometry incident, I've spent the last week at school feeling like nerdy Ronald Miller near the end of that old '80s movie, *Can't Buy Me Love*. Invisible was better.

On Wednesday in geometry—the first day back after my big blowup—Brooklyn had shoved me when I walked through the door. She literally pushed me! And so hard that I ran into the corner of the front table and now have a huge bruise on my leg. For someone so little, she's powerful. It didn't occur to me to push back. The next day, I walked by the water fountain where Brooklyn and some of her pageant friends were taking turns filling water bottles. When I went past, they threw water on me. I was soaked—my hair, my T-shirt, even my shoes. Dizzy was with them, and while she didn't laugh along with them, she turned her back on me.

"Traitor," Brooklyn hissed at me.

"Lifer lover," the other girls chorused.

I want to tell everyone that I'm not a Lifer lover. I let Jesse go. I refused to believe him. To believe *in* him. I can't stop thinking about how hurt he looked that day at the lake. How can I possibly ask for his forgiveness? How can I possibly ask him to believe that I am still me, that I am still a good person, when I couldn't do that for him?

I called him this morning before we left for the park. No answer—just his voice mail, the prerecorded voice of that ubiquitous, electronic phone lady. Not even his own voice. I wanted to hear it one last time.

"This place is so…whimsical," Melissa says after we show our special Quiet High tickets at the park gates.

I roll my eyes at her. "Just say it," I tell her. "It's a capitalist nightmare, a money trap in the guise of amusement."

Melissa pats my back, and whispers in my ear. "Try to have a good time, Daph. Try to forget for at least a few hours, okay?" This advice is very unlike Melissa. It sort of makes me want to look closer to see if this is some Melissa imposter, some pod person who volunteered to chaperone a school event and who encourages her daughter to forget about an issue of social justice—the unfair treatment of predicteds!

It's a bright Friday morning with only two weeks of school left, the briefest hint of summer freedom already in the air. The month of May is always better than real summer, because when the day is done, when the sun sets, there will still be as many summer days left as there were in the morning.

"Why don't you just make sure that nobody gets heatstroke?" Brooklyn's mom—another chaperone—tells Melissa. "You can be the keeper of the water."

"The keeper of the water?" Melissa asks skeptically.

Mr. Oakes comes from around the back of the cotton candy stand, pushing cartons of bottled water on a small cart. He pushes the cart in front of Melissa, and then says, "Go have fun, Daphne. Everybody is heading for the rides."

We all look down the midway where QHers—and all the kids from any number of high schools around central Oklahoma on class trips—are standing patiently in line to go on rides that look old and rusty to me. I hear the roller coaster creaking above us. "I think I'll just give the keeper of the water a hand."

After we grow bored of sitting on benches with the water cart, Melissa insists that we dress up in old-time clothes and have our picture taken at one of the old shops. The black-and-white picture is grainy. Melissa is faking a smile, the right and left sides of her mouth forced up in a painful-looking way. I stare grimly at the camera, my eyes diverted slightly to the left, which makes it appear that I'm watching something in the background. I am not. I am just letting my eyes drift. My hair is an anachronism— no frontier woman would have my updated Louise Brooks do. I feel like an imposter. Melissa manages to pull off nineteenth-century homesteader with grace.

I carry the picture in the small backpack Melissa brought for us to carry our things. In the bag are the necessities: sunscreen, sunglasses, water bottles, a sweatshirt for later, and a cell phone, a gift Melissa gave me this weekend—it's something she knows I've wanted. The irony is that I haven't used it yet. Nobody wants to talk to me.

Melissa gets sick on rides, so while she sits with the

water—handing out bottles to thirsty students and then giving them a lecture on the importance of recycling plastic—I ride alone. I'm paired up on the roller coaster with a chubby girl from Ardmore who cries all the way through the ride. I throw my hands in the air for the first time ever on a roller coaster. Who cares if I fall out? What will it matter if the stupid car derails and sends us all pouring out of the little containers onto the concrete of I-35?

At lunchtime, QHers head for the picnic tables by the water park. Melissa and I sit by ourselves. I eat corn dog bites while Melissa nibbles at her apple. I feel way too old to be here on a class trip with Melissa as a chaperone. She keeps trying to find out what's wrong.

"Why aren't you hanging out with your friends?" She's already asked about ten times now—not just today, but every day since I opened my big mouth in geometry and rendered myself outcast of the century.

"Because I don't have any," I tell her.

"What about silly Dizzy?"

"No, we aren't friends anymore."

"Come on, Daphne. Tell me what's wrong."

I stuff enough corn dog bites in my mouth that I am physically unable to squeeze out words. I shake my head.

Melissa sighs and takes a big bite out of her browning apple. "Suit yourself," she says, but I know that she is frustrated by the way she wrinkles her nose at me. "Do you want cotton candy?" she asks three seconds later.

I've never even tasted cotton candy—how would I know if I want it? It's just like Melissa to skip a key part of my childhood and then try to make up for it ten years too late. Cotton candy can't possibly taste as good now as it would have then.

We haven't talked about Jesse—not since I told Melissa that he left Quiet and moved to live with his mother. She's had the good sense not to ask me about him. It's a subject that's hard to talk about. Naturally, she picks today—when most of QH is swarming around us—to ask the money question: "Do you love him?"

I'm not sure what to say. I fill my mouth again, feeling sick as the breaded, deep-fried hot dog touches the roof of my mouth. I chew and then answer with a question of my own. "Aren't you concerned about the fact that Jesse is predicted? I mean, maybe he didn't attack January, but according to PROFILE, he will. Eventually, he will do something like that. Would you let your own daughter near that kind of person?"

Melissa adjusts her sunglasses and looks up at the rickety roller coaster above us. "Daph, I'm always concerned about you and your safety. And I would never want you to be with someone who could—or would—hurt you. But let me ask you *another* question now." I nod. "Did Jesse ever do anything to make you think he's capable of violence?"

I shake my head.

"Did he ever give you a reason not to trust him?"

I can't answer that. Can I trust him? I shrug my shoulders.

"That's all you can really know about a person."

"But what about the PROFILE results? We know that about a lot of people."

Melissa reaches across the table and grabs my hand. I don't even look around me to see if anyone is watching. "PROFILE might tell us what people are capable of, but only people can tell us what they'll do. Don't let the predicted hysteria fool you, Daphne. People can change."

"But you told me before that PROFILE doesn't lie, that it actually works. Are you saying you were wrong?"

"I don't know," she says after a long pause. "I'm just not sure of anything anymore." This is so unlike Melissa that I feel even more uneasy than I did before.

She sees the tears in the corners of my eyes. "Hey," she says, giving me a fake punch in the arm, "Go ride the Steel Lasso." She tips an imaginary cowboy hat. "I'll guard the water."

I pick up all of our lunch garbage, including Melissa's apple core, and throw it in the trash can next to us. I decide to stand in line for the Mindbender instead—the scariest ride I've ever seen. I am surprised to find myself next to Sam Cameron in the line, sans Dizzy and company. We don't talk, but we wordlessly step into the little car together. Sam keeps his eyes closed throughout the whole ride. I watch him closely as we go up and down and swing back and forth and upside down like a whacked-out pendulum. He's green when we finally set foot back on level ground.

"Hi," he says after we get off the ride.

"Hi," I answer. We part ways without speaking. So this is what it's going to be like for me from now on: visible, but just barely.

After the ride, I feel the greasy blob of corn dog bites moving around in my stomach. I head for the bathroom, hoping that I won't throw up on the midway.

The restroom line stretches outside, and I take my place behind all the girls who have to pee so badly that they hop from foot to foot. All the anxiety about holding it is making my bladder shudder. I find myself shifting my weight, keeping it all in.

After standing in line for a few minutes, my stomach settles down. I'm not going to barf, after all. This is a disappointing development. Right now, I can't think of anything better than expelling all those mini–corn dogs. Instead, I'm forced to keep them—punishment for my own gluttony. The long hallway is cool and dark, and I lean against the dirty wall and let the relief of the cold surface sink inside me. I move with the line, shuffling along with everyone else, listening to the chorus of flushes echo around me. When I turn behind me, I recognize Kelly Payne. She half-smiles at me. I give her a little wave.

"Shhh," she says. "I'm not supposed to be here."

I nod. I remember Mrs. Temple's announcement: "Due to recent changes in school protocol, predicteds will not be allowed on the junior class trip." Something about legal liability and logistical problems. Some bullshit.

"I'm here with Nate," she tells me. I wonder how she thinks she's going to remain unseen, but I don't ask. "We're making a statement," she says. "Kind of like a protest." I nod.

We stand silently, and I let my eyes flutter closed for a second or two. When we round the corner, I open them and see three girls standing at the sinks. They are finger-combing their hair and then messing it up again. They all make faces at their reflections. They block the best sinks, the ones closest to the dryers. Everyone else must fight for the two remaining sinks.

I stare at the three reflections—they look different somehow, even though I just saw them all yesterday. Cuteny's hair is pulled into a very high ponytail. Brooklyn's face is plastered in makeup. Dizzy's tube top is the size of a washcloth. She is smacking her lips at herself in the mirror. I eavesdrop.

Dizzy: "This place is lame."

Brooklyn: "Very."

Cuteny: "Why did we come here again?"

Dizzy: "Boys."

Brooklyn: "Shut up. You have a boyfriend already."

Dizzy: "Oh, yeah."

The line for the toilets moves forward. The next open stall is mine. If I move quickly, head down, they will never notice me. I will leave the bathroom, find Melissa, and tell her I'm done with amusement parks and class trips for today. For forever. We will go home. She can return to the garage, where she wants to be anyway. I can listen to the clock tick or count the number of specks in the speckled kitchen wallpaper. The usual.

That's what might've happened. Instead, a shy girl from my English class who sketches horses on her binder covers steps out of line, stands by Brooklyn at the sink, and hurls with ferocious intensity. Vomit hits the floor very near Brooklyn's shoes—horrific, silver wedge sandals. Brooklyn shrieks, the girls start gagging, Cuteny stifles a laugh, and Dizzy turns the same green as her skimpy tube top. Brooklyn must step over the pile of puke. Everyone gags. We all have to turn away. I feel sorry for the girl. I vividly recall being in her position that day in chemistry.

Some girl with a yellow visor: "Somebody needs to clean this up."

Brooklyn: "Duh. Of course it needs to be cleaned up. She could've gotten that on me! That's so unsanitary!"

An argument begins about what's sanitary and what's not.

While the argument builds, I finally get into a stall and lock the door securely. Long after I'm done going to the bathroom, I wait it out until I can no longer hear Brooklyn or Cuteny or Dizzy. When I emerge, the bathroom is almost empty. A park employee with a surgeon's mask and rubber gloves is mopping the floor. "Gross," I say. She nods. Kelly is washing her hands at the sink next to me.

Outside the bathroom, the air is fresh. Even burned popcorn smells better than the dank smell of a park bathroom. Kelly follows me out the door. Nate is waiting for her. I give him a half-pity smile, my penance for making judgments about people when I shouldn't have, and then I breathe in heavily, turning to walk toward the gift shop. Brooklyn and Cuteny block me when I walk past the giant scale where a scary-looking park employee wants to try to guess my weight. For a small fee. "Come on," he yells at nobody in particular. Dizzy stands behind the other two girls, looking like she is ready to flee. She gives me an apologetic look.

Brooklyn: "I told you it was her. I saw her in the bathroom. She just stood there and watched that fat chick barf. Practically *on* me. She didn't even warn me."

Cuteny: "Figures."

Brooklyn: "I suppose you think this is funny."

I don't answer.

Brooklyn: "Fine. Don't say anything. But I want to say something to you, Daphne. I know you and Jesse had something to do with what happened to January. I don't care if the police cleared Jesse. I don't care if Jesse has left the state and gone to live with his mother. I don't care that January insists it wasn't Jesse who did it. I don't care that she doesn't know what actually happened. I know the truth. We all know the truth. You can't trust a Lifer. And you can't trust a Lifer lover either. Look at you, all best friends with Kelly—someone who has probably already stolen your wallet!"

She yells the last part at me, flinging the words at me like rotten tomatoes. Some people stop to watch us. I hear someone murmur nervously, "There's a predicted here? Where?" Instinctively, people huddle together. "I thought the QH predicteds weren't allowed here today."

"They *aren't* allowed," someone else says. Nate and Kelly stand behind me, as if I am their bodyguard, an African native hired to lead them through a dangerous safari.

Josh appears with a giant bowl of orange-colored nachos in his hands. "What's shakin', bacon?" he asks, chip shards spewing out his mouth.

"Hi, honey," Dizzy says and wraps her arms around his waist. When she unwraps herself, he hands her the nachos.

"What's going on, Gormley?" Josh asks menacingly.

Nate holds up both hands. "We were just leaving," he says. He doesn't seem scared, just anxious to get away. I wonder again about Josh's story—about Nate pulling a gun on him at the Zoo on Monday. Nate got suspended for that, even without evidence of a gun.

Brooklyn addresses Nate and Kelly now. "Nobody wants you here. Nobody wants you anywhere. I don't know why they don't just lock people like you up. I hope they do. Why should we have to wait until you hurt someone? And Daphne, you're just pathetic."

I look to Dizzy for help. *Please?* I say with my eyes.

She looks away. *What can I do?* she seems to be saying.

Cuteny: "I can't believe we let you into our group, Daphne. We were, like, friends with you. And all along, you were like this predicted-loving person. How could you?"

Brooklyn: "I never had a problem with you. Not even when you got Josh in trouble at the diner. But I cannot tolerate a person who knowingly aids and abets criminals!"

It takes all of my strength to just walk away.

I find Melissa spinning a rack of sunglasses inside the shop. "Take me home," I say. "Please, take me home. I'm done with class trips."

"Oh, thank god you said that," she says. "I can't hand out water for one second longer."

"Aren't you the chaperone?"

"They'll live without me."

The phone rings late Saturday morning. "I'll get it," I yell, assuming that it's a telemarketer. I'm that desperate for social interaction.

"Daphne?" a small voice says when I answer.

"Yes?"

"Do you want to come over?"

I still have no idea who it is.

"Ah…" I rack my brain, trying to place the voice. "January?"

"I'm back from the hospital. Home." She sounds different—not her usual brazen self, but like a broken little girl.

"Do you want to hang out at my house?" she asks again. "We have the pool uncovered now. We can lay out."

"Is it warm outside?" I flip up my blinds and peer outside. I squint against the sun.

"Great," she says enthusiastically. She appears to think I've agreed to come over.

I show up exactly one hour later, wearing black shorts and a red tank top. My old one-piece swimsuit is in my bag.

January points two fingers at me when she sees me. She looks like a flight attendant pointing out the illuminated exits. "Daphne!" She limps toward me. Her hair is even shorter now—she looks younger, more breakable. She doesn't look like a girl who got pregnant or who got drunk and passed out on a dirty frat house floor. She looks like someone who could break in the wind. She's wearing blue Old

Navy shorts and a T-shirt, and her limbs look scrawny and bony. Her arm is in a cast covered with signatures and smiley faces.

"January," I say. "How are you?"

She throws her good arm around me. "I'm doing summer school," she says when we are apart, as if I'd asked her that question. "I'm not going back the rest of this year. So I need to finish in the summer. I think that's better. I can't go to the Zoo." She grimaces. "I've heard all about it. And I might need tutors for every subject next year anyway. Doctors don't know how much of the damage is permanent. Lots of head trauma," she says, pointing to her face, and I can see now that it is tinted bluish, the same color as her shorts.

We stand there awkwardly until she invites me to sit down on the water-stained deck chairs. She moves slowly, and I can tell it's hard for her to bend her body. We sit on the edge of the cement to let our feet dangle in the pool.

"Are you okay?" I ask, realizing too late that she is probably not okay.

"I guess. It's all just so weird." She starts talking about the attack just as if we were talking about the weather. She hands me a Diet Coke from the cooler next to her. "The last thing I remember about that night is going to the party. I just needed to escape. Then I remember waking up in that disgusting train car. Everyone thought it was Jesse, you know."

"I know," I say, not bothering to point out that it was all anyone could talk about when she was in the hospital. All anyone can *still* talk about. My skin feels like it's boiling under the intense sun.

"You thought so too, didn't you?"

I don't answer.

"That's what bothered him the most—that you believed he was capable of this." She waves her hand in front of herself, holding her cast toward me. "He could never do this." It's exactly what he had told me himself.

I nod.

"The police couldn't find any evidence that it was him. None."

I nod again. A lot of people in Quiet believe that this just means Jesse covered his tracks well. The newspaper is full of letters to the editor written by people who think Jesse is getting away with murder. Or attempted murder.

Hillary comes out of the sliding doors to join us—she's carrying a book and a Jonas Brothers beach towel. "Jan, do you have to go through all of this again? Can't you talk about something nice?"

"Like ponies?" January asks. "Hilly, go get us a snack."

"If I do, will you stop talking about this stuff?"

"Yes," January says. "Now, go! And tell Mom to stop hovering!" She turns to me, "She can't stop waiting on me."

When the sliding screen door slams shut and Hillary has disappeared, January leans over and says quietly, "I just want you to know that it wasn't his."

I know what she is talking about. I stare up at the sky, hoping for a shimmering cloud to cover part of the sun.

"The pregnancy. The baby. Dizzy told you, didn't she? It wasn't his. Jesse and I were never like that, if you know what I mean. But I didn't want him to tell the real story. He let everyone

285

believe it was him, that the baby was his. I asked him not to tell anyone. Not even you. And he took a lot of heat from everyone, including my own brother, but he never said a word to anyone. He kept my secrets."

Through the slats of the fence, I can see the next-door neighbor, a fat man wearing a sleeveless T-shirt. He's putting hamburgers on a grill. Saturday lunch.

"Why? Why so many secrets?"

She smiles weakly and pushes her hair behind her ears. She crosses her arms and taps her fingers delicately on her cast.

"It's a long story, Daphne."

"Will you tell me?"

The man starts whistling, warbling off key, a hissing sound accompanying every breath he takes. I know the tune from Grandma's old big band records: "Pennsylvania 6-500." Why *not* reveal secrets here?

"Actually, I guess it's not a *long* story. It's more like a very *complicated* story. But you need to know something. Jesse had nothing to do with any of the things that happened to me. Nothing."

In the sunlight, in the Morrisons' backyard, January doesn't seem like that weird girl I first met in the library. She seems like a fragile Barbie doll, the kind that you can pop the head off of, if you aren't careful.

"I know," I say confidently. I say it loudly. But I'm saying it too late to the wrong person.

"There was no reason for me *not* to get pregnant, you know." She looks behind her to be sure that Hillary is still in the house.

"I mean, if it was going to happen, why not happen now? Why prolong the agony? Same thing with the alcohol. Why not drink it all now and just get it over with? That's what I was thinking. In case you were wondering."

I lean back on the cement, feeling the pleasant sting of the sun on the back of my legs. I *was* wondering. I did want to know why January would do these things to herself.

"That's the thing I just haven't figured out," she says, shifting in her chair, holding her casted arm away from her. "If I hadn't have made those things happen, would they have happened anyway?"

"I don't know," I say, and I truly don't. Do things happen no matter what you do to prevent them from happening? Is there some immutable law of the universe that prohibits us from veering off the course of destiny?

"I'm really sorry for what my brother did," January says. She looks sad, but she doesn't cry.

"I can't imagine what this has been like for you. For your whole family."

January laughs eerily. "Fortunately, my mom can just tune out anything that she doesn't want to think about. As far as she's concerned, my brother never existed. And my problems? Well, she blames my dad for those. Bad genes. Hilly is her one last hope."

"That must be hard." I don't know what else to say.

January swats at a fly lazily buzzing above her face. "I don't want to forget that he existed. He's still my brother."

There's nothing I can say to that—nothing that could possibly make her feel better.

287

She crosses her ankles. "I still don't remember much. It's weird. If it weren't for this cast"—she holds up her arm as far as she can—"and the bruises, I wouldn't know anything had happened to me. One minute I was at that stupid frat party with you—I remember that—and the next, I was at the hospital with everyone hovering over me." She looks out at the pool. We hear the fat hamburger man softly swearing at his grill. "But lately, I've started remembering things."

"About that night?"

"Well, not so much remembering as just kind of knowing. You know? Like I just kind of know things."

"What do you mean?"

"I know, like, little details. A red shirt. There was a red shirt. And I close my eyes and see a bat—a baseball bat. But that might just be because the police keep saying that the guy who did it had a bat. Then there's a tattoo."

"What kind of tattoo?"

"I can see it when I close my eyes." She does that now. "A tattoo. But not like on someone—just a disembodied tattoo, floating around out there." She waves her good hand in front of her. "One that you wouldn't expect, like a tattoo of a cartoon character or something. Isn't that weird? That something like this could happen, and all I remember is, like, a shirt and a tattoo?"

"Have you told anyone? Have you told the police?"

"Nah. I'm not even sure what it all means. You're the first person I've told."

We both lie back and close our eyes until hamburger guy calls,

"Come and get it," to his lunch guests, wherever they are. I can only see parts of him through the fence slats.

"Did it make you feel like a different person?" I ask, "When you found out you were predicted?"

"I *was* a different person."

"You think people can change, though, right?" I say this persistently, hopefully.

"We are who we are." It's not what I wanted to hear her say. "I'm trapped in my biology," she says, miming being trapped in a box. "You are the lucky one. Trust me."

"Daphne?" she asks a little bit later when I'm almost asleep.

"Yeah?"

"His name was Tommy."

I know without asking that she's talking about her brother.

"I don't think he was all bad. I think somebody could've helped him. But nobody did. Not even me."

We spend the rest of the day hanging out by the pool, a peaceful silence enveloping the two of us like a big, broken-in beach towel.

CHAPTER 25

I'm sorry.

—Email message from Daphne Wright to Jesse Kable

WRI!" CALL-ME-VIC BARKS AT ME. "IF YOU'RE GONNA SIT there like a lump, why don't you make yourself useful, huh? Wanna head out to the library and do some tutoring? I still gotta get everybody ready for this test. Take Bassy with you. Her brain's half-empty."

I look at Brooklyn Bass, who rolls her eyes at me. "I don't think so," she says.

"Fine. Take Cammo. We got to get him ready for this thing." Sam Cameron doesn't look directly at me, but he does stand up with his book in his hands.

"Don't come back till that kid can name every serial killer who terrorized the West Coast since 1950!" Call-Me-Vic yells after us.

Once we're out the door, I say to Sam, "You don't have to go to the library with me."

"We're cool," Sam says and gives me a tentative smile. "It's really none of my business who you date."

"That's right," I say, not that I'm dating anybody now. "But I'm sure Brooklyn won't like it."

"First, I don't necessarily share the same views as my girlfriend. Second, it's not that she doesn't like you. She just doesn't get you."

"Fair enough." I wipe sweat trickling close to my eye. It's so hot, the hottest day of the year, and the air conditioning isn't on yet. It doesn't help that I am wearing crisp jeans and a white V-necked ribbed sweater. Somehow, I can't seem to pay close enough attention to the weather to dress appropriately. I should never take my cues from Melissa, who can be surprised by the presence of rain after five minutes of standing in it. Today, she left for work wearing a turtleneck and corduroy skirt with thick patterned tights. I'm so hot that I feel like I'm going to melt into a puddle of human goo.

"So you want to skip out of here?" Sam asks suddenly. "Get some cool air?"

"What did you have in mind?"

"Whataburger?"

Why not?

A burger, a mass of fries, a large Diet Coke, and a serious blast of air conditioning later, I'm patting my full stomach like a middle-aged fat guy while Sam runs outside to make a quick phone call. He checks in with Brooklyn like a dog on a short leash.

"Sucks, doesn't it?"

I turn around. It's Nate Gormley, carrying a damp rag and a bottle of blue cleaner. He's wearing a Whataburger uniform. "You live here, or what?"

"I like the atmosphere," I say, pointing at the dead flies on the windowsill.

I see Sam, who is outside, spread out on the hood of his car, his phone attached to his ear. "So what do you do here?"

"Nuclear physics," he says holding up the blue bottle. "What do you think? I'm predicted, you know." He pretends to be outraged.

A man in a stained tank top standing at the front counter yells, "Better not be bugging my customer!"

Nate holds up his middle finger at the guy but keeps it below the table so he won't see it.

I stare at Nate for a second while he fiddles with the sprayer on the bottle—it appears to be stuck or clogged. He turns it to his face and examines it carefully. I wait for the inevitable squirt in the eye, but even he seems to figure out how to avoid that.

"You still tutoring crime?" he asks me.

"I wouldn't put it that way. But Vic is still trying to get everybody to pass his class."

"Dumb class," Nate mutters.

"I don't know. Maybe there's something to learning all about criminals. Helps you figure out who to avoid." I clamp my jaw shut. I don't want Nate to think I'm talking about him. "Sorry."

He slides into the booth across from me. I look out the window and see that Sam hasn't even moved. It looks like he's sunbathing. Nate pulls out a cigarette and then offers me one.

"You can't smoke in here," I tell him.

He lights the cigarette anyway. He has greasy brown hair that looks in desperate need of a good cut. His acne-scarred face

293

sports rivulets of sweat running from his forehead down his face. He swipes at them with his free hand. His fingernails are dirty. Grandma always used to tell me that nobody hires someone with dirty fingernails. Clearly, that doesn't apply at Whataburger.

"What?" he says when he sees me staring at him. "What the hell?"

"Nate, do you ever think about the future?"

He blows smoke away from me. "I'm probably going to Tulsa next weekend," he tells me.

"No," I correct him. "Like what you're going to do in the *future* future? When you're older?"

"I dunno," he says, leaning out of the booth to look at the front counter. He's clearly checking to see if the guy at the counter has noticed what he's doing.

The smell of the makeshift ashtray—a cup lid—wafts over me. Nate's lit cigarette smells like Oklahoma at the end of a humid day—warmed over and old. Like broccoli in the microwave. "I wonder what everyone will do," I muse, thinking about Jesse and all of the other predicteds.

Nate stamps out his cigarette, wipes the tip with his fingers, and then puts it in his front shirt pocket. He blows air in his cheeks and then uses his fingers to pop them. I've never heard one person make as much collateral noise as he does. "I guess I'll just stay here for awhile. I don't know."

"Oh," I say, checking my watch and then sliding out of the booth. "I should go."

"I already done it," Nate says to my back. I turn around to face him.

"Done what?"

"Done *it*. Done a crime."

My jaw drops. "Really?" I feel fearful immediately, as if I've turned around in the bank and spotted a ski-masked man standing behind me.

Nate stands up and stretches. "Nah, just screwing with you." He punches at the air in front of me, a fake right hook followed by a left. He steps ahead of me and grabs my tray of trash from me. He tosses the whole thing—including the tray—into the garbage can and walks behind the counter.

I run into Sam at the door. "Was that Nate Gormley talking to you?" he asks suspiciously.

"We weren't really talking," I lie.

"Good." He puts a shielding arm around me. "I don't want you anywhere near him," Sam says softly.

Dizzy calls me on Thursday night after ten, when I'm rattling around in the kitchen trying to find something to eat. Melissa's favorite dinner—grilled soy bologna on wheat bread with mustard and a slice of Velveeta—always leaves me feeling ravenous at precisely the time the house stops stinking of her culinary creation.

"So you're talking to me now?" I say to Dizzy.

"Come on, Daphne. Be fair. What was I supposed to do?"

"Ah, stand up for me when Brooklyn goes on her rampages. How about that?"

"I'm sorry about that. I should've said something."

She sounds so sad that I soften. "I can understand."

"So you forgive me?" she chirps.

"I said I can understand."

"Well, I'm calling for a reason. Do you want to come to Josh's birthday party? I'm personally inviting you."

"Does Josh want me there? Does anyone else want me there?"

"That's not the question we are discussing," Dizzy says with great authority. "I would like to know if you would like to be my guest at Josh's birthday party. It's his seventeenth, and I'm throwing him a great party. Saturday night. Come at six. I know that's early, but you can help me with the food. It's a pool party. Bring your suit to change into later. It's kind of an end-of-the-school-year bash too."

"And people want me there?"

She hesitates.

"Dizzy, does Josh know you are inviting me?"

"Leave that to me. I'm inviting you. You're my friend."

"And what about being popular?"

"Oh, pish posh. We only have a few days of school left. They'll forget by the fall. Please? Will you come?"

"I won't make any promises—" I start to say.

Dizzy shrieks, "Great! I'm so excited. And Daph, I really owe you an apology about all that Jesse stuff. I'm sorry."

"So you don't think he's a dangerous person?"

She takes a long breath and blows it through the phone. "I think there's a party on Saturday and you're my guest. That's it."

I can live with that. For now. I take a bite out of something leftover in the fridge—something that seems too squishy to be food—and spit it out into the sink.

"Come to Josh's house. You know it, right? It's off Lakeview? At the top of the hill? The big three-story place—you know, Richard Kable's house." Dizzy stops suddenly. "Jesse's old house," she says quietly.

"I know the place," I say, even though I've never been there. You can see it from the road when you drive around the lake. Quiet's very own mansion with its very own royalty. I wonder if there are any signs of Jesse there. Do I want there to be? Or would it be easier to know that everything about Jesse—including Jesse himself—disappeared into the sunny West, where I imagine the landscape is nothing but mountains and tall trees.

"Has Jesse called you?" Dizzy asks, as if reading my mind.

"No. Why?" My heart starts beating quickly.

"Just wondering. Josh said he was thinking of coming back to Quiet."

"For good?"

"I hope not. Nobody wants him here." I say nothing, which prompts a meek and relatively sincere, "Sorry," from Dizzy.

"Why would he come back?" I ask casually. I can't help but wonder if—and hope—it's because of me.

"I don't know. Hey, are you going to wear your bathing suit with a wrap or something, or are you going to change at Josh's?"

"I hadn't contemplated that perplexing question."

Dizzy misses the sarcasm. "Call me if you want to talk about it more," she says ardently. "Anytime."

I hang up the phone and decide to give up on real food. I take M&Ms and a glass of iced tea to my room, flopping on my bed and narrowly missing my open laptop. I set my food and drink down and pull the computer to my lap, arranging myself against the headboard with two old pillows.

My fingers take on a life of their own. I don't even think—I just let them move across the keyboard. It reminds me of the time that my childhood friend Sarah and I found a Ouija board in her basement. We delicately touched the plastic planchette, asking the board to tell us the names of our future husbands. One second, I was fully aware of moving that piece to spell out the letters of Sarah's current crush, *T-A-Y-L*, and in the next, I felt like my fingers were moving of their own accord. There was nothing I could do to control them. And the board ended up telling Sarah that her future husband would be named Taylwart.

The message is short.

I was wrong about you. I don't know how to tell you I'm sorry.

I stare at the screen until I fully realize what I've written. I go back to the top of the email window and type his address. I hit send before I have the chance to change my mind.

CHAPTER 26

It might be weird for you to get this message from me. Honestly, it's kind of weird for me writing it. I'm Jesse's ex-girlfriend. I got your email address from my brother. I'm sorry if this makes you feel awkward or whatever. You're probably a really nice person, and I have no reason to lie to you, so trust me when I say that you are getting in over your head. He has two sides. You've only seen the good side. And I, of all people, know how easy it is to get sucked into the bad side. Be careful.

—Email message from Brit Gormley to Daphne Wright

LIKE A PATHETIC LOSER, I GET UP AT FIVE O'CLOCK ON FRIDAY morning just to check my email. No answer from Jesse. But there are a fair number of people who want to enlarge my penis, sell me porn, or introduce me to hot singles in my area. No wonder old people think the Internet is a cesspool. I check my email about three hundred more times before I leave for school.

During French, Madame Ada sends me to the main office to pick up a stack of handouts. Or maybe she's sent me to Paris for a loaf of bread. I can never tell because my French is so bad. I take the long way, walking just to the entrance of the Zoo.

"Sightseeing?" Nate asks me, his face almost obscured by the hood of his sweatshirt tied tightly around his face.

"Phone home," I say, a dumb reference to *E.T.* It just confuses Nate.

He follows me through the cafeteria as I head to the office. "What are you doing?" he asks.

"Errands," I respond, giving it a thick French accent. "Aren't you supposed to be back there?" I point to the Zoo.

"The cages were left unattended," he tells me, matching my stride.

Just before we get to the glass doors of the main office, he asks, "So you going to Josh's thing?"

I stop.

"You are?"

"Yeah."

"I thought after the gun incident—"

"There was no gun," Nate grunts at me. "You're turning into one of them." He holds his hands up. "Want to send me back to the internment camp?" Nate's reference to World War II surprises me. I guess I assume his knowledge begins and ends with pot and *Star Wars*.

"You were invited to Josh's party?" I ask skeptically.

"An invitation is optional." He pulls his hair back into a slippery, girl-like ponytail. "I'll see you there. Unless you want to drive together?"

I can't tell if he's serious or not, so I don't answer.

That's just what I need: to pull up to a party that I'm only sort of invited to with Nate Gormley. That would do wonders for my already tenuous social status.

"No, thanks," I say. "I'm good."

◼◼◼

Josh's house is up a winding road behind the Walmart. (That's what the locals say here: *the* Walmart, never just Walmart.) The road leads past a large group of new luxury townhouses and single-family homes. No Christmas lights or old toilets left to rot outside these doors. Definitely not college housing. These homes are too expensive for the college professors in town—this is Quiet's top-of-the-money heap.

At the crest of the hill sits a stately house that can only be described as a mansion. It's white and dignified, with green-painted plantation shutters. A delicate picket fence (green, not white) hems the giant house in. Without the fence, it seems like the house would probably spill its guts all over the circular driveway.

Dizzy has pulled in directly in front of me. She rolls her window down and motions for me to pull up next to her. "Just leave your car," she says. "Somebody will be here to park."

I raise my eyebrows. There's a valet?

I follow Dizzy to the front door, but at the last minute she changes course and we go around the house to a gated courtyard where she uses a key fob to open a shining, white wrought-iron gate. The pool is aqua-green and the size of a lake, practically. Nobody is in the pool yet, but two women in matching shorts and aprons are setting up food on a buffet table. "There's a pig!" Dizzy says. "They're roasting a pig." She points to the giant red

301

smoker, placed in the great expanse of a backyard that looks more like a football field than someone's lawn.

In the corner, an older man with glasses is lining up fireworks. I recognize him from the news—it's Jesse's dad. He says something under his breath as he tries to line up bottle rockets. A woman stands over him and pats his shoulder. She turns around to look at Dizzy and me. Her hair is thin and dirt-reddish, the color of dirty Oklahoma windows, parted in the middle and held securely back in a tidy bun, pioneer-woman style. She's wearing plaid shorts and a brown shirt with a big stain in the front. She doesn't look like she belongs with the house.

"Joanna, I'd like you to meet Daphne Wright."

Joanna looks over my head and says hi.

"Joanna is Josh's mom," Dizzy tells me. Then she clears her throat and says, "Richard, this is Daphne."

Jesse's dad looks at me through thick, round glasses. No sign of recognition appears anywhere on his face. Did Jesse never talk about me? "How many knots do you know how to make?" he asks me.

"I'm not sure. At least one," I estimate generously.

"Oh, Rich, not now," Joanna says. To me, "He wrote a book about knot-tying, and he wants to tell you about it."

"That's interesting," I lie.

"There are at least thirty kinds of knots, and I'm always on the lookout for more." Jesse's dad names a few and uses the air as makeshift rope to demonstrate one or two of them.

I stare at him intently, trying to find any evidence of Jesse in this odd man. At last I see it—the way he shrugs his shoulders when he loses his confidence. I give him a big smile. "That's sounds really…useful." He smiles back.

"Dizzy," Joanna says, "help me get the food out. You," she says, looking at me, "Daphne, right? Can you help carry ice?"

I should've known I'd get put to work—like a paid employee—at Josh's party. "Sure," I say, and then I go hide out in the garden for a while.

The guests all arrive between six thirty and seven. By seven thirty, the food tables have been eviscerated. Joanna and Rich are nowhere to be seen, and most of the guests are splashing around in that giant pool. I hide out in the corner, by a changing room, sipping Diet Coke and holding a plate of roasted pig and coleslaw in my lap. Nobody says a word to me, although that's progress. Nobody has thrown food at me or tossed me into the pool either.

Brooklyn sashays past me three times wearing the same swimsuit Dizzy bought at the mall. Standing next to Dizzy, she looks like first runner-up, for sure. She screams when someone accidentally pushes her into the pool. Then she has to be led inside to find a place where she can heat up her hot rollers.

Sam wanders by and sits with me for a few minutes. "This place will be out of control when Heller breaks out the booze. It's pretty tame right now." We watch the floundering bodies splashing around in the pool, the smell of charred pig delicately enveloping all of us.

"Sounds dangerous," I say.

"Nah," Sam says. "This is a nonpredicted-only party."

"Keeping out the riffraff," I say sarcastically.

"Do you believe Jesse did it?" Sam asks me.

I shake my head while I keep my eyes on a game of Marco Polo. "January doesn't think so either."

"How do you know that?"

"She told me."

Sam sits up in his lounge chair. "Since when are you friends with January?"

I shrug. "I don't know. Since I went over to her house."

"What did she tell you?"

"What makes you so interested?"

"Everybody is interested."

"Change of subject," I announce. "Let's not talk about PROFILE for five minutes."

We are silent, the sounds of the party filling in around us. "So," Sam finally says, "there *is* something I wanted to ask you."

I look at him expectantly.

"Do you want to hang out sometime? With me? Just the two of us, I mean."

"What about Brooklyn?"

He scratches his head. "It's over. We weren't good together. She's just so—"

He can't find the right word. I can. But I don't say it.

"So what do you think? About you and me?"

I'm silent for too long, which is pretty much the same as a rejection, only worse. It means I recognize that I'm humiliating him. "Never mind," he says, getting up so quickly that he knocks over his chair. "Have a good time tonight." He leaves to join a game of volleyball. I throw my plate away and return to my seat in the corner.

A few minutes, later Nate appears from behind me. "Hey," he says. "Think anyone will notice I'm here?" He's wearing jean shorts and no shirt. I can't help but stare at his prominent ribs. He's short, hairy, and mean-looking like a catfish. He's drinking something red from a glass pitcher, which he sets by the edge of the pool.

"Wait here," he tells me, and he disappears into the small changing room near the garage. When he comes out, he's wearing long tan swim trunks with white stripes on the sides—the kind that dads wear when they take you swimming at the Holiday Inn. Or at least, I assume that's what they wear. On him, the swim trunks reach almost to his ankles.

"I'm going for it," he says, carefully putting on goggles as if they are part of a complicated disguise. When he's a few feet from the pool, he takes a running jump and cannonballs into the water, splashing to the outer edges of the pool. His foot nicks the pitcher, and it breaks into three pieces. He ignores it and motions for me to get in.

I'm hot and tired of sitting. It affects my judgment. "Hang on," I say. I go into the changing room, pull the tags off the new bikini I grabbed at Maurice's on my way over, and then undress. The suit is the color of green coral and chocolate bars—pretty in the store. When I put it on, though, I realize that the bottom is too tight and the top is too roomy; I should've tried it on in the store. I try to pull the high-cut bottom across as much of my butt as I can, and I cinch the tie on the bikini top as tight as it will go. Without a mirror, I can't tell if I look hideous or not. There's a row of stiff towels on a shelf, and I pull one out to wrap around me. The frayed and shrunken piece of cotton doesn't do much good, but it does make me feel braver.

I walk out of the changing room. Nobody notices me, except for Nate, begoggled and treading water at the edge of the pool near the diving board. I marvel at the fact that nobody seems to notice him or care that he's there. I take the towel off and tiptoe toward the ladder. "Wow," he says. "Daphne, you should wear a bikini all the time. I had absolutely no idea that you were so hot."

"Gee, thanks," I say sarcastically, knowing that I'm ridiculously stupid to be socializing with—let alone swimming with—a gate-crashing predicted. But somehow, being nice to Nate helps me feel like I'm making up for treating Jesse poorly. I sidestep the glass—let the uniformed help clean it up—and submerge myself. I swim away from Nate, who is still under the diving board. The pool feels like bathwater, and the lights at the bottom cast a peaceful, bluish tinge everywhere. Nate follows me and dunks me just long enough to make me nervous.

"Come on," he says when I come up, sputtering water out of my noise. "Let's swim." I watch him swim low and fast around bodies and through legs. Nobody seems to notice that the hairy fish is Nate.

I float on my back, looking at the stars just beginning to light up above us.

"I could live like this," I say to nobody in particular.

The pool roils underneath me as everyone fights for room to spread out, but I keep hold onto my little corner.

"I do live like this," Josh replies, water dripping down his freckled face.

I sit up quickly and start treading water. "Hey," I say, "thanks for inviting me—er, letting Dizzy invite me." I decide to be nice to him. I'm enjoying his pool, after all. Maybe I've misjudged him. Dizzy loves him, right? Certainly that must count for something.

"You like it here, huh?" His eyes seem focused on me, but at the same time, I sense that he is looking through me, not at me. He's not drunk—I know, because he doesn't have the same slobbery, obnoxious air he had that night at the diner. His eyes are warm and conciliatory. I feel cozy in the warm pool. "Hey, Daphne?" he says suddenly.

"Yes?" I tread water slowly, watching the waves spread out around me.

"I wanted to talk about—everything. You're Dizzy's friend, and I don't think I've been totally fair to you."

I look at him skeptically. "Are you drunk again? Is my head injury acting up?" I pat my skull. "Are you actually trying to apologize? To *moi?*"

"Come on, I'm trying to be serious here. I've been a jerk, and I'm man enough to admit it. Friends?" He reaches out a dripping hand.

I grab on to the edge of the pool so I can wipe water from my eyes.

"Tentative friends?" he amends.

We shake on it. "To starting over," he says, holding up an imaginary glass.

"To pool parties," I respond.

"Is that Nate Gormley?" Josh asks me suddenly, forgetting about our mock toast. "Is that little bastard actually at my party? At my house? In my pool?" I follow his gaze to Nate, who is now bouncing on the diving board, preparing for a soaring splash into the crowded water.

In one fluid movement, Josh heaves himself up the side of the pool. "Hey, Gormley!" he shouts. Nate stops jumping, the still-vibrating diving board causing him to lose his balance a bit. He rights himself and looks out at the pool through his goggles.

Josh walks toward the board with his arms half-flexed, held out away from his body. Dizzy told me that he once said he walked that way—half man, half monkey—because his muscles were too big. Josh yanks Nate by the arm and pulls him off the board, scraping Nate's skinny legs against the cement and the broken glass from the pitcher Nate broke earlier. "I don't think so, Gormley," he says. "It's time for you to leave." The backyard has grown so quiet now that I can hear the crickets in the background. Everyone in the pool, including me, stands still.

Nate picks himself up, still hanging from Josh's tight grip, and examines the blood running down his left calf. "Oh, come on," he says. "I thought we had an agreement. I keep quiet, you let me—" Josh yanks so hard that Nate ends up on his side, his arm twisted awkwardly behind his head. "Goddamn it!" Nate yells. "You're gonna break my fuckin' arm."

"That's what I'm hoping for," Josh says.

We all watch as Josh drags Nate down the length of the pool, with the smaller boy struggling to get his feet under him. "This is crazy, man!" Nate keeps saying. "What the fuck? I thought we had an agreement!" And the more Nate talks, the faster Josh drags.

I get up and follow them. "Wait, Josh! He's hurt." Josh stops, and I point at Nate's bleeding leg.

"Oh, Christ! He's bleeding on my patio!" He watches the blood trickle over the shiny flagstones. By this time, everyone has returned to swimming. No one is much interested in watching Josh throw out Nate, a lowly predicted that nobody cares about anyway. "Daphne," Josh says, "get Dizzy." I walk the few steps to the gate myself to examine Nate's leg. I pull gently on a piece of glass stuck in his calf, but it's wedged in there pretty good, and I'm too afraid to go any further.

"Go," Josh tells me. "Go tell one of the waiters. Have them find somebody who can clean this up." He turns to Nate. "I don't care if you bleed to death, but I don't want you bleeding all over my yard." Josh shudders, as if the thought of blood-spattered grass is just too much for him to contemplate. What's up with boys and fear of blood?

"Here," I say, taking my scratchy towel from around my waist. "Let me just pull that piece of glass out. Then we'll wrap it up. It'll stop bleeding."

But by this time, Josh has already walked away. "Get out of here, Nate," he orders as he walks away backward. "I'm not going to warn you twice." Then he says to me, "I'll be back in a second, Daph."

"You better go," I tell Nate when Josh is out of sight. I step over the pool of blood on the patio, and squat to examine the wound more closely. I tie the towel around his leg. The skin is ripped off from his knee to his ankle. The glass is jutting out just above his calf. "We're going to have to pull that out," I say, wrinkling my nose. "Let's do it on three."

"I'll get it," Nate says. He leans over and yanks the glass out, grimacing and then doubling over in pain. The blood pours out. I look around for help, but nobody is paying any attention to us. "I'll drive you to the ER," I tell him. I tie the towel tighter around his leg. "Hold that there," I tell him.

"No," he tells me. "I'm not going to the doctor." He limps toward the gate, faster than I thought someone who was gushing blood could.

"Wait!" I say, chasing after him.

"I'm fine," he tells me.

I bend over to make sure the towel is going to stay.

"Just let me go," he says, ripping his leg away from me.

That's when I see it, glistening with water and covered by droplets of blood.

A tattoo.

It's on his ankle. A little red-bearded Viking with a helmet, holding a club. Hagar the Horrible. From the old cartoon strip.

I used to read it when I was kid—the only part of the Sunday paper I ever looked at. I roll Hagar around in my brain for a second or two, like one of those giant hoppers they use for bingo. The hopper stops. I remember the conversation I had with January just a week ago.

The guy who attacked her had a weird tattoo, like a cartoon character.

"Wait!" I yell. I stare at his ankle, and the mean little Viking stares back at me.

Nate lets the gate slam behind him. "You should take care of that cut!" I call to Nate, pointing at his bloody leg.

"Thanks, doc," he calls over his shoulder.

I know it was him. I'm more sure of it than anything I've known in my life. It was Nate who attacked January.

"I have to go," I tell Dizzy as soon as I'm able to find her. I turn and walk back to my stuff, conscious of everyone staring at me. I grab my bag and a damp spare towel draped over a chair and step through the sliding glass doors into the kitchen.

I have to find January.

CHAPTER 27

Daphne Wright was talking too much, asking too many questions, spending too much time with January. It pissed me off. I knew I should've finished the job on January myself.

—From the Quiet High killer's confession

NOBODY FOLLOWS ME INTO THE HOUSE. I LEAN AGAINST THE shiny, stainless steel refrigerator, breathing in the cool air. I can hear the clock above the stove ticking. The house feels empty. I wonder where Joanna and Rich are.

Why would Nate attack January? I thought they were friends. They hung out together.

I walk over to the patio doors and peer out the windows. It's dark outside, but the pool lights illuminate everyone in a sparkling way. The party has resumed, in spite of the scene with Nate and Josh...and me. I can't see Dizzy in the crowd, although it's hard to take a head count of the pool with so many bodies splashing around, over and under, back and forth.

I reach into my bag for my phone.

Damn it.

Even I have to admire the irony: I finally have a cell phone, but I left it at home.

I see a cordless phone on the counter, but I don't know January's cell phone number, and I certainly don't want to call her house and talk to her mom. I have the urge to call Jesse, a number I know by heart. I pick up the cordless phone once, set it back down. I do this three more times before I decide against dialing. He didn't respond to my email. How many other signs do I need to tell me that he doesn't want to talk to me?

I'm still standing there in the dark when I hear the patio door open again. I hear giggles, then heavy breathing and smacking sounds. It's kissing—long kisses punctuated with strident moans. I find the light switch by the sink. The yellow gleam lights up Dizzy's face…which is attached to Josh's.

I fight the urge to gag.

"Daph!" Dizzy exclaims, running over to give me a soggy hug. "I thought you were leaving." She's been drinking—her pupils are big and rolling around in her eye sockets like pinballs. "We're totally going to do it," she whispers loudly. Josh stands with a smirk on his face, his arms crossed against his bare chest. "It's Joshy's birthday present." She wags her finger at him. "You've been a good boy, right? Right?" She singsongs, "We're going to do it, we're going to do it," until Josh finally tells her to be quiet.

"Isn't your mom here?" I ask Josh.

"Nah, they left a while ago. Went to Tulsa for the night. The house is all mine."

"And mine," Dizzy chimes in.

"Do me a favor," Josh says to me. "Keep an eye on the party while Dizzy and I spend some time in my room."

"In your room!" Dizzy shouts gleefully.

Josh goes to the fridge and pulls out a beer. "Want one?" he asks Dizzy.

"She's had enough," I answer.

"Okay, Mom," Dizzy laughs. "Mom says no. Mom says no. Mom says no." Apparently, drunk Dizzy repeats everything.

Dizzy is too obnoxious to talk to, so I ignore her. Instead, I address Josh. "You'll have to find someone else to chaperone your party," I tell him. "I'm going to January's house."

"Suit yourself," Josh replies.

"January the predicted," Dizzy chants over and over again. I'm about a second away from smacking her to get her to stop.

"Dizzy." I grab her shoulders to give her a shake.

"Whoa!" she yells.

"Dizzy," I say again. "I'm leaving. Are you going to be okay?"

"Oh, I'll be okay. Definitely okay. I'm going to be having sex." She giggles. "It's my first time," she says proudly. "Oops!" She looks at Josh. "Did you know that?"

"Even better," he tells her.

"Maybe we can stay at the party for a while, though," she says tentatively. "We don't have to do it right now, do we?"

"Dizzy, I don't think this is such a good idea. Maybe you should come with me. I can take you home."

"Hey, hey, hey!" Josh yells, slamming his beer bottle on the granite countertop. "You aren't taking her *anywhere*. Dizzy, you don't want to go, do you?"

"Well, I *am* tired," she says, yawning widely. She thinks for a

315

minute. I catch her eye. She's acting drunker than she really is. She's second-guessing this whole plan. "Maybe just a short nap. If Daphne insists."

Josh comes over to her and wraps his arms around her, sliding her off her feet and up against him. "No, no nap. Let's go upstairs." He kisses her hard, right in front of me. I have to turn away.

"Dizzy." I tug gently at her bathing suit strap. "I'm going to January's. I need to talk to her about something. About the attack. About Nate Gormley. Come with me."

Josh drops his arms, and Dizzy stumbles. He's not rough, but she staggers backward, and I have to hold her up.

"What did you say?"

"I just need to talk to January. She remembered something about the attack."

"Oh!" Dizzy exclaims. "We need to go. Talk to Jan. Yes. We should do that." She's definitely not sure that she wants to sleep with Josh now.

"What does she remember?" Josh asks quickly. He knows his night is over. I smile to myself.

"A tattoo. The same tattoo Nate has."

"This is ridiculous." Josh takes a slug from his beer bottle. Then he catches himself. His voice softens. "You're a really good friend, Daphne. But it's late. Maybe this can wait until morning."

"It can't wait. Come on, Dizz."

Josh snaps, "You're testing my patience here, Daphne."

"Come on, Josh," Dizzy says.

He faces her. "What? *You* said the same thing about her.

Remember? She drives you nuts. You called her a Lifer lover." Dizzy looks away from me. "Besides, even if January *did* remember something about a tattoo, that doesn't mean Nate whatever-his-name did it. It just means he has a tattoo. So? Lots of people have tattoos." He finishes his beer and reaches for another one from the fridge. "This is dumb. I'm not going to let this ruin my birthday. Daphne, leave this until morning, and I promise I'll help you figure things out." He seems calm and collected, his face a placid portrait.

It's silent for a moment until Dizzy says very quietly, "I want to go with Daphne."

"Are you serious? After all the money I've spent on you to get to tonight? Are you *kidding* me?" It's like something clicks in his head then, and he knows he's being a dick, because he changes his tone quickly. "Just stay. We'll go upstairs and cuddle—just cuddle. Come on, sweetheart."

She doesn't buy it. "Josh, you're being a real asshole tonight." She's suddenly coherent. It's impressive the way Dizzy can go from obnoxious slob to reasonable, clearheaded person in a matter of seconds. "Let's go," she says to me. "You drive." She hiccups. "I just need to get some clothes." She walks over and puts her hand on the patio door.

"Hold on," Josh says suddenly. "If you're going, I'm going too. Daphne," he says kindly, "why don't you go upstairs and change clothes?" I'm still wearing my suit and that stolen towel. "I'll show you where you can change. Dizz, go get your clothes. You can change in the bathroom down here. I'll grab a shirt."

Dizzy smiles broadly. "Thank you, Joshy. I'll go outside and grab my bag." She opens the patio door. "Meet you back here when you're done."

"Thanks," I tell him. He's not my type, but he's not awful. I'll remember to tell this to Dizzy. I know she desperately wants me to like him.

"This way," Josh says to me, indicating that I should go first.

I turn and walk down a long, narrow, dark hallway. "Up the stairs," Josh tells me.

The staircase curves, and at the top step, I look down a row of closed doors. "Which one?" I ask.

That's when everything turns black.

CHAPTER 28

Help.

—Daphne Wright

THE ROSE-PATTERNED CARPET OF THE ROOM REMINDS ME OF the guest room in my grandmother's house. Maybe this is the honeymoon suite, where guests are encouraged to ignore the sprawling size of the house and pretend they are at a tiny country inn.

The side of my face is smashed against the carpet, and I can feel a hand pressing hard on the other side. "What are you going to do to me?" I ask. My head feels fuzzy, not unlike that night at the diner. A blinding pain radiates from the left side.

"Shut up," he says, but he's good-natured about it, like we're just fooling around.

"Please," I say, and the pressure on the side of my head eases. My vision becomes clearer.

I lift my head as much as I can, my neck straining, my hands bound tightly behind my back.

"Why are you doing this?" I ask.

"We should've known this would happen," he says. "It was predicted. By PROFILE."

"But you aren't predicted."

"You are so naïve, Daphne. Do you think everyone who was originally on the predicted list is actually still on it? Some of us just had enough money to buy our way off it."

"You're predicted," I say, trying it out for size. It makes perfect sense. "But how is that possible?" I say. "Utopia had the list and they—"

"You can't really be this dumb. People will *pay* to get off the predicted list. And there are a lot of people who are happy to accept the money."

Melissa, I think. *Would she do that? Does she know?*

"Jesse," I say. "What about Jesse?"

"Jesse's dad wouldn't pony up the money for him. Sucks, don't it? My mom did it for me. Richard doesn't even know. He's too busy thinking about knots to see that a hundred grand of his money disappeared."

"Where's Dizzy?" I ask.

"She went home."

"No, she wouldn't leave without me."

Josh laughs. "She would if she thought you left her first. She was disappointed that you left without even saying good-bye."

I strain my whole body, listening. I desperately want to hear sounds from the party, sounds from the house, but there is only silence, as if a layer of snow covers everything.

"Don't even think about screaming," Josh says, reading my mind. "Nobody is home. The party is over. It's just the two of us. We have the rest of the night." Josh sits down on the floor, his back against the bed. I wriggle my hands a little bit. I can't see, but I think he's tied them with a bungee cord—the kind you carry in your car. I can feel the hooks on the ends of the cord biting into my skin. If I wiggle, I know I can easily get the cord off. Clearly, Josh didn't listen to Richard's knot lessons. This one feels pitiful.

"I know all about you," I bluff. Josh closes his eyes.

"That's your problem," he says. "You know too much. And you talk too much. I knew you were a problem ever since that night at the diner, when I pushed your head into that window. I should've pushed you harder."

"I knew it. I knew you were evil. You might've fooled everyone else. But you never fooled me." That's not totally true, of course. I didn't know it was him at all. I just knew I didn't like him. And then I blamed Nate.

"You'll tell on me," he says matter-of-factly.

I realize that I'm never going to get out of here if I don't outsmart Josh. "You know, if you let me go, nothing bad will happen to you. Nobody will even have to know. I can keep my mouth shut."

"You'll tell," he repeats.

"I won't. I promise. I'll make sure January never remembers what you did to her."

Josh looks surprised. "You really haven't figured it out yet, have you?"

"What?" I ask warily, trying not to show how worried and perplexed I feel at the fact that my plan to outwit Josh has gone nowhere. He might not be as dumb and simple as I had thought.

"I might as well tell you. It's not like you'll be able to spread this around or anything."

"Don't tell me," I plead, knowing that if he's ready to tell me some big secret, I'm not getting out of here alive. "Let's just not talk. What happened between you and January is your business."

"I thought a smart girl like you would've figured it out. Maybe you aren't as brainy as I thought you were."

"I honestly have no idea what you are talking about."

"I didn't attack January."

"It *was* Nate?" I ask. "See? You're innocent. You can let me go."

"Technically, Nate did it. But it was my idea." His tone changes, becomes more somber. "Poor January. She would've been better off not remembering. Why did you go and help her, Daphne?"

"Why would you want to hurt January?" It's basically a rhetorical question. Even caught up in my own fear, I'm aware enough to know that Josh is psycho. Nate might be stupid and mean and criminal, but Josh is crazy.

"Oh, silly Daphne," he says and runs his finger down my cheek. "That haircut is really cute on you. I should've gotten a hold of you before Jesse did."

He stretches out beside me, using his folded arms to prop up his head. "He might've gotten you, but he didn't get January, and, oh"—he moans as he rolls onto his stomach—"she was a sweet piece of ass. If that dumb bitch hadn't gotten pregnant..." He reaches out, and runs his fingers down my breastbone. "She was stringing me along, making me think she was going to have that baby, and then I'd be trapped. We couldn't have that, could we?" he asks me, letting his hand stop on my stomach. "Kind of like that novel you were talking about in class, huh? Are you appreciating the irony, Daphne?"

"I don't think this is exactly ironic. More like psychotic. But why bring Nate into the whole thing?" I say.

"He wanted the money. I wanted January gone. Easy. At least it should've been. But I guess it's true when they say if you want the job done right, you're better off doing it yourself." He leered at me, his eyes wicked.

"If something happens to me," I tell him, "everyone will suspect you. You know that, don't you?"

"I'm not sure I care. I just want to have a little fun with you, Daph. Doesn't that sound nice?" He tugs at the scratchy towel, miraculously still around my waist. "Nice suit," he says, staring at my bikini bottom. "You know, Dizzy never even found out that Jan and I were hooking up. I'm grateful to you for keeping your mouth shut about that. You're not so bad, Daphne."

"Does Jesse know about all this?"

"I think he knows that my mom paid to get my name off the list. But who's going to believe a predicted if he decides to tell anyone? You can't trust those people." He laughs loud and hard, truly off his rocker. He touches the strap of my bikini top. "Gormley is a problem, and he'll need to be taken care of, but right now I think we—you and me, I mean—should just worry about what *we're* going to do here. Right?"

"I'll scream," I say, wondering if anyone in those houses down the hill could hear me if I really let loose.

"No, you won't." I see his hand coming toward my face, and I feel it connect with my skin the first time. After awhile, I feel nothing but fear.

"You're crazy," I tell him, knowing that I won't be able to reason with him about anything.

"Deal with it."

I scream as loud and as hard as my lungs will allow.

I open my eyes to total darkness. My hands are still tied behind me with the bungee cord. I'm facedown on the bed. I glance around, but everything is blurry—it's as if I'm seeing everything in triplicate. Bodies are moving, but I can't tell how many. I hear heavy breathing, grunting, and punching. There's a fight going on. I try to yell, but nothing comes out. I clear my throat, but all I can do is squawk like a dying baby bird.

"Hold on, Daphne!" someone says, and I can't tell if it's coming from one of the bodies in the room or if it's in my head. I can't seem to get my voice to reach a level of volume beyond a pitiful whisper. Hot tears are streaming from my eyes. "Melissa," I call quietly, even though I know she is probably safely home in bed. "Melissa, help me." I struggle to keep my eyes open, but my eyelids flutter like nervous butterflies.

A long time passes. Or at least it feels that way to me. When I finally open my eyes wide, my vision is normal. The light is still dim, but the bright moonlight is pouring through the windows.

Jesse is standing over me. "Daphne," he says.

I blink once. Then again and again. I am awake. And Jesse is here.

CHAPTER 29

January Morrison tried to ruin my life. She got what she deserved.

—Josh Heller

ARE YOU ALL RIGHT?" JESSE HELPS ME ROLL OVER AND pulls me to a sitting position. He puts a stale towel around my shoulders and then hugs me so tightly that I can't breathe. I stare wildly around the room past his shoulder. I can't speak. "Are you all right?" he asks over and over again, and all I can do is nod my head woodenly. He sits down on the bed, pulling me in his lap. He rocks me back and forth for a long time.

"I'm sorry," I tell him. And I mean for everything.

"I'm sorry I left," he says. "I never should've left you. I knew what he was capable of."

"Josh," I say, moving my head from Jesse's chest and looking around the room. "Where is he?" Suddenly, everything comes back to me.

Jesse grabs my face and turns me back toward him. "Don't look, Daphne." But he's too late. Josh is sprawled across the rose-patterned carpet, blood seeping from his chest. "He had a knife," Jesse says. "We fought. I got a hold of it. And then—"

I start to laugh until I see Josh's lifeless body sprawled on the carpet again. "He's dead?" I ask, sucking my breath in.

"Don't look," Jesse repeats. He's crying now. "I had to do it! He was going to kill you!"

We're still sitting on the bed, rocking gently, when the police arrive.

CHAPTER 30

Not being with her is harder than I thought it would be.

—Jesse Kable

'VE GOT A SURPRISE!" DIZZY DOESN'T BOTHER TO KNOCK. AS far as she's concerned, my room is her room.

I open my eyes and try to see the clock. It's midafternoon. I've been napping for over an hour. It seems like I do a lot of that these days.

Dizzy plops herself on the bed next to me. She's wearing some kind of blue cape. She sees me staring at it. "Vintage," she explains. "Hot as ice, isn't it?"

"Isn't it a little warm for a cape?" I peer through the blinds. The sun is so bright that it hurts my eyes.

"Did you hear me? I brought you a surprise," Dizzy says again. Her eyes are gleaming. She tugs at the two French braids hanging at her shoulders.

"Please," I say, throwing myself back on the pillows, "not another makeover." She's been over here at least a dozen times bearing creamy eye shadow or fake eyelashes or an electric eyebrow plucker.

"Better than that," Dizzy says. She pats my forehead. "I've brought someone who wants to see you." She looks at my half-open bedroom door. I don't see anybody, but I smooth my hair anyway. "I'm really not in the mood for company," I say.

"Don't be silly, Daph." She acts as if I've just announced that I want to join a convent and take a vow of silence. "Come in," she calls to the door.

Sam steps through it. His hands are stuffed in his cargo shorts pockets, his baseball cap pulled low over his eyes. "Hey," he says.

I give Dizzy an *I'm-going-to-kill-you* look, but she can't parse it. "Surprise!" she calls.

"Look, Dizz, I'm glad you came to visit. And Sam, it's nice to see you, but I'm not exactly up to…" I can't think of the right words. "I'm not exactly up to thinking about dating or whatever."

Sam and Dizzy laugh together. They laugh hard enough that I feel stupid. "What?" I ask. "What's going on?"

"Silly, Daphie. I didn't bring Sam here for *you*, like some kind of male offering. Jeez." She chuckles again. "I came here to tell you the news." She grabs for Sam's hand. "We're an official couple!"

Sam turns red, but Dizzy is clearly over the moon. She likes him. That's obvious. I've never seen her look at anyone the way she does at Sam. It's not so much adoration as just general joyfulness. Frankly, she looks at Sam the way I remember looking at Jesse.

"We've kinda been hiberdating. You know, just holing up together. And here we are. Together." She beams. Sam gives me an *aw, shucks* look from behind those long eyelashes.

"I'm really happy for you." I'm sincere, because they're obviously so smitten with each other. She fits in the crook of his arm perfectly—they are like a matched salt and pepper shaker set. "I'm really glad things are going well."

It's something of a surprise to me that the world is going on without me. The weeks I've spent in bed or on the porch reading or watching TV while I listen to Melissa's critical analysis have felt like an eternity. The night of Josh's party seems so long ago. Some days it's hard to believe it even happened.

"Have you seen him?" Dizzy asks tentatively, her mood shifting slightly.

I shake my head. She asks me every time I see her. I haven't seen Jesse. "I don't even know if he's in Quiet." Dizzy opens her mouth, but I cut her off. "And I don't *want* to know. If he wants to call me, he can."

It's been over a month since Jesse and I have spoken. After the police arrived that night, they arrested Jesse for the attempted murder of Josh Heller, his own stepbrother. It was twelve long hours before they sorted out the whole story. I was so tired by that time, I felt delirious. But I wouldn't let myself rest until I knew that Jesse was going to be okay. I spent a day in the hospital. I didn't have any physical injuries, but I was pretty shaken up. That time is blurry now. I really only remember Melissa standing over me, handing me a giant plastic cup with a straw, telling me not to talk. "You can talk later," she told me.

But later, I didn't feel like it.

Dizzy filled me in on the details later, when I got home,

tender and bruised. Josh's stabbing was ruled self-defense. I was just lucky, the police told me, that Jesse found me in time. Josh might've killed me. I didn't mention what else he planned to do. I can barely think the words, let alone speak them. He was going to rape me.

Josh wasn't dead. He spent three weeks in the hospital. He's now in jail, awaiting trial as an adult. I will eventually have to testify. I try not to think about it, though Dizzy loves to talk about him. If only she had known he was predicted, she likes to say, she would never have gotten near him. Dizzy isn't bothered by PROFILE—she's delighted to be part of a world where everything is determined. Or so they say.

"Have you heard all the news?" Dizzy asks now. She brings me gossip like fruit in a basket. It's a peace offering, a token of her affection for me. She tells me she saw January at the grocery store, but she avoided her. She doesn't know that I see January often. We have become friends. I wonder how things will change when school starts again in a month or so. Right now, she's a different girl, more like a clone of her mom, but there are times when I see flashes of the old January—not the one who hated herself, but the one who was wonderfully bizarre and full of life.

"Did you hear about school?" she asks. She's too excited to let me respond. "We're all going to the new private school."

I already knew that. Melissa told me, but I pretend to be surprised. Dizzy's so excited to tell me, and I don't want to ruin it for her.

"My parents don't want me at QH. In fact, hardly anybody is going there except the predicted. And people who are poor, of course." Dizzy adds that last part as an afterthought.

"It's going to be weird," Sam says. "It's our senior year, and we'll be starting over again."

The new school will be open in record time. A group of concerned citizens, led by Brooklyn's mom, started the ball rolling. They remodeled an old Big Lots in a strip mall. That'll be the new school. They won't accept the predicted. Because it's a private school, that's legal. The Bass School, it will be called—named after Brooklyn's parents, because they donated a ton of money to get the thing going.

"You'll be going to Bass too, right?" Dizzy asks. It's not so much a question as a pleading wish.

"Of course," I say.

I feel guilty about lying, but I just don't want to argue with her. She'll never understand. I'm going to QH in the fall, because I don't feel right about going to a school designed to keep people out. Even Melissa thinks I'm nuts. "I know that what they are doing at the Bass School is wrong," she told me, "but I can't send you to QH, not when I know I might be putting you in danger."

I haven't told Melissa yet. I *will* be going to QH. And she can't stop me.

"Sammy," Dizzy says suddenly, "will you run to the kitchen and get us some Diet Cokes?" He smiles at her, happy to do her a favor.

When he's gone, she grabs hold of my hand. "I know you still love him," she says.

"It's not fair," I respond.

"Fair doesn't matter much. We have to be safe. This is the only way things can be," Dizzy says gently. "It's us against them, and that's the way it will always be. I don't care if Jesse is confirmed. There will always be a question mark."

Confirmed. She's speaking the new language of PROFILE. While the test can predict for an extremely violent personal crime, it doesn't necessarily know the difference between self-defense and premeditated murder—a glitch in the system, I guess. Jesse is confirmed, which means he's already committed a crime—a crime of defense. In this crazy new world of PROFILE, that makes him slightly less dangerous than a predicted. He might have committed all the violent crimes he'll ever commit. Or he might not have done so. That makes him a different kind of social pariah—more like an ex-convict than a ticking bomb.

"I'm really sorry about that night," she says.

"I know." And I do know she's sorry. Dizzy has apologized about a million times for leaving without me that night. But she couldn't have known what Josh had planned. She'd been fooled by him. When she went back to the pool that night to get her clothes, she ran into Cuteny and Brooklyn and chatted for a long time about what an asshole Josh was being. By the time she came back inside to change, I was already unconscious in the pink-flowered room. Josh told her that I'd gotten tired of waiting and left. Brooklyn gave her a ride home later that night because Dizzy had been too drunk to drive. How was she to know that Josh had hit me over the head with a heavy stone statue of Buddha, taken from Richard's office, when we were walking up those stairs? "It's not your fault," I say for the hundredth time.

"Sure." She flips through a book on my desk. "You know I want you to be happy, right?" Dizzy's face is inches from mine. She has that look she gets when she's ready to beg forgiveness, whether you want to give it or not. It's not a fight I want to have today.

"I'm happy," I say, grateful that Dizzy can't tell when I'm lying.

"I didn't think a pizza buffet was your thing."

"I'm expanding my horizons," Melissa says, turning her nose up at the vat of gravy in the buffet line. "Pizza and gravy?" she asks.

We're at Pizza Heaven, my first foray into the outside world since the Incident. That's how I think of it—the Incident. That phrase is nonthreatening. It could suggest anything: a flat tire, an unfortunate belch let loose in polite company, a conveyor belt gone wild with too many pies on it. It allows me to think of that night without thinking about Josh—or Jesse.

Melissa selects a seat under a stuffed moose. "I have some news." We haven't talked about PROFILE in ages. "Nate Gormley has been arrested and is awaiting trial."

We've all been watching for his twitching little face. After the night at Josh's, he simply disappeared. But he left behind the bat he'd used on January. The police found it in his bedroom with January's blood all over it.

I gnaw on a slice of chicken wing pizza while Melissa talks: "They found him in Oklahoma City. He confessed everything. He'll probably spend most of his adult life in jail."

I chew slower. The buffalo sauce turns acidic on my tongue.

"His sister Brit admitted that she lied about Jesse. They went out a few times, but he never stalked her, and he certainly never hit her. But Josh convinced her to spread the rumors because he thought it would put even more negative attention on Jesse. Everything Josh did was calculated. It's scary, especially when you think about how many people he was controlling like marionettes."

"Why would Brit lie? That doesn't even make sense."

Melissa chews loudly on a celery stick. "I guess you're too young to realize that there are certain kinds of people out there who can convince anyone of anything. That's what sociopaths are."

"I always hated Josh," I say, trying to convince myself. "He didn't fool me."

"Josh's mom is probably going to get jail time for paying the school district to keep Josh off the predicted list. Utopia, in fact, had the correct list, but nobody bothered to check it against the school's list, not even me. I feel responsible for that. I should've been more careful. I guess I was duped along with everyone else."

I give her a sympathetic look. This isn't Melissa's fault, but I still don't feel like talking. Plus, it's no big surprise to me that Melissa can be a scientific genius and still not understand the first thing about people. She was truly surprised when the news articles started pouring in.

Nate Gormley is completely without a conscience, the reports said. Josh, the armchair psychiatrists told us, is a classic narcissist. The whole story came rolling out piecemeal, an article a day. Josh couldn't stand the thought of looking bad, of having everyone know that he was with January. He had to get rid of her. When January didn't die, Josh was temporarily relieved when he discovered that she didn't remember a thing. By that time, he'd also found out that she'd lost the baby before the attack. No baby. He was safe and didn't need to get rid of her anymore. I feel weird even saying that—*get rid of her*, like she was a bag of garbage or something—but that's how Josh saw her.

"The gravy isn't bad," I note.

Melissa gamely tries dipping a carrot into it. "The superintendent is in some hot water himself, because he accepted the large *donation* that Josh's mom gave him in exchange for losing Josh's PROFILE scores. She'll probably finagle her way out of the mess. She's got a lot of resources and great connections. Nevertheless, Jesse's dad has filed for divorce. I've heard the gossip." It must be big gossip if Melissa has heard it. She once asked me if the Jonas Brothers was a fast-food chain.

I stop chewing at the mention of Jesse's name. I drop the slice. "All I want to know is if things are going to go back to normal now."

Melissa stares at her salad—a pile of bean sprouts on iceberg lettuce. "Once things are set in motion, it's sometimes hard to stop the downward spiral."

"Translation?"

"I couldn't in good conscience work on that project. It's just not right. And it's all bunk, Daphne. The data is there, but we're still

335

a long ways away from ever applying it. If I had any idea what Utopia was going to do with that information, I never would've agreed to be part of this. This data they have—it's useless. We don't know enough yet."

I look up in surprise. I've never heard Melissa say that. "So it doesn't matter? The predicted are just like everybody else?"

She shakes her head sadly. "No, they aren't. Don't you see? The test has *made* them different. It doesn't matter if the science behind it is all hogwash. We can't undo what's already been done. The predicted will become exactly what we tell them they are going to become. That's the tragedy here."

"What can we do?"

Melissa smiles a hopeful smile. "Well, we can try to be decent human beings. We can help people whenever possible. We can eat pizza." She sniffs a piece of bacon ranch. "We can go for a jog immediately following this meal."

I wait until we are almost done eating, until I know the time is right. "Melissa?" I say.

She wipes her hands on a napkin. "Yes?"

"I'm going to QH next year. I don't want to go to the Bass School."

"I understand," she responds, surprising me. "It's the right thing to do."

She holds my hand for just a second across the sticky table. But instead of making me feel like a toddler, I feel like I've grown up. And we both know it.

"You know what?" I say. "I think I'm happy."

And now I'm telling the truth.

CHAPTER 31

I don't know what happens next.

—Daphne Wright

THE LAKE IS THE ONLY PLACE WHERE I CAN THINK. DUSK IS MY favorite time, the best time of the day. On the pier, in the hot, humid breeze, I can think. Sometimes I bring a book. Sometimes I just watch the joggers.

"Can I sit?" The voice comes from behind me. I whip my head around. And there he is. A million times I've imagined it. But he's really here.

"Jesse," I say, trying out his name.

He kneels beside me. He points to the brown lake water lapping at the shore. "Somebody dumped a toaster oven in there. It washed up right about here. I found it last week."

"Oh, yeah? Only in Quiet."

"Only in Quiet," he repeats. He sits down next to me. We don't look at each other, but the smell of him—his cologne mixed with minty gum—makes me picture him as if he's looking right at me.

"Almost time for school to start."

"The summer went by too fast. It always does."

"I'm ready for a change."

I pick up a stick and drag it through the water.

"You like it here? At the lake?" he asks.

"I love it," I tell him. "How'd you know where to find me? Or maybe you weren't looking for me," I add quickly.

"Does it matter?" he says. "Whether I was looking or not? The point is that I just knew you were here. Just like I knew it was you that night. I knew you were in trouble. We're just linked together in some weird way, I guess."

I see his head move in my peripheral vision. "You didn't call."

"Neither did you."

He's right. I haven't known what to say. I haven't known what we are to each other.

Until now.

I know with a sureness that I've never had about anything: we are meant to be together. I turn to tell him. I don't care what PROFILE says. I don't care about anything. Except him. Except us. It just took me a while to realize it. And I just know he feels the same way. It's time to start over.

I turn my head toward him. My lips are ready to speak, but I can't, because his lips are already covering mine. When we move apart, he speaks first. "Don't say anything. We got lost, but we're back where we're supposed to be."

■■■

It's too hot for boots, but I want to wear my new grey slouches with my skinny jeans. I throw on a white tank top with a vintage necklace Melissa gave me as a back-to-school present. "Don't forget that the Perseids meteor shower is tonight!" she'd called this morning when I walked out the door. It's exactly the kind of non sequitur I expect from her, and it makes me smile.

Jessie drives me. When we pull up to the school parking lot, it's eerily empty. Quiet High's population has dropped in half. We still park far from the entrance so we can walk hand-in-hand to the front doors. We pause at the flagpole, where a handful of students are gathered to smoke and complain about the first day.

I stop and turn to him, my hands on his shirt and his skinny tie—he's dressed for work after school. "Do you ever regret it?"

He doesn't have to ask. He knows I'm talking about Josh. About that night.

He stares at the flag, the chain clinking rhythmically against the metal pole.

It all could've turned out so differently. Months later, I'm finally able to think about it. I know that I am lucky that Jesse came home, back to his dad's house, that night. He'd gotten my email a couple of days before. "I needed to see you again," he told me later. He'd left his mom's house as soon as he got it and drove straight through the night. He went to my house first. Nobody was at home, although I'm sure Melissa was probably camped out in the garage, working away. She wouldn't have noticed anyone at the door. He'd come back to his dad's house just after midnight. The house was strangely quiet, he'd told me. He went to his room—down the hall from the rose-carpeted guest room—and fell asleep immediately, with the intention of going back to my house in the morning. He woke up when he heard the scream.

339

"Hey," Jesse says now, "I don't regret anything." He pulls me into a tight hug. "We're going to be fine, you know."

"We're going to be fine," I repeat.

"I still like you, even though you're confirmed." I teasingly poke him in the ribs. And then, more seriously, I say, "And you like me even though I doubted you?" I ask because I still feel guilty about not believing in him. The last few weeks have been amazing, but we've never had this conversation. Coming back to QH brings it all back. We're in the real world again. Not hiberdating, as Dizzy would say.

"Daphne," he says, putting his finger under my chin and turning my face toward him, "don't you know? I love you." My heart turns to a puddle of mush inside my chest.

"I love you too," I tell him. And I mean it. He kisses me gently, his lips softly brushing mine.

"To senior year," I say, raising my copy of *1984*, our summer reading project.

"To us," Jesse says.

"More specifically," I add, "to the real us. The us right here and now. Not to the us that any technology says we may become. Only we can decide who we are."

Jesse looks at me solemnly. "To the us that we are, right at this very second," he says.

We kiss under the flagpole until the last bell rings and we enter Quiet High together, my hand in his, our futures intertwined.

ACKNOWLEDGMENTS

It turns out that writing a book is hard. Fortunately, I had a lot of help. First and foremost, big heaping thank-you's to literary agent extraordinaire Alyssa Eisner Henkin. Her unerring judgment, superb instincts, and endless knowledge should be written about in epic poems. A big hunk of gratitude also goes to the marvelous editor, Leah Hultenschmidt. Not only is she a delightful person, she's a spot-on reader with grace and elegance to spare. The whole Sourcebooks team has been terrific.

Special thanks goes to my employer, Westminster College, who generously gave me a semester of merit leave to write and think. Thank you to my colleagues who let me drone on and on about writing. Drs. Rulon Wood, Janine Wittwer, and Helen Hodgson deserve special credit on that front. Thanks to Elisa Stone, Stacey Winters, Fayth Ross, Dan Boregino, and Camille Etter, dear friends who always encouraged me. Tiffany Dvorske and Sarah Pike were particularly helpful early readers. And thanks to all of my students, who never failed to ask how things were going.

Lots of appreciation for unbridled enthusiasm goes to my terrific in-laws: Ken and Jeanette Twelves, Candie Cox, and Jennifer Jones. Greg Hoverson is still the coolest big brother ever. Thanks also to Taylor Hoverson for reading an early copy and for suggesting that he be a major character in my next book. My parents, Bill and Carol Hoverson, get credit for making me a lifelong reader. They also get all the credit for any other good qualities I might have. Finally, I never would have written a word if not for Robert Seifert, the very best thing that ever happened to me.

ABOUT THE AUTHOR

Christine Seifert, a native North Dakotan, is an Associate Professor at Westminster College in Salt Lake City, Utah. When she's not teaching writing and rhetoric, she's an avid reader and an enthusiastic listener of podcasts (especially podcasts about books). She's a fan of taking long walks on sunny days, browsing through the library on Saturday afternoons, and watching embarrassingly bad TV at any time.